Something's Brewing at Heron House

A Small-Town, Opposites Attract Romance

Tara Ryan

Above Average Press

ISBN 978-1-967758-08-1 (Paperback) 978-1-967758-07-4 (eBook)

Books in the Eastport Beach Series

Welcome to Heron House – Book 1

A Heron House Affair – Book 2

Something's Brewing at Heron House – Book 3

These books are interconnected standalones that do not need to be read in order to be enjoyed. However, for those of us with FOMO, I've listed the order above.

Enjoy!

For my lovely friend, Asher, who has a giant heart made of pure gold. She created a very special ministry for the people of Uganda called Sole Hope. The work they do saves many lives every day.

Chapter One

For most of his life, Seamus McLaughlin hadn't fit. He was bigger than his classmates in elementary school. In middle school, he was the only kid with facial hair. By high school, he'd become obsessed with chemistry, while most of the guys his age only cared about sports. Hell, his name didn't even fit and not a soul had used it since he was two years old and glued to Shark Week on the Discovery Channel. He'd been Sharkey ever since.

He certainly didn't fit in the dollhouse-sized shower inside his camper.

A stream of mumbled profanity stronger than the water pressure flowed from Sharkey's lips as he hit his funny bone for maybe the hundredth time. He was too damn big to live in a house on wheels. Turning the water off, he wrenched the shower curtain aside, popping several of the hooks off the top.

It was only temporary, he told himself again. And again. Once the brewery was finished, he could find a place with high ceilings and doorways he didn't bang his head on every other day.

The mantra started to work. He could feel his breath evening out and his muscles relaxing.

That's when he heard the racket outside.

Dammit! I'm going to catch those bastards once and for all. He raced to the door and flung it open, the cold January air hitting his naked, wet body and prompting him to pull the towel from around his neck and secure it at his waist. For weeks, someone had been making his life hell, basically undoing everything he did. Empty kegs, cut wires, an entire shipment of hops destroyed.

It was why he was living in this damn trailer. To keep an eye on things. To catch them in the act.

Barefoot, he slipped on the plastic steps, which he struggled with on a regular basis, because his feet were bigger than the treads. He nearly landed on his ass, but caught himself at the last second, by sheer will, determined not to make a fool of himself in front of his mortal enemy.

In his effort to save face, he lost the towel. Damn, it was cold.

A quick survey of the area between his camper and the container he would eventually use as the bar revealed no saboteurs. No one to see his pasty white ass. He quickly re-secured the towel and crept along the side of the giant metal shipping container.

For the last week, he'd been working inside the container, running plumbing and electrical. If someone was in there undoing everything he'd just done, there was going to be hell to pay. Sharkey was a pacifist, preferring quiet contemplation over confrontation any day of the week, but he'd make an exception. He was at the end of his rope. This project was already a month behind because of this mess.

When he poked his head around the corner, he didn't see anyone inside the container. Then movement closer to the riverbank drew his attention.

Atop one of his picnic tables stood a small, blonde woman waving her arms and...praying? It sounded like she was asking the Lord to rid her of the evil one.

Sharkey expected to find some punk kids messing with his property, not a possessed young woman dancing with the devil.

As he stepped closer, he finally saw the issue.

Damn gator.

He'd thought between the construction and more people frequenting the area that Stumpy wouldn't want to hang around. That alligator was too dumb for his own good.

Grabbing a stick, he rounded the corner fully and approached the table. Stumpy was acting a fool, snapping the air like he was actually going to eat the scared little waif.

Sharkey shook his head and puffed out his chest. When he was within six feet of the reptile, he slammed the stick into the ground and growled at the scaly interloper. The woman shrieked, and it appeared she didn't know who was scarier, man or beast.

Stumpy wobbled closer to the threat. He was missing most of his front right leg, but from the locals' experience, it didn't slow him down.

"I'm not playing with you today." Sharkey spoke low in tone and volume and banged the stick into the ground again. This time, the branch broke into two pieces. The animal took another step closer, jaws snapping like he was laughing.

The woman was hugging herself, repeating, "Ohmygosh, ohmygosh, ohmygosh," over and over again.

It made it hard to concentrate. "Can you hush for a minute?"

She froze, her eyes growing to the size of sand dollars.

Sharkey tried to think, but between the cold breeze blowing through his partially open towel and the nine-foot gator stalking toward him, it was difficult. He wished it had been a couple punk kids instead.

Slowly, he backed toward the container, to the giant hole he'd cut in it to use as a serving bar. He reached his hand through the opening, keeping his eyes on Stumpy, trying to find anything he could use as a weapon. He had plenty of options in the camper—although right now he was wishing he'd grabbed pants.

Finally, his fingers wrapped around the handle of a cordless drill. He lifted it and was relieved to feel the weight. He hadn't put the battery on the charger last night. Throwing up a prayer that it still had juice, he brandished it at the gator.

Whirrlllll.

Stumpy took a step back.

Sharkey advanced, waving the power tool through the air.

The beast turned toward the woman on the table, snapped his jaws, and then fully turned around, heading back to the river. Just as he slid into the water, the drill died.

The blonde pixie started back up with her "Ohmygosh" chant, looking from the river to Sharkey and back again.

"Ma'am, you can get down now."

Arms flailing, she shook her head, her short bob swishing from side to side. She muttered something incoherent. Just what he needed. A woman with the vapors.

Sighing, he set the drill down and reached his hand out.

"He probably won't come back today." He didn't want to lie to the woman, but he also wanted her to get off his table before she fell and broke her neck and held him liable. Of course, getting eaten by an alligator could also cause liability issues. He made a mental note to check with his insurance company about coverage for wildlife attacks.

The woman looked like she was struggling to choose between being eaten alive or canoodling with King Kong. Sharkey had heard the comparison before. Just because he was big, hairy, and grunted a lot, people compared him to an ape. Whatever, let people think what they want. It didn't keep anyone from buying his beer.

"I need you to get off the table, please." He spoke slowly, hoping the words would penetrate her fear, and she'd see that this particular ape was literate.

Clutching her chest with one hand, she reached toward him with the other, a look of sheer terror on her face. She was lovely, really, once you got past the horror. Delicate features, striking hazel eyes, full lips.

Well, hell.

He tried to soften his face—appear less threatening—but he was a big dude, and she was a tiny thing that he could crush just by hugging her too tight. Not that there would be any hugging. Or kissing, despite the kissable lips. He still didn't have a good reason why she was there in the first place. On his property.

"I'm not going to hurt you." Sharkey wasn't used to doing the talking. Usually, he left that to other people, preferring to only speak when necessary.

Finally, she placed her hand in his, and his heart stilled. Her hand was tiny, almost fitting in his palm, the fingers slender and delicate, the skin almost as pale as his Irish complexion. Carefully, he pulled her off the table, to the bench, then down to the ground. As her feet hit the dirt, she stumbled.

He caught her as she fell against him, and that's when his towel hit the ground for the second time.

Chapter Two

I t wasn't the first time Hope Seaton had been chased by a wild animal. Heck, she'd grown up in a place where a mosquito could kill you. But it was definitely the first time her rescuer was scarier than the creature chomping its jaws in her direction.

The man was huge. And hairy. And naked. Encountering a totally nude man was more intimidating than meeting Sasquatch himself. At least Bigfoot had hair *everywhere.*

"Ohmygosh, ohmygosh, ohmygosh." She staggered back, unable to avert her eyes. *Stop staring, Hope. It's just a penis. You've seen a penis before.* Things must really be bad if she was lying to herself.

Her brain couldn't form a coherent thought, and her mouth wasn't cooperating anyway, so she did what any sane person in her situation would. She turned and ran. As she darted between live oaks and hanging moss, she began to seriously reconsider this trip. Maybe she should go back to Chicago. To her aunt's house, where there were no giant reptiles trying to eat her and certainly no giant men showing off their impressive physique.

Between checking the shores of the river for the three-legged alligator and looking over her shoulder to see if the naked Sasquatch was chasing her, she completely missed the hammock strung between two trees. Like a slingshot, the hammock pulled her forward before it shot her backward, causing her to land on her butt in the soft sandy peat.

A tear leaked out of her eye. Angrily, she swiped it away. This was nothing. She'd endured far more than a dirty pair of dungarees and a bruised ego. Flopping back, she squeezed her eyes shut, willing her traitorous tear ducts to cease production. She'd been lying there several minutes when it occurred to her that her current position would make it much easier for the alligator to have her for lunch.

She had every intention of getting up and hurrying back to the house, but when she opened her eyes, Squatch was standing over her, his towel barely covering anything, holding her purple sparkle journal and matching pen.

"I'd lose my head if it wasn't attached," she muttered as she jumped up from the ground, wiping the dirt from her backside.

"You may lose it if you lie that close to the riverbank. The hammocks are much safer." He handed her the notebook and pen and turned to leave.

Hope gathered her wits enough to yell, "Thanks!"

She watched his retreating back with interest. As hairy as the front of him was, his back was all muscle, smooth skin, and a tattoo of a shark fin on his shoulder blade. Just as he was almost out of sight, he whipped the towel off, looked back at her, and winked.

Winked!

"Argh!" she huffed and clenched her free hand into a fist. *How dare he? What kind of man just walks around the woods naked?* She spun around, sidestepping the hammock this time, and stomped toward the Heron House. What kind of place was this? She'd come to Eastport Beach for peace and quiet, not naked Yetis and three-legged alligators.

As she rounded the corner of the house, she heard music and laughter. Her mother would call it hippie music. To Hope, it sounded like what the airline played after they put her on hold when she was trying to track down her lost luggage. As it was, she'd had to pack and leave in a hurry, forced to leave behind most of her belongings. Just her luck that her suitcase got permanently rerouted. At some point, she'd have to shop. But she'd save that for another day. There was only so much embarrassment she could take in such a short time.

Just past the fountain, spread out on the grassy lawn, were about a dozen ladies on yoga mats and five or six puppies running between them. The women were all bundled up in hoodies and sweats, items that even if she had her luggage, she wouldn't possess. There hadn't been much need for warm clothes at home.

Home. She didn't even know where that was now.

Riley, her host, popped up from one of the mats and ran to meet her. Her sweatshirt looked well-worn and cozy. It featured an album cover and the word "Journey." "Hey, Hope! Do you want to join us? We're doing puppy yoga. The dogs are so freaking cute."

Everyone looked like they were having fun, striking poses while furry balls of adorableness licked their feet. She wiggled her toes inside her sneakers. Nope, it was way too cold for bare feet.

She started to tell Riley about her terrifying encounter—and the alligator. But who was she kidding? She'd never complain to Riley about anything. Hope had learned a long time ago to go with the flow. Besides, the story didn't really reflect that well on her.

"I'd love to, but I don't have a yoga mat." Hopefully, she'd struck the correct balance of accepting hospitality while ducking out of joining in.

Riley grinned. "No problem, we've got extra." She jogged up the porch steps and grabbed a yellow mat with large blue flowers on it. Returning to where Hope stood, Riley grabbed her arm and pulled her toward the grass, spreading the mat out beside hers.

The woman was a force of nature, and it was hard to tell her no. Hope had only been at Heron House for a day, and she'd already figured that out. "I haven't really done—"

"It's my first time, too! And puppies!" Riley scooped up a fluffy brown one and thrust it in Hope's direction. His curly hair flopped over his eyes, and his tiny pink tongue licked the air. And he wasn't even the cutest furry thing she'd seen today.

She took the puppy from Riley and tried to focus on what the teacher was saying about bridge pose, but between the sloppy kisses and thoughts of the scary, hot man she'd left in the woods, she wasn't winning at yoga. After Hope fumbled through several poses, the instructor asked them to lie down on their mats and focus on their breathing.

Closing her eyes, Hope slowed her breathing and paid attention to the air filling her lungs. She must have been really in tune with her body, because she could feel her stomach doing somersaults, or maybe cartwheels. *Stop thinking about Squatch. You don't have time for distractions. Even if he is the hottest man you've ever seen in real life. They don't make men like that in Uganda. And besides, lust is a sin.*

So far, this trip wasn't at all what she'd planned. If she didn't buckle down and find a way to string together approximately seventy-five thousand words into something resembling a story, she was screwed. It was time to get serious. *As soon as this puppy stops pulling on my pant leg, I'm going inside and filling up at least five pages. Any words will do.* The publisher had paid her handsomely for a story, and if she didn't deliver, she'd have to find a way to pay the advance back—because that money was long gone.

***

The view from the gazebo was stunning. The wide river flowed past the property, branching into a small inlet in front of the hill the gazebo sat upon. Tall grasses lined the banks, and she'd already seen a number of waterbirds wading through the mud and fishing in the shallow depths. Hopefully, they were better at evading alligators than she was. The mast of a sailboat was visible over the trees, bopping occasionally as the river rocked it.

It was a picturesque vista that had likely inspired many artists to create masterpieces—watercolors, charcoal, sculpture. Was it too much to ask it to inspire a few thousand words?

Hope looked down at the journal in her lap. Instead of a blockbuster story, she'd filled the page with a drawing of a certain big, hairy gator whisperer. She'd heard about monster romance on that blog she wasn't supposed to read. Maybe she could write a love story about a woman lost in the woods who's rescued by Bigfoot himself.

Only her contract wasn't for a romance, or fiction, for that matter. She was supposed to write about her life. Or, more precisely, how her parents had mucked it all up.

News of her parents' fall from grace traveled quickly across the Atlantic. Soon, an aunt she barely knew was picking her up at O'Hare, telling her stories of two sisters growing up on a farm outside the city. Stories that, under normal circumstances, Hope would have gobbled up, begging for more.

But after what happened, that person—the woman who birthed her and raised her—felt like a stranger. Had it all been a lie? And why did Hope think it was a good idea to tell the world about it? To share her shame with millions of strangers?

But what other choice did she have? She had no skills, no proper education, no means to pay for anything. All she had was her story.

And it was as elusive as the real Bigfoot.

Chapter Three

The sun was just peeking over the horizon when Sharkey left the camper to start work that morning. He wanted to get a jump on finishing the electrical and plumbing in the container. The county inspector would be in the area later in the day and said he'd try to stop by. If Sharkey missed this chance, he'd likely wait weeks for another inspection.

The morning air had a bite to it, like maybe winter would show up at some point, but he was originally from the mountains, so it rarely got cold enough here for him to notice.

He'd barely taken two steps when he saw it.

If any birds were up early trying to get those extra worms, they got an earful from Sharkey. He used words he hadn't pulled out since his early twenties when he was a very angry, lost young man in hostile territory. The years had dulled that anger, and now most people would describe him as laid-back or chill.

But the graffiti decorating the side of his container had steam rising off his head. The punks had painted "Bite Me" in neon orange and drawn a passable picture of a shark. If he wasn't so pissed about the further delays it would cause, he might have appreciated the humor. He'd already pushed his opening twice, so he wasn't finding much funny these days.

It'd have to remain for now, because he was on a schedule, and "remove graffiti" was not penciled in.

His phone rang, and he aggressively tapped the screen to answer it. "What?"

"Whoa! Did you bump your head when you got out of bed again?" His cousin, Maverick, was the only person in his family Sharkey spoke to regularly, so he had heard many rants about the cramped quarters in the camper. "Sorry, Mav. It's stupid early here, I just found another mess at the work site, and yes, I hit my fucking head on the ceiling again." He snapped a picture of the "art," and sent it to Maverick.

There was a low whistle, then a long sigh. "Have you installed those cameras yet? Or maybe get a big ass dog."

"There's already one too many big, hairy creatures living in this cracker jack box. And I ordered the cameras, but I had to send them back because they weren't wireless." Moving onto the work site had not deterred this "mischief" (what the sheriff called it) one iota. "It's just one setback after another."

"That's it. I'm coming out there early. I can hear the stress in your voice."

His cousin could read him better than anyone, well, other than Eve. "You've got, what? Three festivals lined up in the next month? No, I can manage. I've got an inspection for the electrical and plumbing today. Smooth sailing from here on out."

"Are you lying to me, or yourself?"

"What did you call so early for, anyway?" Duck, weave, redirect.

"I had to get up to marinate some pork. Sun's not even up here. I can't keep up with what time zone either of us is in." Maverick traveled all over the country, setting up his food truck, Nacho Average Taco, at festivals.

Sharkey laughed. "I've been in the same time zone my entire life. You're the moving target." Other than his deployments.

Maverick grumbled. "Yeah, yeah. Mr. Dependable. Anyway, I couldn't go back to sleep, so I invented a new taco." His truck specialized in non-traditional taco fillings, like bacon cheeseburger and veggie supreme pizza.

Sharkey's stomach rumbled. The tiny refrigerator in his camper barely held any food, and all he had for breakfast was a banana. "I'd kill for one of your taco mcmuffins right about now."

"Hmm, yeah, I haven't done a breakfast menu for a while. Picture this: A Thanksgiving Taco—turkey, stuffing, gravy, topped with cranberry sprinkles. Soft shell, obviously."

Sharkey would throw that down right now. "It sounds freaking delicious, but it's January. You might be a little late on that one."

Maverick groaned. "I know. I'm always a day late and ten bucks short."

He wasn't kidding. The man was constantly borrowing "a couple bucks," despite the fact that he had a successful food truck, which dealt mostly in cash. Sharkey was convinced his cousin had a stash of cash buried somewhere, maybe on his parents' farm back near Ashford. "I do a pumpkin brew in the fall. That will pair up perfectly."

"Fire! Remind me I had this genius idea around August."

"I'll be sure to make a note in my planner."

"No need for sarcasm. I'll set a reminder on my phone." Maverick was meticulously organized when it came to his business, so it was almost like he didn't have the bandwidth left for any semblance of order in his personal life.

"It's a great idea, Mav. I've got to get this pipe run before the inspector gets here. I'll see you in a couple weeks." Sharkey would have loved to have his cousin's help and support, but he also knew how important the upcoming festivals were for him. They were the last events Maverick had scheduled before he retired from the road and set up shop at Shark Bite Brewing. The income from them would help him float for a couple months until Eastport Beach discovered how amazing Nacho Average Taco was.

"Peace."

Sharkey and Maverick had vended at the same festivals in the past, and it was a great collaboration. He was confident having the taco truck permanently stationed at his brewery would be the perfect fit for both of them.

He just had to push through all this bs and get the place open. The neon orange words mocked him as he rounded the side of the container. He stuck his middle finger up at them and got to work.

Chapter Four

Hope woke up determined to find a spot that would kick her writing brain into gear. She grabbed a pastry from the kitchen and sat at the long dining table, notebook and pen at the ready.

Half an hour later, she had an adorable sketch of a giant gray cat. He seemed content to pose in the middle of the table, just out of reach. Tail twitching, he surveyed her with interest but didn't seek to advance their relationship with physical contact. Like most men she met.

They'd had a cat back at the house in Uganda. Her mother had named her Ruth. Hope always assumed it was because her mom wanted the cat to like her best. Turned out Ruth didn't like anyone. She would hiss and lash out at anyone attempting to pet her, and she always looked malnourished, despite being fed regularly—both cat food and people scraps.

This cat wasn't missing any meals and had a similar look of disdain on his face.

Under the scrutiny of the feline's condemnation, Hope gathered up her supplies and went in search of a more inspirational locale without so much pressure.

Maybe doodling was part of her process. *What does a silly cat know, anyway?*

Across the hall in the parlor, she found Riley curled up at one end of a velvet sofa, reading. She was so engrossed, she didn't notice Hope or the cat, who had decided to take his disapproval on the road.

There was a small desk along the front windows. Sunlight shined through the glass, sending prisms of color across the wooden surface. It was hypnotizing, and exactly the sort of distraction Hope needed to avoid.

"Hope! Hi." Riley held up the book. "Sorry if you've been standing there long. I can't put this book down."

"What is it?" The cover had daisies all over, but she couldn't read the title from where she stood.

Riley stuck a bookmark in the thick book and gestured to one of the chairs facing the couch. "My sister sent it to me and said I *had* to read it." She glanced around furtively and dropped her voice. "The cover may look innocuous, but it is steam-y!"

She matched Riley's hushed tone. "Do you mean, like sex?" Hope had never read a romance at all, let alone one with sex scenes. Her mother would be appalled.

Her host nodded enthusiastically. "Like dirty sex." She fanned her face with her hand. "It'll take the chill off a cold winter morning. You can borrow it when I'm done." Hope's face must have shown her shock because Riley clutched her chest and looked stricken. "Oh, I'm so sorry. I hope I didn't offend you."

Hope shook her head. "No, not at all. I've just never read a romance before." Or had a romance, for that matter. "My mom was super strict about what I was allowed to read or watch."

"Oh, that makes sense. Your parents were missionaries, right?"

Her chest constricted, and suddenly, it became difficult to pull air into her lungs. All she could do was nod. Eventually, she'd have to find a way to talk about what happened. That's what the whole book was supposed to be about. But it was physically painful to even think about it.

Riley slapped her forehead. "Gosh, I've done it again, haven't I? Just ignore me."

"No, it's fine. Really." Hope took a deep breath and focused on how the air traveled through her body. When she'd first moved back to the states, her aunt had found a therapist for her, and they still had remote appointments. She'd given Hope exercises to help her deal with the anxiety around what had happened. "It's hard to talk about, but I have to learn how to do it. And it's much less scary to talk to you than a crowd of people." That was the worst part about her book deal. She'd be traveling after the release, giving talks and answering questions. So incredibly out of her comfort zone.

Riley patted Hope's knee. "I'm here if you want to talk, but don't feel like you have to."

"Can I ask what you know?"

Her host cringed, looking decidedly uncomfortable. "Well, I heard that your parents used some contributions to fund expensive travel and luxury items, like fancy cars."

Hope wondered if Riley was downplaying her parents' offenses, or if that was the extent she'd heard through social media and the news. "That's part of it. I knew they travelled a lot to speak about the work we were doing in Uganda. What I didn't know was that they were basically living a double life." She bit her bottom lip. "And I wasn't part of the fancy one."

"How did you find out?" Riley scooted to the edge of the sofa, enraptured.

"My aunt called to tell me they had been arrested in Chicago. Tax evasion. Apparently, they weren't claiming most of the money they raised and since their ministry was founded in the U.S., they were required to report everything to the IRS." That call would be forever etched on her memory. "I had just walked back from a neighbor's house after helping them with a pregnant goat. She delivered twins, which was really dangerous. I had afterbirth all over my clothes and my hands were bloody, but our neighbors didn't have running water, so I rushed home to clean up." She'd answered the call and put it on speaker, listening to her aunt as she scrubbed the blood from her hands. What an appropriate metaphor.

Riley's eyes widened. "You know how to deliver a baby goat?"

"Not really, but my neighbor was in her seventies and needed a cane to walk, so she couldn't physically do it. She talked me through it, although the twins thing was new to her as well."

"Aww, I bet the babies were so cute."

"Once they got cleaned up, yes."

"Sorry, I guess that's not really the point of your story. I'm the queen of tangents."

Hope smiled. "Yeah, but it was a nice distraction." She fidgeted with the metal buckle of her overalls. "They wouldn't let my parents fly back to get me, so I had to pack up the house and move back to the States."

"How long were you in Uganda?"

"We moved there when I was five, so basically my whole life. I barely remembered my aunt, but I needed a place to stay close to where my parents were being held." In the beginning, she had believed them when they explained it was all a minor accounting error, and they would get it cleared up quickly. "After the trial, she offered to let me stay on, but it didn't feel right to be there. She'd help them set up the ministry, so she was also charged, but ended up testifying for the prosecution."

Riley wrinkled her nose. "That must be so hard. Do you have any family you're close to?"

Hope shook her head. "Not really. I have a cousin on the west coast, but the people who worked on our property were my family. I couldn't afford to keep the place after the U.S. government froze my parents' assets, so I had to leave." *That was the hardest part—realizing that in their eyes, I was just as guilty as my mom and dad. I was foolish, naive, believing every day that we were really helping people.*

"Well, I'm so glad you're here. I believe everyone who stays at Heron House becomes part of our family—my uncle's legacy. I didn't know him, but as I learn more about him, I'm proud to follow his lead and open our home to anyone who needs a place of refuge." Riley squeezed Hope's hand.

"Thank you," Hope choked out the words, her chest filling with emotion.

"Anyway"—Riley clapped her hands together—"we've got to catch you up on all the meaty stuff you missed! Starting with a good, sweet romance. Come with me." She jumped up from the couch and grabbed Hope's hand, pulling her toward the stairs.

They climbed the main staircase, passing Hope's room and continuing down the hall. At the end, there was a door she hadn't noticed, with another set of stairs behind it. On the third floor, there were nine doors in total, four on each side, and one red door at the end of the hall.

"There are a few guest rooms up here, but we've got the other rooms set up as studio space—one for painting, one for sewing and one for writing—and..." She swung open a door dramatically.

"A library!" Hope was delighted to see the cozy room full of books. It was a corner room, so it had two windows, and sunlight filled the space, making it cheery and well lit. A comfy upholstered chair sat between the windows to take advantage of the light.

Riley pointed to one of the bookcases. "We've got all kinds of books in here, but this is the romance shelf. You are welcome to read in here or borrow the books for as long as you need." She trailed her finger along a row of books with blue covers and pulled one out. "These are Harlequin romances. I think this is a good place for you to start. Sweet, quick reads with no spicy parts."

Hope took the book from her and scanned the back. "It sounds cute. I'll give it a shot. I need something light and easy to read in between writing sessions." If she ever got any actual words down on paper.

"Yeah, it sounds like your book will be a little intense. It'll be good to break up the heavy stuff with some fluff. And I'm always down to watch a romcom." Riley pulled Hope into a hug. "I'm here. Whatever you need. I always wanted a younger sister."

That broke her. For the first time since all this happened, she felt like her name. Hopeful.

Chapter Five

Sharkey hated asking for help. But no matter how much he could bench at the gym, he couldn't move these picnic tables by himself. So, he lured his friends over with the promise of free beer. As much as he considered himself a loner, Ben, Trip and Chesnee were good guys, and he enjoyed their company.

He wasn't ready to share his deepest thoughts and worries, but he'd happily throw back a brewski with any one of them. As he waited for help to arrive, he surveyed the area once more, trying to determine the best placement for the half a dozen tables. The truck that delivered them had a crane that took them off the bed and plopped them in their current position—bunched up along the riverbank.

After the incident with Stumpy and Tinkerbell yesterday, the farther they were from the river, the better. He chuckled to himself, remembering the look of sheer terror on the tiny woman's face—and he was pretty sure it wasn't because of the alligator snapping in her direction. Not that he got his jollies from scaring random women. He was a warm-blooded man. He enjoyed the company of a lady. Once upon a time, he'd even loved one.

Now, it was a rare occasion for him to have more than a couple casual dates. No one could begin to fill her shoes. So, he kept things light and unattached. Mostly, he kept to himself. Just him and his beer.

But last night, lying in bed, he'd thought about her. Not HER. No, the tiny imp dancing atop his table. She couldn't have been much taller than five feet and likely weighed about ninety pounds soaking wet. He'd bet money she wouldn't be wading into this river to get an accurate weight after her introduction to the locals.

Her short, blonde hair was straight and fine, cut in a no-nonsense type of way, like she didn't invest too much time in worrying about her appearance. Her face was clean and fresh, free of makeup and wrinkles. He guessed she was pretty young, maybe early twenties, but her overalls and plaid shirt made her seem younger than she was. There was no denying she was a grown woman though. Those overalls didn't hide her figure completely.

She was cute as a button, flapping her arms around like she was trying to take off to get away from both beasts stalking her.

He'd watched her run away, zigging and zagging through the trees, like they teach in self-defense courses. After she disappeared from sight, he'd looked back at the table to discover her notebook and pen. Worried she'd be too scared to come back for it, he decided to go after her. It wasn't a stretch to assume she was staying at Heron House. There wasn't anywhere else for miles.

When he'd come upon her laying on the ground, his first instinct had been to rush to her side and make sure she wasn't injured. But as he got closer, he could see her lips moving, like maybe she was giving herself a pep talk, or possibly praying again.

Praying had been second nature to him once upon a time. Before real life intruded and he learned that all the prayers in the world couldn't save everyone.

"Sharkey! What up?" Chesnee's voice boomed through the trees, shattering the peace of the woods and forcing Sharkey back to the present.

The trio appeared, Trip and Chesnee pushing at each other and all three of them laughing.

"Sharkey, man, settle a bet for us. Which of us wins a triathlon?" Trip jabbed his finger into his own chest.

He knew Ben swam in the river almost daily when the weather allowed, but Trip practically lived in his kayak year-round. Chesnee, on the other hand, spent several hours a day chasing a small yellow ball around a tennis court. They were all healthy, fit men. "Why don't you enter one and find out?"

Chesnee scrunched his face up. "Ugh, who has time for that?"

Ben and Trip mumbled their agreement.

These guys certainly kept things lively, if you liked that sort of thing. They'd be excellent plants once he got the brewery up and running. Trip and Ben were educated and personable, and Chesnee would talk to a wall. Sharkey could serve his beer and let them socialize. "How about a beer before we get started?"

"I'm never gonna say no to that." Chesnee rubbed his hands together.

Trip tried to lift the corner of the closest table. "Yeah, I'm happy to put off this hernia waiting to happen."

Sharkey had set up a small keg before they arrived, so now he filled four glasses with his latest formula and the perfect amount of head. He passed them out, and they all clinked their glasses.

"To Shark Bite Brewing Company," Ben cheered and everyone echoed.

Trip held up a finger as he swallowed. "Is that a bit of orange I taste?"

He bobbed his head. Trip was pretty good at figuring out Sharkey's new flavors. He loved creating new blends and toying with the ratios of hops to yeast to water. Every day was basically playing around in a lab, but instead of scientific discoveries, he made people happy with beer.

Case in point, Chesnee was currently up on a picnic table dancing to a rhythm only he could hear. And Stumpy wasn't in sight.

"So, Ben, is the house still full up now that the holidays are over?" Sharkey pointed at the idiot on top of the table. "My insurance doesn't cover stupid, Chesnee."

Ben chuckled. "It's definitely dropped off since the new year, but we have one gal who's staying for two months. She's real quiet, keeps mostly to herself. I think she's writing a book."

Sharkey had flipped through the purple glitter notebook before he returned it to Tink, but it was just doodles and marked out words. Hopefully, she was writing a book with mostly pictures. He held his hand chest height. "Tiny thing? Blonde?"

Chesnee leapt from the table into the middle of their conversation. "What's this about a blonde?"

"Maybe we're talking about you." Ben smacked the back of his assistant's head playfully. "Stop stalking our guests."

The younger man pouted and took his indignation to the riverbank where Trip was standing, probably texting Ada. The two had moved in together just before Christmas and were rarely apart. Sharkey was happy for them. Love was great. For everyone else.

Ben continued, "Her name is Hope. Riley is desperately trying to be her best friend, but she startles easy from what I can tell."

Sharkey stroked his beard and nodded. She was definitely jumpy. "Well, she had a run-in with the local wildlife yesterday."

"Damn Stumpy. We need to buy him a muzzle."

"I might have to think about putting a fence along the river. Keep the gators out and the drunks in." At that moment, Chesnee grabbed a vine and swung out over the river. It was January, and the water was probably about fifty degrees.

"Sad thing is, he's only had a half a beer." Ben shook his head.

The nut swung back to the shore, where Trip grabbed him before he landed in the water.

Yup. Definitely need a fence. "Let's get these tables moved before Chesnee's five-second attention span expires."

"Yeah, some of us need to go back to work." Ben raised his voice loud enough for his employee to hear. "Preferably with dry clothes."

Sharkey slapped his neighbor on the shoulder. "Thanks. I know you're busy."

"It's nice to get out of the office and outside. The water's too cold for my daily swim, so I need to get this energy out somehow."

He grunted with a smirk. He'd seen Ben's boat rocking enough times to know how he and Riley got their energy out.

And he wasn't jealous at all.

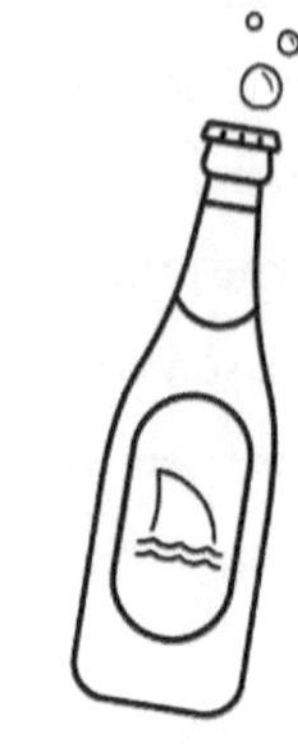

Chapter Six

For the past few days, Hope had tried various locations on the property to find inspiration. Between the scaly beast and the sasquatch, she wasn't sure she should go back to the picnic tables. Today she was trying the dock. She was too nervous to hang her feet over the side, so she had her legs stretched out, notebook in her lap. A skinny white bird landed in the grass near her, poking its head between the reeds. Soon, her page was filled with doodles of the bird instead of words.

Hope leaned back, closed her eyes, and soaked in the warmth of the sun. It was chilly, maybe in the fifties, but nothing like a Chicago winter. It had been years since she'd spent any significant time there, but she remembered the snow from before they moved to Uganda. This was the warmest time of the year there, so she was still adjusting to the change of seasons in the states.

Her phone buzzed in her pocket, startling her. She still wasn't used to the device. Her parents had cell phones, but she'd never had a use for one. In Uganda, her world was small, her friends just a bike ride away. Adjusting to life here was harder than she'd expected, especially because she didn't feel settled. Her aunt's house felt foreign, and she was always asking about the book and how it was coming.

That's how Hope ended up at Heron House. She was used to quiet, to entertaining herself and figuring things out on her own. Her parents had always been busy. Jetting around the world, raising money for their ministry, speaking about all the good they did for the people of Uganda. The reality was Hope rarely saw them.

She reached for her pen, feeling like she was on the brink of something insightful, when her pocket vibrated again.

It was a text from her agent. Nadine had seemed like a savior when she approached Hope about writing a book. The article she'd written for *Time* after her parents' trial had garnered a lot of attention. It had been easy to write a thousand words. Those words only skimmed the surface of what Hope was going through. She needed to dig deeper for the book, and she was terrified of what lay under all that dirt.

She shot a quick text back to Nadine—cheery words about Heron House and how inspiring it was. More lies. She'd spent the first twenty-three years of her life following all the rules—never lying, never talking back to her parents, never getting in trouble. What had following the rules gotten her?

A whole lot of nothing. She had no home. No future. No purpose.

Who wanted to read a book about being lost?

Hope didn't know who she was anymore. Until a few months ago, she'd felt honored to call herself the daughter of missionaries. She was proud of the work she'd done. But now all that was tarnished, a dirty spot on a clean, white dress.

Finally, her pen moved across the page.

> *If you give ten cans of vegetables to the food pantry, but then steal twenty boxes of macaroni, does it negate all the good those vegetables will do? I was there. I saw the good with my own eyes. The people we fed, the medicine we delivered, the homes we built. Does that count for anything now?*

She sat back, staring at the page. The words felt raw, like a paper cut, stinging with the slightest movement. Had it all been for nothing? Could she have grown up in America, gone to a regular school, played soccer and video games? Dated, gone to prom, kissed a boy?

Anger and resentment roiled in her chest like the indigestion from the deep-dish pizza she'd had her first night back. Her chest constricted, her breathing becoming labored. This was too hard. How could anyone possibly understand when she couldn't even put her feelings into words?

Or when those words tore a hole in her chest.

She closed the notebook against the offensive thought, stuck her pen in the spiral spine, and laid back on the wooden dock.

Above, the sky was clear, save for a smattering of thin clouds. It was a brilliant blue, like it had been painted the exact, perfect color.

Are you still there, God? I don't know what is true anymore. I don't know what they lied to me about and which parts I can cling to. I need something, because I'm free-falling. The ground has shifted under my feet and I'm on the precipice of a deep chasm.

In that moment, it occurred to her that maybe she should be writing all this down, but was it a prayer anymore if someone has paid for your words?

A heron flew overhead, his wings appearing to stretch for miles. She was trying to figure out what the Lord was showing her when a splatter of white landed right beside her head. The message was clear. Her life was complete crap.

***

When she walked back to the house after another failed writing session, Riley was out on the porch reading in one of the rockers. Frustrated, Hope wanted to just go up to her room, bury her head under the covers, and take a nap. She wasn't sleeping well. Her brain continued all night long, churning, but not producing any usable thoughts. As a distraction, she'd been reading into the early hours of the morning. Inhaling all the books upstairs. Putting language to feelings.

"Hey, Hope. I saw you down on the dock. Were you able to get a lot done?" Riley closed her book, sticking her finger in the pages to keep her place.

"Yeah, it was great. Listening to the water lap against the shore was really good background noise." Hope tapped her journal. She had actually written something today, even though she doubted she would keep it. "This is a great place for inspiration."

The elation on Riley's face made the fib worth it. She'd known her host for less than a week, but she didn't like to disappoint people.

The front door opened then, and a group of senior citizens filed out of the house. They weren't typical elderly people with walkers and orthopedic shoes. Hope had seen them outside earlier this morning doing some kind of martial arts on the lawn. Between that and the puppy yoga, she wondered if she'd accidentally booked a spa.

"Riley, don't wait up. We're heading to Myrtle Beach for the *Rocky Horror Picture Show*." A lanky gentleman waved a curly black wig through the air.

A purple-haired lady wearing a gold sequin top hat sang, "It's time warp time!"

Another couple waved their arms up and down like the Thriller dance, but Hope didn't remember that being part of the song.

As the crowd moved down the steps, a rotund fella sang out in a screechy voice, "Don't mind my pelvic thrust!"

Soon the entire group was dancing toward a party bus pulling down the driveway.

Riley laughed and waved at her guests. "Have a good time! Make smart choices!" She turned to Hope. "I hope I'm that energetic when I'm their age."

"They certainly looked like they were having fun, and they aren't even at the show yet." She hoped Riley wouldn't notice that she didn't have a clue what they were talking about.

"I've seen the movie, but I've never been to a live performance. I'm way too shy to do anything like that." Riley watched the bus as it pulled away, her expression wistful.

Hope certainly understood wishing she had the nerve to do something everyone else seemed to be doing. "Sounds like it will be a quiet evening in the house." She was the odd man out staying at Heron House. The older folks had an annual tradition of meeting up somewhere for a week, and they had taken over most of the rooms on the second floor. Hope was lucky she'd been able to snag a suite for her two-month stay. It had taken the last of her advance money, but she knew she wouldn't get anything done with her nosy aunt breathing down her neck.

Not that she was banging out pages.

It had only been a few days, she tried to reason. Meanwhile, it felt like the world was crashing down on her.

"You can join Ben and me for dinner, if you'd like. Nothing fancy, just grilling some burgers." Riley was back in her rocking chair, a hopeful expression on her face.

She'd already put off several invitations to eat with her host, so maybe this was a smart time to accept. With the other residents of the house gone for the night, it should be low pressure. "That sounds great. I might take a little nap first if I have time."

Riley beamed. "Of course. Ben won't be home until close to six, and I'm not allowed to touch the grill." She laughed. "Or the oven."

Hope figured there was a story there, but she still needed to mark "bury head under covers" off her to-do list. "Great, I'll see you around six." She reached for the screen door as Riley opened her book back up. "And thanks for the book recommendations. I'm really enjoying them."

"Just let me know when you're ready for the big guns." She waved the heavy tome through the air.

Hope was a little curious about what came next, but just reading about attraction and longing was intense and a little over her head. Plus, she could hear her mother's disapproving tone in the back of her mind. She needed to find a way to excise that demon.

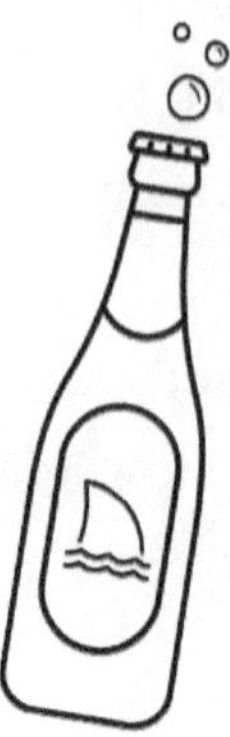

Chapter Seven

He always said no to things like this. But Ben had taken time off a few days ago to help him, so when he asked, Sharkey felt obligated.

That's why, against his better judgement, he was dressed in pants that didn't have paint on them and a shirt with buttons and a collar. The damn thing already felt like it was choking him.

He made it to the spot where he'd found Tink, or Hope, he supposed, on the ground, and the pounding started in his head. Pulling his phone out, he pulled up the text screen, ready to beg off the dinner. His fat, clumsy fingers left the text unintelligible. *Wimp.* He erased the text and shoved the phone back in his pocket. She probably wouldn't even be there. It wasn't like Ben and Riley fed all their guests.

For all he knew, Chesnee would be there, and poor Riley would have to suffer through a sausage fest. Or maybe Ada and Trip were coming. He adored Ada—she'd taught him how to line dance. *Yeah, it'd be fine. Fun, even.*

When he rounded the corner of the house and didn't see any cars parked out front, his pace slowed.

Maybe he was early. Maybe he should hang on the porch until everyone else got here.

"Sharkey, hey." Ben held open the screen door and gestured for him to hurry. "I just lit the grill. Come out back."

He followed Ben into the house, and down the hallway to the kitchen, where he stuck his growler in the fridge. It was rude to show up to a meal without a contribution. Surprise, surprise—Sharkey always brought beer. "Should I pour a couple glasses?"

His friend looked to the ceiling, like the answer would be written there. "I'll have one, but only one. I've got court tomorrow. The girls have lemonade—Riley swears it's a year-round drink because it's been such a mild winter."

Riley's lemonade was legendary, and the running joke was that it was the only thing she was allowed to make in the kitchen. *Wait, did he say "girls?"* Maybe Trip had parked around back, like he used to do when he lived at Heron House. *Yeah, that was probably it.* So, why did his feet suddenly feel cemented to the floor?

Ben handed him two pint glasses from the pantry. "I've got to tend to my coals, just come out when you're ready." He disappeared through the door, followed closely by Ansel, the house cat.

This is ridiculous. It's freaking burgers and beer. I'm a brewer. This is literally my wheelhouse. Shake it off, dumbass. Sharkey grabbed the beer out of the fridge and calmed himself with his pouring ritual. When he had two perfect glasses of ale ready, he stuck the remainder of the brew back in the fridge and dragged the dead weight he called legs toward the back door.

As much as he hoped one of these beers was for Trip, or even Chesnee, he knew he wasn't that lucky, so he took a fortifying sip out of one of the glasses.

His pep talk had failed. He could feel sweat pouring down his back, and it was fifty-five degrees outside. Damn collared shirt.

Through the window in the door, he could see Riley facing away from him, gesturing wildly with her hands. He couldn't see who she was talking to, but logic would dictate that it was someone on the small side, because Riley was petite herself. Chesnee, Trip and Ada were all of above-average stature. Which left Hope.

Ben was manning the grill, spatula at the ready, as burgers sizzled on the grate. Nothing like grill-marks on a hamburger. A lot of people preferred smash burgers, but Sharkey was old-school. Not much beats the taste of a flame to go along with a hearty beer.

Riley spun around when he stepped outside. "Sharkey! Welcome!"

He froze, echoing Tink's stance as their eyes met.

Their hostess plowed ahead, not noticing the discomfort of her guests. "Hope, this is our good friend, Sharkey. He lives behind us." She gestured in the general direction of his property. "He's opening a brewery further up the river." She yanked the poor woman forward. "Sharkey, this is Hope. She's staying with us for a couple months."

Months. He dipped his head and held out his hand. "Nice to meet you."

She slid her hand into his, craning her head back to see him. "Thanks for saving me from the alligator."

"Say what?" Riley shrieked like a little kid who wanted a toy she couldn't have.

"Stumpy." He shrugged, figuring that explained everything.

While Hope was relaying the story to a captivated Riley, Sharkey studied his damsel in distress. Between the gator, his nakedness and her fleeing the scene, he hadn't really taken stock.

She was wearing the same overalls, but instead of a plaid shirt, she had a plain white long-sleeved tee underneath. Her short hair was simply styled, and while she talked, she kept tucking the strands behind her ears. She was again make-up free, but her cheeks were rosy from the chilly air and her eyes sparkled as she told her story. He couldn't make out their shade from this distance, so he stepped closer.

Hope glanced his way, long enough for him to see her eyes were blue, then she slid to her left. Away from the giant man. Surely, she wasn't still afraid of him. Ben and Riley had invited him to dinner. How bad could he be? Yeah, he always brought beer, so that probably got him more invitations than, say, an insurance salesman, but he was a likeable guy. Right?

Maybe if he sat down, he'd look more approachable. Smaller.

He scanned the intimate backyard space. There were a couple loungers—men looked ridiculous on those unless there was a pool nearby, and even then, it was sus—a couple small stumps that his left butt cheek wouldn't fit on, and two plastic Adirondack chairs. With any luck, it would be big enough. Ben was sitting in one and he was almost six feet.

Hope was telling Riley about running into the hammock as Sharkey lowered himself into the chair. Ben was watching the ladies, sipping his beer. Riley gripped Hope's arm in apprehension, and Hope might as well have had a spotlight on her. Her whole face was lit up with excitement. She was radiant.

Crack!

No, no, no. Sharkey tried to jump up before he landed on the ground, but the way the chair was angled, he struggled to get up quickly, then his hips snagged on the arms of the chair and by the time he got to his feet, the damn thing was stuck to his backside like some comedic parody of a turtle.

All eyes were on him. Hope's mouth hung open, and for once, Riley was speechless. Ben jumped up from his chair—the way a normal sized man would—and helped Sharkey out of his plastic prison.

In an effort to appear less threatening, he'd only managed to make a mockery out of himself. "Sorry about the chair," he mumbled to Ben, and ducked into the kitchen.

Chapter Eight

After Sharkey fled into the house, the three of them stared at one another in disbelief. Hope felt awful for the man. Obviously, he was big, but breaking-a-chair big? He wasn't fat. She'd seen most all of him—and it was pure muscle. The only comparison she could make would be a football player—American, obviously—not that she had watched any sports regularly.

At their home in Uganda, they'd had several people who helped with the upkeep of the property and the men enjoyed watching the Super Bowl, so they would come to the main house and gather around the only television set. Hope had watched in awe as the men battered into one another, pushing and pulling their opponents to the ground.

The men she'd been around growing up were typically lean—likely from poor diets and manual labor. So, even as a teenager, she'd been fascinated by the muscle-bound men chasing a brown ball.

"Excuse me." She stepped around Riley, who was still staring at the back door, and past Ben, who was tending to the grill. Like she was being pulled by a force outside herself, she climbed the two steps and pushed open the back door.

The kitchen was empty—the house quiet. She stepped lightly down the hallway, peeking through doorways, like she was looking for an injured animal and didn't want to startle it. She had zero plans about what to say to him if she found him. Her heart hurt for him, and she had to at least try. He had saved her from an alligator, after all.

He wasn't in any of the rooms on the ground floor, and he wasn't staying at the house, so she doubted he'd be upstairs. It was possible he'd just gone home.

She found him on the porch, leaning against the railing, staring a hole in the floor. His hands were stuffed in his pockets, and he had unbuttoned most of his shirt like it was choking him. She'd only seen him in (and out of) a towel, so she had no idea how he normally dressed, but she was guessing it was more casual than the khakis and button-up shirt he had on tonight.

His whole body jerked when the screen door squeaked. He lifted his head and transferred his stare to her face, his eyes expressing more than words could possibly convey.

She didn't know the man, heck, she was slightly terrified of him, but she wanted to hug him, reassure him, tell him it was just a stupid chair. Then she wondered about the mechanics of it. Would her arms even reach around him? If he wrapped her up in his embrace, would she disappear entirely?

It wasn't necessarily an unpleasant possibility.

He tracked her across the porch, where she sat in a rocking chair opposite him. She rocked. He watched. Minutes passed in silence.

Hope had never minded the quiet. Growing up, she spent a lot of time alone, left to entertain herself with a single baby doll, a Bible, and the collection of rocks she hid from her mother. When she was sick, which had happened on more than one occasion, she'd lie in bed for hours, reciting Bible stories from memory because she was too weak to pick up the book. She would close her eyes and try to picture what was happening and add little innocent details, like giving Sarah a dog to keep her company during the decades she longed for a child.

But feeling Sharkey's gaze on her was different. Like the air was pressing down against her skin, generating heat inside her body. It was a completely foreign feeling. She wondered if it was what her mother had warned her about. Lust.

Suddenly, the silence was oppressive. There was no way she'd win this staring contest. He might as well have bored holes through her skin. "Did you ever play football?"

He flinched, his eyes flashing away from her for mere seconds, breaking the spell.

She missed the heat.

Regaining his composure, he stroked his beard and slowly nodded his head. The heat was back in full force.

Huh, a beard. She never would have thought she'd be into a man with a beard, but her body was definitely responding in ways she'd never experienced. This was outside her ilk. Sure, she had a rudimentary idea of where babies came from, and her mother had been forced to explain some things when "she experienced Eve's curse," but she was not prepared for this. Was this what those romance novels had been describing?

Her cheeks heated up, likely turning bright red, giving her away completely. She bowed her head, suddenly finding the stitching on her dungarees quite interesting and complex.

"Why do you ask?" His voice was raspy, like maybe he was also struggling to maintain his breathing.

"I was raised in Africa. Uganda." She shook her head, regretting her verbal diarrhea. That wasn't at all what he asked, but it was like she didn't have control of her mouth. She peeked up from her lap, catching his confused expression. *Dummy.* "We would watch the Super Bowl sometimes. The men in my village were slender but worked hard."

Sharkey's brow furrowed.

Yeah, not any clearer. "You're a big, strong man. Like a football player." *Yeah, that was better. At least it made sense.*

A chuckle rumbled in his chest, so low she almost couldn't hear it. But his torso shook, and his lips stretched under that beard. He braced his hands on his knees, his shoulders heaving, the chuckle morphing into a full-blown, audible, laugh.

It was exactly how one would imagine Bigfoot laughed.

Hope's cousin, Bridget, used to write her letters when they were young. Her mother called them pen pals. It was her only connection to life in the states for many years, and as they got a little older, sometimes her cousin would send her books, or CDs with secular music. Their family lived on the west coast, where apparently, the legend of Bigfoot was taken pretty seriously. Hope had become mildly obsessed with a series of books about teenage boys searching for the mythical being. She identified with Sasquatch a bit. Where she lived, she was an outsider—a pale-skinned girl surrounded by rich, dark-skinned people. Eventually, some accepted her, but to many, the Christian family who lived in "the big house" were not welcome and in fact, feared.

Was she supposed to meet this man? First, the Bigfoot books, then football? Her mother would say she was being ridiculous.

Hope couldn't help but join in his laughter. His low and rumbling, hers sharp and tinny. Discordant, but somehow melodic.

The screen door flew open, popping the magical bubble of mirth they had created. "What's so funny?" Riley stepped out onto the porch, her face bright with anticipation.

Sharkey and Hope simultaneously quieted, sharing a covert glance.

"You had to be there." He pushed off the railing. "Are the burgers ready?"

She looked disappointed but nodded her head. "Yeah, Ben needs to know if you want cheese. We have American and Swiss."

Sharkey turned to Hope. "Well? What kind of cheese do they put on burgers in Uganda?"

She shrugged. "Goat, usually, because it's made in the village."

"Well, Riley? Got any goat cheese?" He held the door open for the girls to pass through.

"Yeah, let me go out back and milk one real quick," Riley threw over her shoulder as she led the way back to the grill area.

Sharkey and Hope shared a smile as they followed her down the hall.

There it was again. That not entirely unpleasant feeling of heat. Hopefully, the book she was reading could explain what the heck this Squatch was doing to her.

Chapter Nine

Riley single-handedly kept the conversation flowing all evening. Sharkey was grateful, because despite the moment they'd shared on the porch, there was still an awkwardness between him and Hope. She joined in the conversation when warranted, but avoided looking directly at him.

By the time they'd gone back outside, Ben had located a chair sturdy enough to bear his mass. The four sat around the fire pit, eating and talking until most of them were fighting back yawns. Sharkey bid his farewell, thanking Ben and Riley and telling Hope good night. Then he headed back to his camper, using his phone as a flashlight, feeling very different than he had on the way over.

Hope had grown up in Africa, a world away from the States. Her parents were missionaries, but when Sharkey had asked where they were now, she went quiet, and Riley tried to do some covert charades crap behind her back.

He really didn't understand women. He knew how to make a woman come, but he didn't get the way their minds worked 95% of the time. In order to keep his size fourteen foot out of his mouth, he usually avoided deep conversation.

He still wasn't sure why the parent question wasn't appropriate, but knowing Riley, she'd fill him in the next time he saw her. He could always count on Riley to provide too much information. After tonight, he was craving more info about their new guest.

The woods were dark, save for the moonlight filtering through the trees. The cypress had dropped their needles in the fall, making the ground soft, almost bouncy. Because the live oaks didn't lose their leaves until closer to spring, there was still a decent canopy overhead to block out the light from the moon. So, when Sharkey saw a light moving up ahead, he stopped abruptly and strained to hear any sounds that didn't belong. Over the crickets' midnight melody, he could just make out a scraping sound.

His chest swelled and his pulse quickened. That wasn't Stumpy chasing an innocent woman onto a picnic table—that was someone up to no good.

Clicking off his flashlight, he moved to the right, hugging the bank of the river instead of taking the path that had become worn between the two properties. He was less worried about wildlife and more worried about his livelihood.

The growler he carried was still about half full, so it could function as a blunt instrument if needed. Of course, his actual weapons were in the trailer. Lot of good that was doing him now.

The scraping noise grew louder as he approached, and whispered voices floated to him on the light breeze. By the time he got to the first picnic table, a sheen of sweat coated his forehead, and his jaw ached from gritting his teeth together. He almost felt sorry for the poor fools that were now laughing inside the metal container.

For the slimmest moment, he considered calling the sheriff, but so far, he'd brushed off his concerns and said it was probably just kids messing around.

Well, they aren't going to mess around with me anymore.

He slipped past the container, making sure no one was near his camper. Should he take the time to get his gun out of its lockbox, or attack with his growler? It'd be a sweet irony to take them down with his product, since they seemed hellbent on screwing up his operation.

Obviously, he wouldn't shoot anyone, but wielding a gun could send a clear message that he wasn't playing around. Then a thought gave him a momentary pause.

What if they had weapons?

He slipped behind his camper and pulled out his phone, shooting off a quick text to Ben. At least someone would know what was going on in case things went sideways. It didn't hurt that Ben was an attorney.

Considering a multitude of possibilities, Sharkey decided to get the gun. He was one person and from the racket they were making, there were at least two of them, if not three. Creeping back to the front of the camper, he climbed the tiny stairs and unlocked the door. Just then, a gust of air swept between the two structures, grabbing the storm door and slamming it against the camper.

He heard someone cuss, followed by a bang and then running. Before he made it ten feet, he saw the taillights of a truck light up and a cloud of dust as it sped away.

Dammit.

Inside the camper, he quickly located his high-powered flashlight and grabbed his gun just for good measure. Untucking his stupid button up, he shoved the weapon in the waistband of his pants. Better safe than dead.

By the time he rounded the corner of the container and could see what the miscreants had been up to, Ben appeared, tennis racket in hand.

"Sorry, man. The match is off. Our opponents hightailed it out of here."

As Ben moved closer, his eyes widened, and he cursed under his breath. "I know you'd like to handle this on your own, but I think you've got to call the sheriff."

Sharkey nodded, the light feeling he'd had upon leaving Heron House replaced with a deep, dark dread. This wasn't a group of bored teenagers.

Through the opening he'd cut for a pass-through window, he could see all the wiring he'd just installed and had inspected pulled off the walls and cut in multiple places. And stuck to the wall with a large knife was a small tiger shark and a note that read "Die Shark Bite." The poor animal was still twitching. Sharkey's heart split in two.

Chapter Ten

The first light of dawn was peeking through the transom window over the front door when Hope crept down the stairs. She'd been so swept up in the book she was reading, she'd only slept a few hours. But she'd set an alarm, hoping to leave the house before anyone else was awake.

She filled her water bottle, cringing at the clamor the ice cubes created. She knew Riley and Ben's bedroom was off the kitchen, though she had never seen it. Heron House was a bit of a puzzle, with doors seemingly leading nowhere and rumors of secret passages. But she had a bigger enigma to focus on. A big, hairy enigma.

Snagging a banana from the fruit bowl, she tiptoed down the hall and slid out the front door. She was a grown woman, and a guest paying to stay there, but her heart still raced with excitement. At home, she'd never had a reason to sneak out of the house, nor would her parents have even noticed from halfway around the world.

Her brain was zinging with the stories she had devoured over the last couple days. The books Riley had shared with her were short and engaging. She found herself racing to the end, where so far, every couple had lived happily ever after. This morning, she even felt inspired to write. Somehow reading these made-up stories knocked something loose in her mind. Now she could imagine her life as a story, one she could step out of and look at from a distance. Time would tell if her story had a happy ending.

Right now, she felt stuck in the middle part, where it looked hopeless for the characters. She thought that maybe if she got the story down on paper, she could somehow get to the end faster.

It was still dark under the trees, so she picked her way carefully over roots and around depressions in the squishy ground. Along the way, she picked up a large stick, just in case her three-legged friend decided to pay her another visit.

When she broke through the woods into the clearing, she noticed the picnic tables had been rearranged and moved further from the shore of the river.

Quiet blanketed the area, like an oasis in the middle of a forest, even though she knew Heron House was only a few hundred feet behind her. Squatch was nowhere to be found, and she couldn't decide if that was a good thing or not.

She sat at the furthest table from the river, fussing with the position of her water bottle and notebook. Flipping past a series of drawings, she arrived at the passage she'd written that day on the dock. Reading it now, she feared the logic that made sense in her head wouldn't translate to the general public.

Ripping the page out, she crumbled it into a ball and shoved it in her pocket. This would be the last day she'd have to wear these dungarees. Riley had offered to take her clothes shopping this afternoon, since it appeared the airline had given up on locating her luggage. Everything else in her life had to start over, so why not get a new wardrobe?

Riley assured her they would hit the outlet stores, which offered inexpensive options. Hope would be getting some money from the airline for their mistake, but she only had a couple hundred dollars left from her advance check, and she had to eat for the next two months.

When she turned her manuscript in, she would get another chunk of money. If that wasn't motivating, nothing would be.

She turned to a fresh page and started writing the goat story she'd told Riley. It had occurred to her in that moment that maybe what she had to say could be interesting. Riley had certainly seemed engrossed.

One of the romance books she'd read was about two people who were best friends growing up and then falling in love when they got older. The book jumped around in time, showing their relationship throughout the years. It made her realize that she didn't have to start chronologically at the beginning, because honestly, she didn't know when all this started.

Her parents had yet to fully admit their wrongdoings to her, so all anyone knew was what had come out in court. She wondered if they'd been crooked her whole life. Had they created the ministry to help people or to help themselves?

After talking to Riley, she realized that her beginning was the day her aunt called. So, she started there. It was easy to write about her neighbor asking for help, about the goat in labor, and about the twin kids she delivered. She could take herself back there and feel the rush of blood and sticky goo of the afterbirth. Hope had stayed calm and likely saved the three animals.

She filled pages of the notebook talking about the village where they lived and the people who would come to their property and till fields, cook meals and play games with a young Hope. Her heart swelled with love as she wrote about Cali, the woman who took care of her when her parents were out of the country.

Writing about her life in Uganda was easy. Her memories were happy. She couldn't get the words down fast enough. Her pen flew across the page, her chest loosening with every word.

"What are you doing here?" The voice boomed, startling her.

She slapped the book shut, holding it to her chest as if she could protect all those precious memories.

Squatch wore a white t-shirt that strained across his chest and a pair of gray sweatpants. She thought they'd had a breakthrough last night, but today he looked like he was angry at the world.

"I-I didn't think you'd mind if I wrote here." She hated that she'd stuttered, because she had promised herself she would be brave around him. But the big, angry Yeti was intimidating.

He raked his hand down his face, tugging on his beard.

Her stomach flipped like a fish flopping on the dock after falling for the bait on the hook.

He sighed and sat down opposite her, closing his eyes like he was mentally preparing himself for something. "Of course you can write here. Just not alone." His eyes opened.

She hadn't noticed the deep green of his irises before. She'd never seen eyes that color.

"It's not safe."

Grabbing her stick, she wielded it for him to see. "I'm ready if Stumpy comes back."

He rubbed his temples. "I'm not worried about the alligator."

Having a conversation with this man was like waiting for water to boil. He spoke deliberately, like every word cost him something, and he had to figure out if it was worth the price.

"I've been having some trouble around here. It's probably nothing, but I'd feel awful if something happened to you."

Studying him, she realized he was exhausted. His eyes were bloodshot, and his neck could hardly support the weight of his head. "You're not sleeping."

"Not much."

"Maybe I can help keep an eye out. I like writing here, so I can be your lookout while you get some rest."

He shook his head, his mouth set in a firm line. "Give me your phone."

It was an order, not a question. Hope had always been a rule follower, so she slid it out of her pocket and across the table, wondering where this was going.

Tapping the screen, he cursed under his breath, then started over. He looked like he was playing with a toy, the tiny electronic device nearly disappearing in his giant hand. He pulled his own phone out of his pocket and typed something. "That's my number." He returned her phone. "I'll let you know when I'm out here working, and you can come write if you want. But only when I'm here."

She stared down at the number displayed on the screen. She tapped add to contacts and entered "Squatch."

"Got it?"

Hope nodded. Part of her wanted to assert her independence, but mostly she liked the idea of him being around. "Is there anything I can do to help?"

He sighed as he rose from the bench. "No. Just ignore my language while I'm rewiring the container."

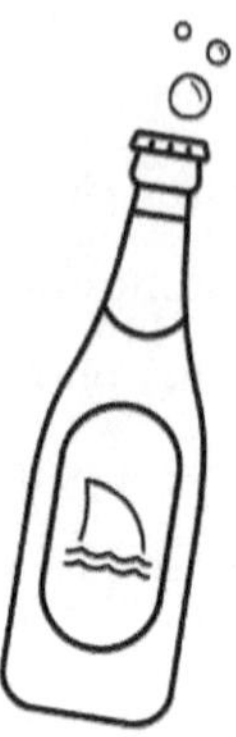

Chapter Eleven

It was well past lunchtime when Sharkey finally threaded the last wire through the plastic sleeve. He was sweaty, hungry, and seriously annoyed. After the less-than-helpful sheriff left early this morning, he'd tossed and turned until after the sun came up. Two hours of sleep made him a grumpy dude. He regretted taking it out on Hope.

Actually, he'd been happy to see her sitting there, pen racing across the pages. He could tell she was writing instead of drawing, so he almost hated to interrupt her. But when he thought about those miscreants coming back—and potentially hurting her—he lost it.

Peeking out the window of the container, he found Hope in the same spot, furiously writing in that purple sparkly notebook. She'd been there for hours, and all he'd seen her eat was a banana. No wonder she was so tiny, if that's all she ate.

His own stomach chose that moment to growl, because the protein shake he'd had earlier was wearing off. Picturing the contents of his pocket-sized fridge in his mind, he realized he had nothing to offer her. Most days, he picked up something at one of the local spots, not having the energy or space to cook inside his camper.

He wasn't leaving her here alone, but if he asked her to lunch, would she think it was a date? Sharkey didn't date. Sure, he occasionally hooked up with a woman, but he didn't wine and dine. He never wanted anyone to get the wrong idea about what he could offer. Especially not this woman, who looked fragile enough to break if he so much as looked at her wrong.

He was standing there deliberating when she jumped up from the table, slapping her journal closed and stuffing her phone in one of her many pockets. "I'm late! See you later."

Before he could react, she was dashing off into the woods, leaving Sharkey rather unsettled. He'd been seconds away from asking her to lunch. And now he was alone. Abandoned. Rejected.

You can't feel rejected when you never even asked the question, dumbass. He was still berating himself when he stepped out of the container and noticed a piece of trash on the ground. Near the table Hope had just vacated lay a piece of crumpled paper. He bent to retrieve it and started to toss it into the trash bag with his construction debris, but something stopped him. Looking back toward the woods, he made sure he was alone before he spread the paper open, smoothing out the wrinkles.

If you give ten cans of vegetables to the food pantry, but then steal twenty boxes of macaroni, does it negate all the good those vegetables will do? I was there. I saw the good with my own eyes. The people we fed, the medicine we delivered, the homes we built. Does that count for anything now?

This is what she threw away? He'd expected to see one of her doodles, and while there was a small sketch of a bird, the words he read sucker punched him. And he wanted to know more.

After one last look at the spot where Hope disappeared between the live oaks, he grabbed his bag of trash, the paper she'd left behind, and his drill. Inside his camper, he set the drill battery on the charger, added his bathroom trash to the bag, and carefully placed Hope's writing in the top drawer of his small dresser.

A glint of glitter caught his eye from under a stack of boxer briefs. *Not now.* He shoved the pile of underwear over, covering up the sparkle trying to escape its hiding place. He'd never thought this drawer would share space with another woman.

He was too damn hungry to consider the implications.

He changed clothes, grabbed an apple, and jumped in his truck. First food. Then he had a lead to track down. If the sheriff's department wasn't going to take this matter seriously, he'd just figure it out on his own.

As he drove toward town, he couldn't help but wonder if Tink was eating something for lunch. It'd been a long time since he worried about anyone besides himself, and certainly not a woman. Thinking about what she'd written, he realized Hope was a hell of a lot more than she seemed on the surface.

As a man who rarely revealed anything personal to anyone, he recognized the signs of deep trauma. And being really good at hiding it.

***

After inhaling a reuben from The Spicy Mermaid, Sharkey headed across the street to Manny's Bait & News. Their newspapers might be a week old, but Manny and his cronies always had their ears to the ground.

"Sharkey!"

The shouts rang out like he was Norm from *Cheers* entering the bar.

He tipped an imaginary hat at the group of older men who spent their days shooting the breeze. The inside of the store was part convenience store/part newsstand/part bait and tackle. The sales counter extended the length of the building, with bar stools pulled up at one end—each belonging to the regulars who came daily to scratch off lotto tickets, drink bad coffee, and tell tall tales to anyone willing to listen.

Sharkey had never seen anyone else sitting on one of the stools. It was an unspoken rule that those seats were always reserved—even if the men were outside in their folding chairs on a sunny day.

Dickie mimed cracking open a beer. "When is your place going to be ready, Shark Bite? We're thinking about moving this dog and pony show to somewhere a little classier."

Manny narrowed his eyes at his friend. "Well, Dick, if you don't like my digs, take your stool and go on home to Carol. We can manage just fine with four."

The other men watched quietly from their stools like they were at a Wimbledon match.

"Don't get your knickers in a wad, Manny. We'll still buy your scratchers. I'd just rather drink Sharkey's beer than this slop you call coffee."

"Beggars shouldn't be choosers. Where else are you going to find a cup of joe for a buck? You want some half pump hazelnut, skim almond milk latte, head on down to The Coastal. But you'll have to take a second mortgage out on your house."

Sharkey was enjoying the show as much as the other fellas, but he needed to get back to work before the sun went down, and it was well known that these two could drag out an argument for days. "The brewery should be open by the beginning of February. If I can keep the troublemakers away."

That got everyone's attention.

"Is someone giving you grief, Sharkey?" Irwin leaned forward, a concerned look on his face.

Ralph stood up, sticking out his barrel chest. "You need some help with security?" He'd been a damn fine football player in his time, and a solid coach after that, but he had to use a cane these days.

"I appreciate the offer, Ralph, but I'm installing some cameras, so I think it'll be fine. Just let me know if you guys hear anything. I'm having trouble imagining who would want to sabotage my business."

"Everyone loves your brews. No way it's an Eastporter doing you harm." Earl swiped his nose with a bandana from his pocket. The thing was threadbare and likely as old as he was.

The other men nodded in agreement.

Manny stroked his chin. "You know, I had someone stop in here last week asking for directions. He was a little cagey about exactly where, but he mentioned River Road."

"I remember him, stuffed shirt with a fancy tie. I bet my left nut he was looking at that property for sale across from Heron House." It wasn't the first time Irwin had bet his genitalia on something.

Earl piped up again. "You can't trust those corporate types. He's probably gonna build some big housing complex and ruin Eastport Beach."

The men started debating the merits of Earl's theory. Sharkey listened for a few minutes, but then he got an idea. If someone was looking to build on that land, they might not like the idea of a brewery right across the street. Since there was only one realtor in Eastport Beach, he knew just who to ask.

After a few attempts to break into the conversation and thank them, Sharkey gave up and left with a wave. He'd have to buy a round of scratch offs next time.

Chapter Twelve

Hope had never seen so many options. Rows of stores ran in various directions, like the spokes of a wheel. "We only had one clothing store in my village. I don't know where to start."

Riley's eyes widened, matching the round "O" her mouth formed. "One place to shop?"

She shrugged. She'd never been concerned about what to wear, but she knew things were different in the states. "I just need some basics."

"We'll start with the Gap Outlet and spread out from there." She grabbed Hope's arm and dragged her toward one end of the outlet mall.

They passed a bookstore, a candle store, a fudge shop, and a place that only sold hot sauce. "There's an entire store for hot sauce?"

"Crazy, huh? Wait until you see the Beef Jerky Outlet. Speaking of which, I promised Chesnee I'd stop at for him." She chuckled. "Dill pickle beef jerky. Can you imagine?"

Hope had never been to Myrtle Beach, or any American beach, for that matter. She hadn't seen the ocean yet, as they were currently traversing what must be the largest outlet mall anywhere. "Do people come here because this mall is so big?" Maybe it was a bigger tourist attraction than the actual beach.

Riley quirked an eyebrow at her. "Yeah, I guess if you're used to one store, this seems like overkill. But this isn't a particularly big outlet mall. Most people come to Myrtle for the beach, golf or buffets."

"Buffets?"

"Yeah, all you can eat crab legs, shrimp, steak—anything you could want for the low, low bargain of $49.95 per person."

Yet another thing she would never understand about Americans. Eating enough in one meal to feed an entire family for a week in Uganda. "I'm not sure I'll ever get used to living in the States. Everything is so over the top."

Riley laughed. "Honey, don't judge the whole country based on Myrtle Beach. Over the top doesn't even begin to describe it. It's like Vegas with water." She hooked her arm in Hope's. "I promise we'll get back to Eastport Beach as soon as possible. Quiet, cozy and a little crazy in an endearing way."

"Okay." Hope didn't know what to think, but she needed to replace most of her wardrobe, and she was relying on Riley to be her guide.

The women pushed through the doors of the Gap Outlet and Hope didn't feel any less overwhelmed. A row of a dozen mannequins greeted them—all decked out in revealing swim wear.

"It is still winter here, right?" Hope asked, rubbing her arms.

"I haven't figured the Eastport winter out yet. Some days it's forty. Some days it's seventy-five. I'm just glad there's no snow." Riley fingered a gauzy blue coverup. "We'll get you some jeans and some shorts, just to cover the bases."

Hope hadn't worn shorts since before they moved to Africa. She'd gotten used to the convention to keep her legs covered with pants or long skirts. She wasn't sure she wanted to show off her bony, white legs.

Before she could respond, Riley started piling clothes in Hope's arms. "And leggings. Do they wear leggings in Uganda? I swear, leggings changed my life." She continued to ramble about crop tops and hoodies and boyfriend jeans.

The entire afternoon went by in a blur. By the time they walked to the parking lot, Hope couldn't even remember what was in the bags they carried, and she was worried about having enough money left to eat. Riley had even managed to talk her into a couple sets of matching underwear. Hope didn't see the point of having frilly undergarments when no one would ever see them, but she was a tad bit excited about the emerald-green lace bra and panties. They were exactly the same shade as Sharkey's eyes.

They had dinner at a seafood place on the way home in a small town called Calabash. It wasn't all you could eat, but the fried shrimp were very tasty, and Hope experienced her first key lime pie for dessert. The tartness, combined with the smooth, creamy consistency delighted her—and she'd never really been one to eat sour things.

All in all, she'd had a fun afternoon with Riley. She was easy to talk to and always rambling about something interesting. "Thank you so much for taking me shopping today," Hope said as they pulled down the long driveway leading to Heron House. "And dinner," she added belatedly. "I've never really done that before."

Riley gave her another shocked look. "Done what?'

Hope shrugged. "You know, like a girls' day out."

Her new friend giggled. "Honey, we just bought you some new jammies and underwear. If you want a girls' day out, say the word. There'll be pedicures, movies, and margaritas involved!"

Hope smiled, feeling warm inside. "That sounds fun, too." Maybe moving back to America wasn't so bad.

The car looped around the fountain, and Riley parked at the bottom of the porch steps. "Let's get your bags out and then I'll pull the car behind the house."

The screen door opened, and Ben rushed out, a huge grin on his face. "You ladies have a pleasant afternoon?" He ran down the steps, kissed Riley on the cheek, and grabbed all the bags before Hope could even react.

"Can you believe Hope has never had key lime pie before?"

It seemed like every day she was experiencing firsts. The pie definitely topped the list today.

"Did you like it, Hope?" Ben effortlessly ascended the stairs, his arms full of her packages.

"Very much. Are you sure I can't take some of those bags?" She trailed behind him as Riley jumped into the car to move it.

Once inside, he headed straight up the stairs and paused outside the door of her suite. "I'm fine."

She caught up with him and unlocked the door. "Just drop them on the bed. I'll sort through them. Riley has a couple in here."

"So, what did you think about Myrtle Beach?" Ben leaned casually against the doorframe after he deposited the bags on the bed.

Hope thought about it for a few minutes, while she sorted through the bags. "I had no idea there could be that many putt putt places in one town."

He laughed. "Yeah, it's kind of a ridiculous place. But it can be fun sometimes."

Riley poked her head in the door. "I told her we'd go back to play mini golf."

"I'd like to try to hit a ball through that giant shark skull." It reminded her of Sharkey's logo—that he had recently attached to the side of his new bar.

"Pirate ships, plane crashes, octopi—there are plenty of options." He wrapped his arm around his girlfriend's shoulders and whispered in her ear.

A blush crept up Riley's cheek. "I had a great time today, Hope." She grabbed her bags and gave her a quick hug. "See you tomorrow."

"Thanks. Night." Hope watched as the couple descended the stairs, holding hands and whispering to one another. Her chest tightened, so she rubbed her knuckles against it. Probably just the fried seafood she ate for dinner. Definitely not a pang of jealousy.

The house was quiet as she sorted through the clothes she'd purchased at the outlet mall. It was probably more than she needed, but she was a little excited to wear the short sundresses and capris when it got warmer.

Her phone chimed with a text.

Squatch

> Did you get home safely?

Hope's brow furrowed. She'd left his place many hours ago.

Hope

> Yes, but how did you know I was gone?

Squatch

> Had a beer with Ben. He said Riley took you shopping. Hopefully she fed you too.

Was Sharkey worried about her? *Huh.*

Hope

> Fried shrimp. And key lime pie.

Squatch

> Best dessert on the planet.

Hope

> My first time, it was delicious.

Little bubbles appeared on the screen. Hope thought that meant he was writing her back, but then they disappeared, and no text came through. She stared at the screen for a few minutes, then felt silly, so she went back to unpacking her bags and putting away her new clothes.

She got ready for bed, dressing in her new pajamas with surfing dogs on them. The design made her giggle, and Riley had assured her that they weren't just for kids. She'd just snuggled under the covers when her phone chimed again.

Squatch

See you tomorrow.

Well, that was weird. But she assumed it meant she was free to come write in the morning.

Hope

Good night.

Chapter Thirteen

Sharkey woke up kicking himself. His reaction to Hope's text about her first time was sinful. And it was just damn pie. Why the fuck had he texted her at all?

Because he'd spent the afternoon before obsessing over whether or not she'd eaten lunch.

After he'd checked on his beer and spent another hour scrubbing graffiti, he ambled over to Heron House with a growler of his winterberry cider. When he arrived, there were several very fit senior citizens in the parlor debating the merits of parkour versus power blocking. As interesting as that conversation seemed, he continued down the hall to the kitchen, where he found Ben strangling a chicken.

"Is this a bad time?" Sharkey held up the brew with an eyebrow raised toward the helpless poultry.

Ben chuckled. "It's never a bad time when you bring delicious refreshment." He nodded toward the kitchen table.

He knew from countless visits with Archie, the home's former owner, that these chairs were sturdy enough for his bulk, so he grabbed a couple pint glasses from the pantry and sat down. "What did that chicken do to you?"

"Murrays got a couple in from a local farm, so I thought I'd try one. But I'm used to my easy, deboned, skinned breasts. By the time I finish prepping it, I could have cooked a twenty-pound turkey."

Sharkey glanced around the room, trying to seem casual. "Riley around?"

Ben shook his head, then jumped back as the raw chicken spewed juice at him. "She took Hope to Myrtle to shop. Apparently, the airline lost her luggage."

That explained her repetitive outfit of denim overalls. "So, just you and the old folks tonight?"

Wiping his hands on a paper towel, Ben leaned closer to the table. "Those people are nuts. I heard them talking about holding up a liquor store in the Bahamas last year. I sent out a few texts warning the businesses on Main Street."

"As an officer of the court, don't you have a duty to report a crime?"

"Not in the Bahamas. I'm just glad they're checking out tomorrow. They're going on our 'never again' wall."

Sharkey poked his head around the doorframe to check the hall. All clear. "There's a wall?"

"Yeah, Archie started it back in the 80s when Andy Warhol pissed in the hall closet."

He chuckled. "Anyone else famous on Archie's shit list?"

Ben slid a knife into the chicken, expertly skinning it, despite his assertions. "Annie Leibovitz was up there for a while after she tried to jump off the second-floor balcony, but Archie said she 'made it up to him' and took her off." He lifted one hand off the chicken long enough to make air quotes.

"Man, Archie had quite the life, didn't he?" Sharkey had always respected the man who lived by himself but was never alone. He didn't care what anyone thought of him, and he never judged the people who came to stay at Heron House.

"Yeah, he did. I wish Riley could have known him. The way she treats her guests reminds me so much of her uncle. They cease to be a stranger once they walk through that door."

"Are she and Hope getting close?"

Ben shot him a knowing glance. "I think she's warming up. Riley can be persistent."

"Don't I know it," Sharkey grumbled as he poured them each a drink. "This is something new for winter." He rose and slid the glass across the counter to his friend.

After washing his hands, Ben took a long drink of the smooth cider. "Excellent change of subject." He tipped the glass in the brewmaster's direction before drinking again. "Very refreshing. Crisp."

"It should pair well with chicken." Sharkey took his own swig. "If you ever get it cooked."

"I didn't realize I'd have audience. But I will conquer this slimy beast." He raised his glass in a cheers gesture and then downed it. "Are you just going to watch me choke my chicken, or can you peel a couple potatoes?"

Sharkey laughed. Ben was not your typical strait-laced lawyer, and he was one of the best people he knew. "I was on mess duty more times than I can count. Where's a peeler?"

Ben got him set up with a peeler, a trashcan, and a pile of potatoes that would feed an entire unit.

"Are you feeding the senior delinquents?" He gestured toward the parlor.

"No, but I'm making extra in case the chicken is inedible. Figured I'd take advantage while you're here priming me for information about our reserved houseguest."

Busted.

Now, in the light of a new day, Sharkey worried about how Hope would interpret last night's texts. He expected she'd show up at some point to write, but would she read too much into his words? Hell, he didn't even know what it meant. He just knew the tiny woman had worked her way under his skin like a chigger and he was determined not to let her stay there.

After mixing up a quick smoothie, he threw on a hoodie, laced up his sneakers, and headed over to the production building at the back of the property. He'd built this structure first and moved his equipment from the warehouse he rented near Bluffton almost three months ago. Production had taken a hit for a couple weeks until he was up and running again, and his lager was only about halfway through its process. The quicker ales and ciders had come back online almost immediately.

Just as he raised his hand to type in the security code, he noticed scratches on the door frame near the lock. A slew of select obscenities flowed from his lips and he chucked his half-drunken smoothie across the grass in frustration. His Irish grandfather would be proud of the sheer variety of curse words. Da had the dirtiest vocabulary of anyone Sharkey had ever met. And he also appreciated a fine Irish Ale.

After calling his security company, he learned that no one had made entry. The alarm hadn't been tripped at all.

Grumbling, he called the sheriff again. If he hoped to hold these people accountable, he had to follow the letter of the law, even if it felt like the department didn't take the pattern of destruction seriously. So far, they had only targeted the current building site—where the tasting area would be—because it was an easy mark since a security system hadn't been installed yet. But if they managed to break into his main production facility...he didn't even want to consider the damage that could be done.

Not trusting Barney Fife to do his job, Sharkey took pictures from several angles and studied the tool marks. This wasn't a criminal mastermind, that was for sure. But even a bumbling fool could wreak havoc if they got inside the building.

It'd only take the twist of a couple dials, or introducing extra oxygen into a brew at the wrong stage, and months of work would be down the drain.

He was going to have to ramp up security until these pricks were caught. It wasn't something he'd budgeted when he bought Riley's land and planned for the new brewery. Eastport Beach was hardly a big city, and typically crime was limited to Edna Windsor cheating at bingo or a little public nudity by Captain Percy. Never in a million years would he have imagined this kind of campaign against Shark Bite Brewing Company.

Eastporters had been happily drinking his beer for almost a decade. He couldn't figure out why having a permanent location would upset anyone. But someone was clearly out to destroy his livelihood.

A car pulled into the drive, and he was relieved to see it wasn't Sheriff Morgan. Instead, a woman stepped out of the patrol car, her hair pulled back in a tight bun at the base of her neck and the buttons on her shirt straining a bit. Her posture, gait, and well-built physique screamed military. He'd never seen her before.

She checked her notepad as she strode in his direction. "Mr. McLaughlin?"

He held out his hand. "That's my father. I'm Sharkey."

"Deputy Klein." She shook his hand firmly, then made a note on her pad. "Dispatch said you had a possible break-in?"

"I don't think they were successful at getting inside, but I didn't touch anything."

She assessed the scene and took a few pictures with her phone. "Did the alarm activate?"

"No."

"What do you do here, Sharkey?"

"I make beer."

Her lips curved up slightly and she nodded. "You got any ideas why someone would want to break in?"

"No, but I've had a series of incidents lately—mostly over at the tasting area I'm currently building." He gestured over his shoulder. "It's on the other side of my camper."

"Have you reported those incidents?"

"Yes, multiple times. To Sheriff Morgan himself."

Her face remained impassive, but something flashed briefly through her eyes. Intelligence, for one thing.

Maybe he wasn't completely on his own. "How long have you been with the department?"

"Just transferred from New Hanover County. I inherited some property down here a couple months back."

"Well, it's great to have you."

That hint of a smile returned. "Give me a few minutes." Back at her car, she slid into the front seat, grabbing her radio. She mostly listened, her expression revealing a hint of frustration. She scribbled more notes on her pad, then got out, slamming the door behind her. "Does your security company register failed attempts?"

"Yeah. But they said no one had activated the keypad since I was in here yesterday."

She nodded at the keypad and pulled on a pair of disposable gloves. "Go ahead and type in the code. I'll open the door. Please stay back." She was on the tall side for a woman and plenty fit, plus she had both a gun and a taser.

Sharkey tapped in the code and stepped back, confident in her ability to do her job. More confident than he'd ever felt about Dirk Morgan.

After a few minutes, she called him inside. "Anything look out of place?"

The building was quiet—all gleaming metal and clean surfaces. He let out his breath, silently thanking God no one had made it inside. "No, everything looks normal."

After checking his office and the lab, the two of them sat down at a small conference table. Deputy Klein took out her pen and notepad again and faced him. "Tell me about these other incidents."

Chapter Fourteen

Hope slept well after her busy day, but she woke up with a sense that her dreams were intense. She couldn't remember what she'd dreamed, but she felt...good. Happy.

Yesterday had been productive—she'd nearly filled her journal and today she was ready to try to transcribe some of it to the computer. She was probably the only twenty-two-year-old on the planet that didn't feel comfortable using a computer every day. They'd had a desktop back in Uganda, but she'd only used it occasionally to chat with her cousin under strict supervision from her mother. Surfing the Internet was not allowed.

Having endless information at her fingertips was still wild to Hope. There was so much she wanted to explore, but she got overwhelmed easily.

She got dressed in a pair of leggings and the new boots Riley had talked her into. The pants were tighter than she was used to, but once she slipped on the baggy green sweater, she felt more comfortable. She'd been amazed to find there was a whole section in the store for short people and thrilled to find clothes that didn't hang off her. Normally, she had to roll up her sleeves and pant legs.

Standing in the full-length mirror, she was delighted to find that she looke d...cute. Put together. Except for her hair. It just hung there, straight as an arrow. Boring. Not like she could do anything about it right now. It wasn't long enough to pull up, and she didn't have any accessories or the knowledge of how to use them. She shrugged. At least the clothes were a step up. One thing at a time.

Grabbing a bag, she stuffed her journal and laptop into it, then bounded down the stairs.

Riley was heading out the front door, but she ground to a halt when she saw Hope. "Girl! You look fantastic. I should have gotten some of those boots, too. They're so cute."

"I do love the clothes, but now my hair feels, I don't know, blah."

"I like your hair, but if you want me to drive to the salon, I'm happy to."

Hope shrugged. "I'll think about it." She didn't even know if a haircut would help. Her hair had always been straight and fine.

Riley gave her a quick hug. "Have a great day. I'm heading to the market for supplies."

She watched Riley skip down the porch steps, then headed for the kitchen. It was serve yourself for breakfast, and now that the wild seniors had left, she was the only guest in the house. Since she wasn't sure how long she'd be gone, she scrambled a couple eggs and slathered some wheat toast with homemade local jelly. With her parents gone all the time, she'd been cooking for herself since she could reach the stove.

The other purchase she'd made yesterday was a large water bottle, so she could stay out longer and not get dehydrated. When she got into a groove yesterday, she hadn't wanted to stop, for fear that the words would dry up. She was still learning how to be a writer and when the words were flowing, she needed to take advantage of it.

Her stomach full, she filled her water bottle with ice and water, stuck it in her bag, and headed toward Sharkey's. It was a sunny day with a light breeze, and her lightweight sweater was perfect for the temperature. The only issue was that it kept slipping off one shoulder. After pulling it back up several times, she gave up. Sharkey was a grown man. He'd probably seen a bare shoulder before, and maybe even a bra strap.

Hope wasn't used to wearing loose clothing for fashion's sake, but Riley had assured her it was the trend to wear loose tops over tight leggings. She had to admit it was comfortable.

When she got to the picnic tables, Sharkey wasn't around, so she set up her workstation and poked her head around the container to look for him. It was well after eight, so she was surprised he wasn't working. His truck was pulled next to his camper and a knock on the camper door went unanswered.

Maybe she'd misunderstood his text, because yesterday he'd insisted she not be there alone. They hadn't made definitive plans, like a time, but it was later than most days she'd come over to write. She pulled out her phone to send him a quick text but then heard a car door shut somewhere on the other side of the camper.

She rounded his truck and saw a large metal building that she'd never noticed before. Sharkey was outside speaking to a woman in uniform. They were in front of a sheriff's car, engaged in a conversation. Had something else happened? She knew he was concerned about people up to no good, but he hadn't really given her any details.

Hope started to approach the pair, but the deputy suddenly laughed and reached out to touch Sharkey's arm in a very familiar way. He was smiling—well, as much as Sharkey smiled—and his relaxed posture indicated everything was likely okay.

She didn't feel comfortable inserting herself into their conversation. What purpose did she even have there? *Hey, I'm interrupting you so I can sit at your table and scribble in my journal.* It seemed silly.

She backed away, but while her attention was on fixed on Sharkey, and the woman obviously flirting with him, she didn't see the tree root that sent her flailing. A shriek escaped before she could help it, and she ended up on her bottom once again.

She wasn't sure what was worse, her new leggings getting dirty, her first bout with the sin of jealousy, or the taser pointed at her.

"She's not a threat! She's just a kid." Sharkey threw himself in front of the weapon, bending low to get on her level. "Are you okay?"

Hope was physically fine, but her ego was black and blue, and if the sheriff's deputy didn't haul her off to jail, she was going to set Sharkey straight. She was no kid. "I'm fine."

Before she could protest, Squatch scooped her off the ground, checking her over for injuries. "You don't have enough padding to fall as much as you do." His eyes sparked with a little humor, some compassion, and something else Hope had never seen before. He handled her with such care, truly concerned for her well-being.

The deputy sheathed her weapon and stepped back to give them a little room. "I take it you know this woman."

"Yes, she's a guest at Heron House." He set her gently on her feet, hands held out like he thought she might collapse.

"Sharkey, I'm fine." But she had to admit she enjoyed the attention.

"I'm sorry. Heron House?" The deputy had a small notepad in her hands, likely recording Hope's embarrassment to share with the department.

Squatch gripped Hope's shoulder and bent to look her in the eye. "Go have a seat at the tables. I'll be there in a minute."

Whatever warm feelings she'd had evaporated. She might as well have been sent to her room. "I'm not a kid," she grumbled under her breath, but she doubted either of "the adults" heard her, because they had their heads bent together once more, likely discussing grown-up things.

On her way back to the picnic area, she kicked at a clump of dirt and nearly fell again. *No wonder he treats me like I'm a fragile doll.* She huffed, and her breath formed a little cloud of vapor. It was colder than she'd planned for, so she gathered her things and headed back to the house. Maybe she needed to stay seated today—indoors—before she hurt herself.

She was cursing her clumsiness when a large hand clamped down on her shoulder, halting her forward motion.

"I told you to wait at the picnic tables."

Hope froze, something foreign bubbling up in her chest. She'd been taught to respect her elders and never sass anyone. But, by gosh, she was an adult and so was he. Her hands flew to her hips, and she spun around to face the yeti. It felt like someone, or something, had possessed her. "I'm. Not. A. Kid!"

"Woah!" His hands went up in a defensive stance and he stepped backward. It was like Goliath had seen little David standing below him wielding a rock. "I just wanted to make sure you're okay. I wasn't trying to order you around."

"Well, that's how it came out!" She didn't know why she was still screaming, except her heart was racing and the palms of her hands felt like they were on fire. What were the signs of a heart attack?

He crouched down, like he was trying to make himself smaller. "Hope, I'm sorry. I shouldn't have said that. I was scared."

She took several deep breaths, her heart rate slowing marginally and the tightness in her chest lessening. This giant, intimidating man was scared? "Okay." She knew she should forgive him, but she wasn't ready yet. All her life, she'd been treated like a little kid. Even when she was basically raising herself. Being all alone in the world wouldn't be so scary if she was still in *her* world, but moving to the States might as well have been moving to another planet.

"Okay." His eyes pleaded with her. For what, she didn't know. There was so much she didn't know.

"I'll see you tomorrow." She had so many questions pinging around inside her mind. Did someone break into his brewery? Had they damaged anything?

Had someone tried to hurt him? Did he like that deputy? She was closer in age and height and likely worldliness. Was Hope misreading Sharkey completely? Was she just a silly, naive, little girl?

None of those answers mattered right now. She couldn't face him for another second. Her anger threatened to bubble to the surface again, yet, somehow, at the same time, she feared she'd burst into tears.

He made her feel...too much.

Chapter Fifteen

Sharkey watched Tink walk away, her posture sagging in defeat, her too-big sweater sliding off one shoulder. A thin bra strap on display, reminding him loudly that she was not a kid. Even louder than she reminded him.

It was a defense mechanism. He knew that. If she was a kid in his mind, he could convince himself that she was off-limits.

Because she should be off-limits.

His body knew Hope was a woman and calling her a kid was just his fruitless attempt to dial back his growing attraction to her.

But when that deputy pulled a weapon on her—time suspended, the world stopped turning. Everything adjusted into perfect focus. He'd protect her at any cost, whether from a taser, a punk, or a gun.

Tomorrow. His punishment was not seeing her. Not hanging out with her while she wrote, not making sure she had something to nourish her. He'd gone grocery shopping last night and stuffed the tiny kitchen in his camper with healthy food, so he had something to offer her.

Because of his stupid mouth, he wouldn't see her for twenty-four hours. He knew it'd feel like an eternity.

The attempted break-in had messed up his whole schedule—hell, his psyche. Sharkey had his life together. He had a successful business, never had trouble finding a casual date, enjoyed his alone time. He was content. But two forces had wreaked havoc on his peaceful existence.

Whoever was trying to kill Shark Bite.

And Hope Seaton.

He'd known her less than a week, but she had burrowed through his thick skin and settled in somewhere around his heart. A place strictly off-limits. A place reserved for only Eve.

He'd barely thought of her since the tiny blonde imp had shown up. A different woman haunted his dreams for the first time...ever. That was the main reason he was fighting it so hard. He wasn't ready to give Eve up. It'd been fifteen years since he'd seen her face and forgetting her would be the worst kind of betrayal.

His phone buzzed in his pocket, startling him out of his reverie. He was sitting on the soft earth, live oak trees soaring to the sky above him, Hope long gone.

"Yeah?" He squinted, certain he could just make out her figure near the corner of the house, when an egret took off, shattering his vision.

"Mr. McLaughlin, Deputy Klein here."

At first, he'd been hopeful a real law enforcement professional would finally take him seriously. He'd been impressed with her keen intelligence, her open mind, and her military background. But the moment she'd pulled a weapon on the sweetest, most innocent person on the planet, Deputy Klein had moved to Sharkey's shit list. "What?" He'd given her a piece of his mind about her actions once Hope was safely out of earshot, but he hadn't waited around for anything else, eager to check on the victim in all this.

"First, I want to apologize to the young lady for drawing my weapon on her, but I didn't get her name or where to find her. Second, I was hoping to send a crime scene tech over to dust for prints on that door."

"The county has a crime scene tech?"

"No, but I know a guy."

Okay, maybe she wasn't too bad. His rational side could understand instincts kicking in. "That would be great. I won't touch anything." He rose from the ground and dusted his pants off. "Heron House is the property right next to mine. It's basically an inn. Hope is staying there. And I wouldn't call her a young lady if I were you."

"Roger that."

He disconnected the call and deliberated the wisdom of giving Hope a heads up about the deputy possibly visiting her. In the end, he decided Deputy Klein was on her own.

Since he couldn't work in the production building until the door had been dusted for prints, he decided to finish removing the graffiti on the back of the container. Scrubbing it off would be a great stress reliever. Lord knew he wouldn't be getting another type of relief anytime soon.

***

Several hours later, he dropped onto a stool in the bar at The Landing. His back was killing him, he'd missed a critical window of time for his latest batch of specialty cider while waiting for the crime scene tech, and his container would have to be painted to cover the graffiti he couldn't get off.

Nic, the best bartender in Eastport Beach, raised an eyebrow from the end of the bar, and Sharkey gave him a quick nod. Within minutes, he had a pint of his

33rd Parallel IPA in front of him. There was nothing quite like a beer drawn from the tap. If he ever got the tasting area finished, he'd be able to replicate this himself whenever he wanted. After closing out another customer, Nic leaned on the bar in front of Sharkey. "You eating?"

"God, yes." With everything that had happened today, food had been way down the list of priorities, and by the time he finished, he couldn't bear the thought of cooking inside the sardine tin he called home. "Fish and chips. And fried pickles." He took another swig of his beer. "And mozzarella sticks."

Nic snickered as he typed the order into the system. "Rough day?"

"Nothing this won't fix." He drained his glass and then slammed the empty on the table. "Keep them coming." Sharkey rarely drank to excess, but he knew his limits, and between his size and the amount of fried food he'd just ordered, he'd be fine having a few beers.

The bartender leaned against the opposite counter, settling in. "I heard you've had some trouble at the site."

A waitress slid two baskets of sizzling goodness in front of him. Sharkey popped a pickle in his mouth before he answered Nic. "Yeah, what have you heard?" The two had become friendly when the restaurant started carrying Shark Bite, and he was second behind Manny for information about anything happening in Eastport Beach. So many locals treated him like their therapist, he should be charging a co-pay for visits.

Nic's casual posture changed, and he glanced around before leaning down to dunk dirty glasses in a bath, putting him closer to Sharkey. "You know Brightside up in Wilmington?" He kept his voice low and his head down like he was just washing dishes.

"Yeah." Brightside was one of the shiny new corporate breweries popping up all over the country. It'd opened about a year ago, and Sharkey had heard rumblings that it wasn't doing as well as the local places.

"I used to work with the GM back when he was a mere lackey like me. He's pretty rough around the edges. His brother did hard time, not sure exactly for what, but I wouldn't put it past Craig to color outside the lines to keep his cushy gig."

"That's an hour away." Surely, a small brewery in an even smaller town wasn't a threat to a mega-brewery with a budget to match.

The bartender shrugged. "How many places up there have Shark Bite on tap?"

Sharkey did a little mental math. "Shit. You really think he's trying to take me out?"

Nic plucked a fried pickle from the basket that had gone untouched since they'd started this conversation. "I'd watch my back if I were you."

The waitress reappeared, sliding a platter overflowing with French fries and breaded cod in front of a stunned Sharkey. "Can I get you anything else?"

For as hungry as he'd been, now his stomach churned at the sight of the artery-busting spread. "A box, thanks."

Chapter Sixteen

Anger had sustained Hope's brutal pace when she got back to Heron House. She'd transcribed everything from her notebooks into a Word document. If she really learned how to type, she could probably do it in half the time.

Riley had checked on her multiple times, but she was on a tear and barely acknowledged her hostess. If she started talking, she'd spill what happened. And then she'd lose the anger.

She wasn't interested in what lay beyond that.

Closing her computer, she realized she'd worked straight through lunch. She vaguely remembered Riley offering her something.

In the kitchen, she found egg salad on the top shelf of the fridge with a post it note that read "Eat me!" A loaf of bread lay conveniently on the counter. Hope fixed a quick sandwich, cut up an apple and poured a glass of Riley's amazing fresh-squeezed lemonade. She carried everything up to the third floor and eyed the lone chair in the library. Setting her lunch on the windowsill, she leaned down to select a new book from her favorite shelf.

She'd flown through all the ones Riley had pointed out, so now she grabbed a book with a different colored spine. The couple on the front was embracing, their lips just inches apart. The man had a dark beard. Hope felt that weird flutter in her stomach again. She briefly wondered if this story would go further than the hand holding and gentle kisses of the books she'd been reading.

She's just a kid. The words echoed through her mind, playing on repeat. Would she be able to unhear them?

Settling into the chair, she kicked off her boots, tucked her feet under her, opened the book and picked up her sandwich. She'd just drown them out.

An hour later, she looked up from the book, her breath coming in short bursts. Her body was on fire, the sweater suddenly too hot and the leggings melted into her skin. How did people read stuff like this? This couple was so desperate for each other, passionate kisses leading to caresses, then they were ripping their clothes off.

It was like she was there, like she was the one the bearded hero wanted, the one he desired. Heat raced through her body, and she wished she were in her room so she could strip down, possibly find relief from the fire ripping through her belly.

If reading about sex was this intense, how could she ever possibly handle the real thing? She was certain she'd combust.

What would it be like for a man to want her like that? To be so desperate to touch her?

It felt impossible. She'd never even been kissed.

Closing the book, she tried to compose herself, then gave up, abandoning her empty plate and glass, padding barefoot down the stairs to her room. As soon as her door closed, she stripped naked, but it wasn't enough. She was still burning inside and out.

She turned the shower on, letting the water run cold, then stepped under the stream. Her eyes drifted closed and she allowed herself to imagine how it would feel.

Her mother had told her it was a sin to touch herself. Turned out her mother was an expert on the subject of sin.

In Hope's mind, the bearded hero kissed along her bare shoulder, sending goosebumps down her arm, over her chest. She groaned—although she didn't know if it was in the fantasy or in real life. His hands danced over her stomach, then up to her breasts, stirring that feeling deep in her gut. Her nipples peaked and the man bent his head to take one in his mouth. The hair of his beard ticked her sensitive skin.

She fisted her hands in his hair, pressing him toward the other side, needing to repeat the sensation. Her moan turned to a giggle as he circled his tongue around her areola. His lips vibrated against her skin as he chuckled, and when he looked up at her it was Squatch.

Hope shrieked—most certainly in real life—and she jolted out of the spray of water, pressing her hands against the tile, drawing deep breaths into her lungs. Something had been building in her gut, tightening, like when she overcranked her music box.

If she hadn't snapped out of it, would she have broken like the tiny ballerina that never danced again?

Suddenly she was shivering, trembling like she'd never stop. She wrenched the water to hot, knowing that all she needed to warm up was to go back to the story in her mind. Jumping out of the shower, she wrapped her body in a towel before leaning back in to turn the water off. She sat on the edge of the tub and prayed until she had no more words.

***

Hope woke up, her bottom aching and a crease on her face from where it had rested against the wall. She'd fallen asleep on the floor of the bathroom, still in her towel, propped up in the corner. It was dark outside the window, so she'd been there a while.

She slowly rose, shaking her limbs out, trying to uncramp her muscles. The mirror over the sink revealed her hair had dried in limp strands around her face, which was red and puffy. Apparently, despite her best efforts, she'd still cried. The anger coursed back, so she yanked a brush through her hair and pulled a nightshirt on. No sense going downstairs to find dinner. She didn't want to see anyone anyway.

Grabbing a fresh notebook, she pulled back the covers and was just climbing into the big bed when she remembered the mess she'd left upstairs in the library. She didn't want to leave it overnight, or worse, make Riley clean up after her, so she wrenched open her door to run to the third floor.

Since the spirited seniors had checked out, she'd had the second floor to herself, so she was shocked to find a man in the hallway. He was average height and thin, with a ponytail and wire-rimmed glasses. His arms were full of books, and he was struggling to open the door to a room across the hall.

Part of her wanted to duck back into her room and hope he hadn't seen her—she was barely clothed, after all. But her upbringing, even by charlatans, had taught her to help others in need.

"Can I get that for you?"

The man started, the top book from his stack sliding to the floor. "I'm sorry. I didn't realize anyone would be awake."

It must be even later than she realized. She bent to retrieve the book, praying her shirt covered everything. "I didn't realize anyone else was staying here."

"Just got in a bit ago. Decided to unload the car after Ben and Riley went to bed. I didn't want to bother them." His gaze raked from her toes to the top of her head. "Did I wake you?"

Her skin heated from his perusal. She tugged her shirt down, then remembered he'd asked her a question. She wasn't sure what had awoken her, other than her awkward position on the floor. "No, I was just running up to the third floor."

The two stared at each other, awkwardness stretching between them. Finally, the weight of his load seemed to shake the man out of his stupor. "Yes, it would be helpful if you got the door."

He reminded her of a boy that had once visited their home in Uganda. He'd stayed for nearly a month, helping on the property and studying under her father. Carl, if she remembered correctly, was so painfully shy that he'd spoken maybe three words to her the entire time he was there. She wondered what happened to the young man who'd come to learn from a missionary who turned out to be a fraud.

"So, that's why I have so many books."

Too late, she realized he'd been talking to her while she'd dwelt on the past. She nodded, hopeful that was the appropriate response to whatever he said. "I love to read. Riley has a small library set up on the third floor. People who stay here leave books, so it's growing all the time."

He pushed his glasses up his nose, assessing her from behind the thick lenses. His eyes were the color of molasses. "Maybe you can show me sometime."

She flushed again and yanked the hem of her shirt even lower. "Sure, maybe tomorrow." Suddenly, she felt practically naked standing in front of this stranger. "Um, good night." She slid the book on top of his pile and hightailed it back to her room, holding her shirt over her bottom. Once safely inside, she leaned against the door, feeling completely flustered for the second time that day. Hope Seaton had just had a conversation with a man while not wearing underwear, she was pretty sure he'd flirted with her, and she hadn't even helped him get the door open.

***

Hope was sketching the view from the porch. She'd started a fresh notebook, and the blank page was daunting. An egret glided over the river, skimming the water.

"Wow, it's beautiful here." The screen door banged behind Aiden.

"Definitely." So much so that it was distracting.

He took the rocker next to her and leaned over to peek at her journal. "Are you an artist?"

She blushed. He was close enough she could smell his cologne, something woodsy but not overbearing. "No, I just doodle."

"Looks pretty good to me." He settled back in his chair and sipped from his mug.

"I'm supposed to be writing."

Aiden's face lit up. "What do you write?"

At this point, any words would do. "It's a memoir, but I'm starting to wonder if anyone will even want to read about my life."

"I'm sure you've just got imposter syndrome."

"What's that?" Sounds like what her parents were doing.

"It's basically doubting yourself—thinking someone would do it better than you."

There was probably a bit of truth to that. "My agent sends me encouraging texts, but I think she's just trying to keep me on schedule." The schedule didn't include time for doodling.

"Wow. So, it's a project you've already sold? That's impressive."

"It'll only be impressive if I actually get it done in time."

He stopped rocking and turned toward her. "What do you think is holding you up?"

Painful memories. Fear. Feeling like an idiot who didn't see what was right in front of her. "It's about my family and the way I was brought up. I'm worried how it will be received." Particularly by her parents. Hopefully they don't have books in prison.

"I had an article published in a trade journal once, but only about a hundred people in the world would even understand what I was talking about. I'm sure your book will have a broader appeal."

"My publisher thinks so. I just keep telling myself they know what they're doing, even if I don't."

Aiden chuckled. "I'm guessing most of this is in your head. I'm sure it will come out the way it's supposed to, and it will be a huge success. I'll be able to say I knew you when."

He was almost convincing enough that Hope believed it. "I don't know about all that, but hopefully it will mean something to people who read it." Writing it was cathartic for sure. Maybe her story will help someone else find a little hope in their hard times.

"I know it will." He rose from the chair. "I'm going to set up at the dining room table. I'd love it if you joined me. We'll do writing sprints. It always helps me focus."

"Sprints? I don't think I can run and write at the same time."

Laughing, Aiden threw his head back. When his eyes crinkled up like that, he was quite handsome. "No running, I promise. We'll set a timer and write as many words as we can. Like a little race for motivation."

She was learning new stuff every day. "Oh, that sounds great." Maybe it would keep her from drawing instead of writing.

He held the door open for her and as she ducked under his arm, she felt a little tingle down her arm as it brushed against him. What a nice man. And he hadn't called her a kid even once.

Chapter Seventeen

It'd been two days. Two days without seeing Tink. Not tomorrow (which was now yesterday). And with the sun setting in the sky, apparently not today either. Sharkey was ready to crawl out of his skin.

Occasionally, he'd anticipate a new concoction. Rarely, he'd look forward to an event that might elevate his brand. Never had he lost his mind over not seeing a woman for forty-eight hours.

He'd typed a dozen lame texts, deleting them immediately. He'd skipped appointments so he wouldn't miss her. He painted three coats on the container when two would have done, because he'd see her from there.

But she didn't show. She didn't text. She didn't yell at him for calling her a kid. Hell, he'd take anything at this point.

He'd been reduced to one of those weak, desperate men. And he'd barely touched her.

Before he knew what he was doing, he was halfway to Heron House. His long strides ate up the distance quickly, giving him zero time to come up with a viable excuse for popping in. He considered texting Ben for an audible, but that seemed even more pathetic.

As he neared the house, he heard voices, so he slowed his pace and hugged the side of the building, eavesdropping, like the spineless simp he'd apparently become.

It was definitely Hope, but the guy she was talking to wasn't Ben, and as far as Sharkey knew, there were no other guests staying at the house. His first thought was that Chesnee's single-woman radar had honed in on a new target, but he knew that fool's voice, and he seriously doubted he'd ever read the Canterbury Tales.

Not that Sharkey could talk—literary genius he wasn't—although he enjoyed a good thriller occasionally.

But this conversation would bore his high school English teacher, and that woman was obsessed with Dickens. So, there was obviously nothing to worry about. Hope hadn't missed two days of visiting with him for this nerd.

Except...their voices were awfully close. Like they were sitting on the porch swing close. Porch swings were notoriously romantic, right? He didn't know much about that shit, but he'd seen Riley and Ben out there a million times holding hands and making goo-goo eyes.

Book Boy better not be holding Hope's hand.

Fire rose up Sharkey's chest. It became hard to catch his breath. This was so bad.

After a few more minutes of mindless drivel about stanzas and verse—this was all from *him*, Hope wouldn't talk about something so pedantic—he felt like he would combust. Jogging toward the riverbank, he vacillated between jumping into the river to put himself out or running to the front of the house with a fake emergency.

He settled somewhere in between.

Pulling out his phone, he sent a quick text to Ben.

Sharkey

Stumpy headed your direction. Just in case you and Riley are on the porch.

He berated himself all the way back to his hiding place beside the house.

The storm door creaked open. "Hey guys, apparently our reptilian neighbor is heading this way, so you might want to come inside."

Sharkey's triumph over footsteps flying into the house was short-lived. At least on the porch, Hope would have been worried about impropriety. Inside could mean a bedroom. Privacy. The house was mostly empty. Plenty of opportunity for a sleazy academic to take advantage of a sweet, innocent girl.

Fuck. He was so screwed.

Without thinking, he rounded the corner of the house and flew up the stairs. He was inside the foyer before he could talk himself out of it. His jeans were ripped—not in the on-purpose way—and his sweatshirt splattered with paint. He raked a hand over his face and cursed under his breath. He hadn't trimmed his beard in days.

Riley spotted him first. She jumped up from one of the sofas in the parlor. "Sharkey, hey! Is it Stumpy? Is he hurt again?"

"Uh." *Think, fucker.* "No, I just wanted to make sure Ben got my text."

At this point, everyone in the room shared the same dumbfounded expression. Everyone included Ben, Riley, Hope and a little skinny shit with a ponytail and glasses. Exactly how he pictured Book Boy.

"My signal's been so bad lately, I couldn't tell if it went through." He mentally slapped his palm against his forehead.

"Yeah, I got it." Ben stared at him like he was on the witness stand, and the attorney planned to destroy him. "Why don't you join us, since you're here?"

The way the furniture was arranged, he could sit on one of the velvet couches, which each currently housed two people, or he could sit in an upholstered chair that was facing the fireplace and not in the "conversation area."

He made a beeline for the sofa where Hope sat mere inches from Book Boy. And wedged his massive frame in between them.

The couch was old, maybe even Victorian, so it wasn't built for three modern adults—especially when one of them shopped at the big and tall store. Hope's delicate frame was plastered to his side, and he immediately saw the error of his tactic. Adjusting his jeans, he turned to the other side and thrust his hand at the trembling geek next to him. "I'm Sharkey. Nice to meet you." He gritted the words out, his teeth grinding together painfully.

Book Boy gulped, his Adam's apple too big for his scrawny neck, making it look like a small animal had burrowed in there. "Aiden." He shook Sharkey's hand—his handshake damp and limp.

This guy was not good enough for Hope.

Sharkey wasn't deluded enough to think he was, but he'd move heaven and earth to keep this creep away from her. "What brings you to Eastport Beach, Allen?"

He didn't bother to correct the bigger man, obviously too much of a weenie to defend himself—even more proof of his inadequacies. "I'm working on my thesis. The apartment complex near Duke is just too noisy."

The little shit was going to use writing as a way to connect with Hope. Hell, maybe he already had. It'd been two days since she'd stormed away from him. "Well, don't let us keep you from it."

Nervous laughter rippled out of the scared little boy. "I'm taking a quick break."

Sharkey felt a small hand on his arm, squeezing his bicep. It's possible he flexed a little before turning toward Hope. "Yes, darlin'?"

She narrowed her eyes at him and leaned close, whispering so only he could hear. "Don't be a bully, and don't call me darlin'." Her grip on his arm released, and he missed the heat from her hand.

Okay, so she's still mad. And my current behavior probably isn't helping. But he couldn't just give up. Let this scrawny little grad student have his way with her. He needed to deflect. "Riley, Ben, are you going line dancing tomorrow?"

The hostess clapped her hands together in glee. "I'd forgotten all about it. Hope, Aiden, you should definitely go. Our friends Trip and Ada have a dance studio downtown, and they give free lessons weekly. Sharkey's really picked it up. I, on the other hand, tend to trip over my own feet. But it's a lot of fun!"

"You dance?" Book Boy had the nerve to croak out the question.

Sharkey tipped his head. "I do. I guess I'm just naturally agile. Too bad you'll be busy writing your little paper."

The ponytail bristled, his neck turning a concerning shade of red. "I'd hardly call a doctoral thesis a little paper."

Sharkey shrugged. "If you say so. Too bad you'll be writing your long, boring paper." He turned to Hope to ask her to go with him, but the withering look on her face indicated that now might not be the best time. He just had to keep her away from Book Boy long enough for her to realize he was a pompous blowhard. It seemed obvious to him, but Hope wasn't attuned to the ways of the world. Especially here in America where these professional academics were a dime a dozen and never actually contributed to society. Then inspiration stuck. "Actually, Riley, I was hoping you'd have a room for me. My heater in the camper gave out, and it's getting pretty chilly at night."

Ben narrowed his eyes, likely remembering that Sharkey was basically an oven at night, and he never used a heater. But like a good friend, he kept quiet.

"Of course. It's just Hope and Aiden, so you can have your pick of the remaining rooms. Did you bring a bag?"

He could feel Hope practically vibrating beside him, so he hopped up and headed for the door. "No, I wanted to make sure you had room first. I'll run over there now and drive back." Without waiting for a response, he threw open the storm door and skipped most of the steps going down.

"Hold on a minute, buster."

Buster? He almost laughed, but Hope was actually speaking to him, so he didn't want to push his luck. Turning around, he found her at the top of the porch stairs, hands on hips, a scowl on her pretty face. He bit his lip to keep from cracking a smile.

They were almost eye-level at this point, and if there weren't five steps between them, he could kiss her. He hadn't realized until this moment how much he wanted to kiss her. Had she ever been kissed before? "If you're going to continue to be rude to Aiden, you can just go back to your trailer and freeze your hiney off."

Why did hiney almost sound sexual coming from her? Because he was a horny bastard, that's why. This idea was getting worse by the minute. "I didn't realize I was being rude."

She rolled her eyes and huffed.

Sharkey burst out laughing. Which just made her more indignant.

"Are you laughing at me?" She crossed her arms over her chest, her bottom lip puffed out slightly.

He would take that lip between his teeth and... *Pull it together, man.* "Is that the first time you've ever rolled your eyes?"

Her nose scrunched up and she bit that lucky lip. "So, what if it is?"

God help him. Another of Hope's firsts. He was ready to be her first everything. Sharkey moved closer to the steps, stepping onto the bottom thread, setting them face to face in the fading light. He dropped his voice. "If my staying here makes you uncomfortable, I won't."

She popped her lip back out. "I don't care where you sleep."

Little Sharkey rose to attention. He couldn't resist it anymore. He couldn't resist her. His hand stretched toward her mouth, like a starved man reaching for a steak. His fingers grazed the soft skin of her bottom lip. He leaned further into her orbit. "Have you ever been properly kissed, Hope?"

Her chest rose and fell rapidly, her eyes growing round and full. She shook her head ever so slightly. Subtle enough, he wondered if he'd imagined it.

It took every ounce of resolve to keep from grabbing her, wrapping her legs around his waist, and stealing her away. He pulled his hand back, bringing his fingers to his lips, tasting her for the first time.

Her gasp was audible, and her hand flew up to cover her mouth.

"Tell Riley I won't be getting cold tonight." Then he turned and walked away from the woman that would be the end of his content, solitary life.

Chapter Eighteen

Her legs supported her just long enough for her to save face. As soon as Squatch rounded the side of the house, Hope crumpled onto the top step.

She couldn't tell him she'd never been kissed, period. Couldn't tell him how her heart raced from just a simple touch. She couldn't tell him how he made her feel.

Because she didn't understand it herself.

"Hope? Are you okay?" Aiden poked his head out the door, looking both directions before stepping onto the porch. "Who was that guy?"

She pressed her fingers to her mouth, trying to seal the sensation in, remember how it felt. Was it pathetic? To react so strongly to the mere suggestion that he might kiss her? She couldn't think of anything she wanted more. And that terrified her.

"Did he hurt you?" Aiden slipped past her to descend the steps, then turned to face her, ironically standing exactly where the yeti had. He didn't have nearly the same presence. "Hope?"

Shaking her head, she struggled to speak, to act like she wasn't affected. Not only had her parents betrayed her, but now her body had as well. She didn't understand all these new feelings. Yearnings. "I'm fine." She also didn't routinely lie.

The storm door opened behind her. "Is Sharkey back yet?" Riley asked, like the universe wasn't collapsing in on itself.

Hope swallowed, willing her voice to sound normal. "He said he wouldn't be back tonight." At least that's what she thought he meant. To be honest, she didn't understand anything that had happened in the last hour. It was almost like Sharkey was jealous. Of Aiden? She hadn't been back to the brewery since "the kid" incident, so how did he even know Aiden existed?

"Okay, well, good night, then." The door closed again, and Hope was alone with Aiden, and the lingering sensation of a confusing encounter with the yeti next door.

"I'm going to stay up late and write. Will you join me?"

One time, a carnival had set up in a city close to their home and Hope had gone into town with a group of kids from church. They had maybe five rides, and one was a tiny rollercoaster that went up and down around a rickety track. It wasn't anything like the giant coasters she'd seen in movies, but it still made her stomach queasy and her head spin. One minute, Sharkey's calling her a kid and the next he's threatening to kiss her. *Guess that's what the books mean when they say love is an emotional rollercoaster.* Hope wasn't much of a thrill seeker.

"Hope? Did you hear me?" Aiden snapped his fingers in front of her face. Slowly, he came into focus, a concerned look on his face.

His previous question penetrated her confused state. "Huh?"

"I asked if you wanted to stay up and write with me. I'll make some popcorn and find a jazz station on my phone."

A tingling sensation lingered in her fingertips from Squatch's magnetic presence. She had half a mind to go after him, but Aiden was still talking to her. "Sorry, no. Thank you, though. Bed." Was she making any sense at all? She couldn't tell at this point. Her head was spinning and she needed to lie down.

"Are you sure you're okay?"

Hope wasn't sure she'd ever be okay again.

***

Sleep had been elusive as Hope vacillated between anger and lust. Sharkey was unlike anyone she'd met before. Mysterious, brooding, intimidating. Alluring, thoughtful, a protector. No one had ever made her feel the things he made her feel.

After tossing and turning, she'd grabbed another romance from the collection upstairs. She'd moved on to the steamier books, and the sex scenes were not helping her current state of horniness. When she finally did drift off, her mother was there condemning her.

As the early morning light filtered through the curtains, a battle waged inside Hope. Her emotions, the physical yearning that was so new, guilt as her mother's warnings and what the Bible had taught her about relationships echoed in her mind. It was all so confusing.

She quickly dressed and headed outside, desperate to find some sort of peace about the state of her heart and mind. As she walked briskly down River Road toward town, she talked to God. He'd been the only constant in her life. The only one she could always count on. Which was why her parents' scandal had rocked her very existence.

A few months ago, her world revolved around helping others in the small villages around their city. She volunteered at food banks, orphanages, and another non-profit that focused on the jiggers that were such a problem in Uganda. Maybe people, especially children, didn't have shoes and the parasites would burrow into their feet.

On Sundays, people came from all over to worship on their property at a small chapel her father had built. If her parents were in town, her dad would preach, but usually, that was left to a local man who had studied under Pastor Seaton for many years.

It was Hope's understanding that the work her parents did traveling around the world was to support all of these ministries. In an area that poor, a little money went a long way. To find out what her parents had really been doing—living lavishly while people unnecessarily starved—made her question everything they taught her.

She'd hoped to stay in Uganda, maybe work for the local non-profit. She'd known the director for years and thought they had a good relationship. But the stain of her parents' sins spread to Hope, and no one wanted the blood on their hands.

Since then, she'd been asking God to explain everything to her—to make it clear what her next steps should be—how she could move on from this travesty.

Hope was no clearer on that now than the day of the shocking phone call that changed everything. It was like God had abandoned her as well.

So, she mostly talked to him out of habit.

Her childhood had been lonely, so she'd learned to entertain herself with books and make-believe. She'd use items around her yard to act out stories from the Bible, sometimes putting on plays for smaller children from the villages. Most of the locals were friendly, but no one got too close to the white girl. Hope had never had a best friend, a confidant. The closest thing she had was her cousin on the west coast—which was a world away. They wrote letters mostly, which eventually changed over to emails.

Once she'd moved back to the States, they'd started speaking on the phone, but she didn't have the money to fly out there. Besides, it scared her a little. What if they didn't get along? What if Bridget didn't want to see her? What if she was also ashamed?

Hope missed the confidence of her youth. So far, adulthood was proving to be far harder than she'd ever imagined. She wasn't just facing new challenges that came from growing up, she was facing a whole new world—literally. And she felt woefully unprepared.

Chapter Nineteen

Sharkey had acted like a boor last night. Hope deserved so much better. He used to be a good guy. Growing up, he practically lived at his church, between youth group, Awana meetings and volunteering to help senior congregates. At one point, he thought he wanted to pursue a role in the ministry, possibly as a youth leader. He had a lot of friends, he was happy and confident that God watched out for him, and he had Eve.

When she passed away, his entire world splintered—and his faith was the worst causality. Ever since then, he'd felt a hole in his heart. He'd never been able to determine if the missing bit was his first love or God. If he was honest with himself, it was probably a much bigger hole, and both were contributing factors. But Sharkey didn't want to dig that deep. He wanted to make beer and sit by the river.

Until Hope walked into his life.

Now he found himself wanting so much more.

She'd shown up early today, sitting quietly at a picnic table, scribbling away in her journal. It was downright pathetic how many times he'd spied on her, poking his head around the container just for a glimpse. He was too chickenshit to speak to her after his jealous exhibition last night.

His behavior proved he wasn't good enough for her.

But that didn't make him want her less.

His parting words to her had become an oppressive reality overnight, as he tossed and turned, his dreams fixated on her, causing his body to overheat to the point that he opened all the windows in his trailer—in the middle of winter.

No, he didn't deserve her, but the memory of grazing that full bottom lip still heated his whole body, to the point he was working in gym shorts and a tank on this forty-five-degree day.

Disgusted with himself, he dunked a roller in the paint. He had a laundry list of tasks to complete, but right now, he needed something mindless, so he wouldn't be tempted to pick up where he'd left off last night with Tink.

He'd been painting for over an hour when he realized how little progress he'd made. Coverage on the inside walls was splotchy at best, due to the corrugated design of the metal. He'd have to go back over it with a brush to fill in all the gaps missed by the roller. Sweat streamed down his face, so he swiped his tank off and wiped his overheated head. Hardly felt like January. As he grabbed a bottle of water from the cooler, he heard Hope's sweet giggle. Sharkey downed half the bottle, then sidled up to the pass-through window to see what had garnered the reaction.

The hairs in his beard tingled when he saw Book Boy sitting across from *his* Tink, that stupid ponytail swishing from side to side as he echoed her laughter.

Without thinking, he tore out of the side of the container and rounded the front. "Well, now, what did I miss?" He crossed his arms over his bare chest, only flexing a little. A sane man would be embarrassed to be standing in mixed company in only a pair of basketball shorts on a mild winter day.

But sanity had fled the day Sharkey rescued Tink from the jaws of death. He was even embellishing it to himself. *Pathetic.*

The laughter stopped, and Hope and the ponytail stared at the interloper like Bigfoot himself had walked out of the woods.

Sharkey could feel her gaze on him like a soft breeze blowing against his sweat-soaked skin. Following the goosebumps and raised hairs, he could almost map out everywhere she looked. And it was *everywhere.* Of that, he was certain.

"Oh, you wouldn't get it." Book Boy tossed his head back, puffing his chest out, trying to appear bigger than his flagpole frame.

Narrowing his eyes, Sharkey leaned on the picnic table, invading their space. "Try me."

Hope cleared her throat. He knew before he looked—she'd be scowling at him. So much for swearing to do better. Still a boor.

"Sorry to interrupt." He stood tall, swiping his balled-up shirt across his torso. Tink followed the motion, her accusing glare morphing into some-thing resembling lust. Bet she hasn't looked at the ponytail like that. He turned to leave, but glanced over his shoulder, catching her staring at the expanse of tan skin and muscles of his back. "Hope, would you like to ride with me to line dancing tonight?"

"That's okay, Starky. I'm taking her. Same place and all that."

The little prick had preempted him. *Well played, Book Boy.* "Great," he gritted out. Flinging his shirt over his shoulder, he pinned Tink with a smile and a wink. "Save a dance for me, darlin'." He turned and left before Hope could give him another "Hey, Buster" speech. He couldn't be held responsible for his actions this close to a king-sized bed.

***

Dressed in his best blue jeans and a shirt with buttons, Sharkey headed to The Landing to have a decent meal and an above-average pint before the dancing commenced. As usual, Nic held court behind the bar, the single ladies of Eastport Beach pining for his attention. The bartender had a few years on the brewer, and he whole-heartedly embraced his stature of most eligible bachelor. Sharkey preferred to remain in the shadows and simply provide the best ale this side of the Mississippi.

"Eating?" Nic slid a perfectly-poured 33rd parallel IPA into Sharkey's waiting hand.

"Give me the flatbread. Nothing too heavy tonight."

Nic nodded. "Dancing, huh? Guess this place will clear out in an hour and I can catch a nap before they come roaring back in full of piss and rhythm."

Sharkey sipped the cold beer, savoring its flavor and feeling a rare moment of pride. He was damn good at what he did and would be damned if someone was going to try to take that away. "Or you could come over and join in."

"The only dancing I'm interested in is the horizontal kind." Nic winked at a blonde within earshot. She blushed and whispered something to her friend.

The two had never shared their deepest, darkest traumas that kept them happily single, because they were men, not girls at a slumber party. But Sharkey recognized the facade Nic wore convincingly well. There was a story there. Maybe one day they'd share a kumbaya moment around a campfire with massive amounts of alcohol. Until then, Nic was a great friend who never judged other people's crap.

His meal arrived and as he bit into the crispy flatbread loaded with shredded pork, slaw and the secret mustard sauce that no one could figure out, Nic leaned against the bar and dropped his voice. "Any more mischief your way?"

Sharkey tapped the bar twice with his knuckles. "Been quiet thankfully."

"There were some suits in here the other day, meeting with Piper. I heard them mention the River Road property."

He'd been planning to talk to Eastport Beach's only realtor, and this reinforced the urgency. Piper was a straight shooter. She'd helped him purchase the land for the brewery. She cared about their community, he was certain, but she also cared about supporting herself and her teenage daughter. A sale was a sale—even if it jeopardized what Eastport Beach should be in a perfect world.

His cousin and he had vended at a local festival many years ago and Sharkey had immediately decided this was where he'd open his brewery. The small town was the perfect blend of people caring about one another and knowing when to leave someone alone. The community had welcomed Shark Bite Brewing with open mouths and wallets.

Located on the water, nearly perfect year-round weather, and pride in maintaining American values made Eastport Beach immediately feel like home. And Sharkey hadn't felt that since Eve died. He couldn't stay in the town she had lived so vibrantly in, and after multiple deployments, he was ready to be in one place.

"I've got to get the tasting area open before they bankrupt me. I sunk most of my capital into buying the property. I can't keep hemorrhaging money." He tossed the last bite of flatbread into his mouth.

Nic nodded. "I get it, but I also know once you're open you'll stay very busy. People are tired of looking at this ugly mug just to get a cold pint." He winked at the blonde who fell into a laughing fit.

"Yeah, you've got it rough." Sharkey slapped a couple bills on the counter, shaking his head. "I'll catch up with you later if it's not too busy." Or if he was lucky enough to get some alone time with Tink after the dancing.

The bartender waved as he headed toward a new group of admirers that were hovering at the other end of the bar.

He didn't know how Nic did it. That amount of attention made Sharkey's skin crawl. Maybe he needed to hire a full-time bartender, so he could remain in the production building away from the masses. Or cuddled up in bed with a certain blonde imp.

Chapter Twenty

Hope slipped one foot into her boot and laid back on the bed, yanking the faux leather to pull it up. She repeated the process with the other side. These fancy boots were a far cry from the army green wellies she'd worn around the property in Uganda. Standing, she appraised her outfit in the mirror. "I don't know, Riley. Are you sure this looks okay?"

Riley jumped up from the armchair she was lounging in to join Hope at the mirror. "You look amazing. I wish I could get away with this look. Here, try this." She unbuttoned the bottom of Hope's plaid shirt and tied the tails into a knot that fell right at the top of her snug jeans.

Hope turned sideways in the mirror. She'd always worn baggy, practical clothes before. It was foreign to see the shape of her legs, hips and bottom. "I don't know." She fidgeted with the knot. "I've never even been dancing before.

My friends and I learned the Thriller dance one year, although my mom said it was devil music."

Her hostess's eyes widened. "It's a classic!"

"My parents didn't allow secular music. I doubt we'll be dancing to 'Amazing Grace' tonight."

Riley laughed. "Probably not, but it won't be anything crazy either. Not like we line dance to gangster rap or heavy metal."

"What if I make a fool of myself? With my luck, I'll trip over my own feet."

"Trust me, no one will bat an eye. The first time I went, I ran straight into Ms. Windsor and we both ended up on the floor. Thankfully, I was on the bottom, so she didn't break anything."

Hope took one last look in the mirror. Her heart fluttered in her chest. She'd been feeling conflicted all day. "Can I ask a favor?"

"Anything." Riley hooked her arm in her friend's.

"Can I please ride with you?"

"No sense taking two cars. You and Aiden are welcome to ride with us."

She blew out a breath. "Thanks. Now I can just worry about the dancing."

***

The studio was buzzing with activity. People of all ages milled about, waiting for the class to start. Music thumped, a beat Hope could feel in her bones. She loved the energy of the place—smiling faces, townsfolk hugging and catching up on the latest gossip, an elderly couple already dancing in the far corner. Notably absent was the towering Squatch. Disappointment settled in her chest, which made her feel guilty, because Aiden was right beside her, talking excitedly in her ear.

Riley introduced both of them to everyone they encountered, and the people of Eastport Beach were incredibly welcoming. They asked how long she'd be staying and if her book was coming along well. Obviously, news traveled fast in this small town and people weren't strangers for long.

A tall, lean couple held court near the back of the space. Gracefulness exuded from the woman, a clear sign she was a dancer. "Hope, Aiden, I want you to meet Ada and Trip. They'll be leading the class tonight." Riley leaned closer to Hope's ear. "They met at Heron House last fall and now look at them!"

Ada chuckled, and even her laughter was elegant. "Yes, we are a Heron House success story. You'll love your time there. I certainly did."

Aiden stepped closer to Hope and whispered. "Maybe we'll be the next success."

Hope did not know how to respond to that. Luckily, Trip stepped forward and shook both their hands, then addressed Hope. "I heard you've been helping feed Riley. I swear when I moved out, she lost ten pounds. She can't be bothered to stop and eat."

"I had to lose weight because I put on twenty pounds when Trip was living there. He still sneaks a lasagna in the freezer from time to time." Riley smiled at her former employee and he returned her obvious affection.

Ben pulled Riley close. "It takes a village to keep her fed. And I prefer her a little meaty." He squeezed her side, producing a giggle.

Hope loved the easy affection among the group of friends. She wanted that so deeply. Not too long ago, she'd had a group of friends in her community in Uganda. She never would have guessed how easily those ties could be severed.

"We'll get the class started in a few minutes. I'm so glad you're here." Ada smiled, then something caught her eye near the front door. She waved. "Excuse me, one of my favorite pupils just arrived."

Before she even turned around, Hope knew Sharkey had arrived. The energy in the air changed, like pinpricks of lightning bouncing off her skin. The scowl on Aiden's face confirmed her assumption. The two men were like two roosters in the same pen, feathers bristling at the mere sight of the other. It didn't make any sense to her. It's not like she was anyone's hen.

Aiden wrapped an arm around her shoulders. The contact surprised her, but it wasn't altogether unpleasant. "Let's find a spot."

She let him lead her toward a back corner. The crowd was lining up in rows, with Trip and Ada directing. Squatch caught her eye over the room of people, half a smile lingering under his beard.

Gosh, it's stuffy in here.

Someone turned the music down and Ada addressed the eager dancers. "What a terrific turnout for our third line dancing night! Now, last week we focused on the Electric Slide, which is a classic dance everyone should know. Tonight, we're going to learn a newer dance called Give Me Shivers to Ed Sheeran's hit song."

"We had a special request for this dance, from someone who gets the 'Shivers' whenever a special lady is around. I certainly know how he feels." Trip grabbed Ada and spun her around, then dipped her.

The crowd cheered and an older man up front whistled loudly.

Ada smoothed her dress down as she stood straight, her cheeks flushed from the quick kiss Trip had planted on her mid-dip. "This dance is a lot of footwork and hip action, so let's do a bit of stretching before we get started. Don't want anyone pulling a muscle or falling down tonight."

Someone elbowed Riley and she chuckled. "I never claimed to be graceful."

Trip led the group in a few stretches. As Hope twisted to the right, she spotted Squatch, who had moved from the back of the crowd to one row behind her. He straightened and caught her staring. Heat traveled up her torso and suddenly her shirt felt like a winter coat. Like you'd need in Chicago in January. She pushed at the sleeves, shoving them up to her elbows, while she faced the front again and tried to focus on what Trip was saying.

"Everything okay?" Aiden whispered from beside her.

Hope glanced around the room where everyone but her was arching to their left, arms stretched overhead. They weren't even dancing yet, and she was already behind. *Focus. Focus. Focus.* "Yeah, I'm fine." She was getting pretty good at this lying thing.

Ada clapped her hands from the front. "Okay, let's get moving. This dance starts on a jump and then we're going to work those hips." She demonstrated the first eight beats, ending with her butt sticking out toward the crowd.

Hope was intensely aware that she would be shaking her bottom right in front of Squatch. Would anyone notice if she ran for the exit?

Riley giggled as she popped her hips in a circle. "This is way more fun than the Electric Slide."

"It's more fun to watch too." Ben patted her lightly on the behind.

Hope stood frozen to the spot. Why had she let Riley talk her into these tight jeans that made her bottom stand out? And now she was supposed to wiggle it right in front of Squatch? Whose very presence was already doing things to her heartrate and deep in her gut.

Ada had moved on to the next eight count, and Hope hadn't done so much as a shimmy. Aiden was following the instructions and kept glancing at her—likely wondering if she'd become spontaneously paralyzed.

A large, warm hand landed at her waist, and the hair on the back of her neck jumped to attention as Sharkey leaned in to whisper in her ear. "Relax. Just have fun. It doesn't have to be perfect." He squeezed her side lightly before returning to his spot.

Easier said than done. Hope said a silent prayer that she wouldn't embarrass herself too awfully bad, then focused back on Ada as she demonstrated the steps.

"Okay, we're going to try it with music now."

The song started, an infectious beat that had Hope tapping her foot within seconds. Ada signaled the start and everyone jumped forward and rotated their hips in a circle. It was a bit harder to follow the next few steps because she had been so distracted when Ada was giving the rundown, but she tried to follow along.

Riley was singing along to the song, stepping right and then left and shuffling her feet. Her moves didn't always match Ada's, but she appeared to be having a blast.

Hope tried to loosen up and feel the rhythm, but she was always a few steps behind. The only part she had nailed was the hip part and when she realized they were slowly turning in a circle, it occurred to her that she'd be shaking her butt at Aiden on the next pass. Maybe her mother was right about secular music. As far as Hope could tell, the song was about a person making you horny and she was literally shaking her behind in front of half the town of Eastport Beach and more specifically in front of two men who gave her a funny feeling in her gut.

They turned again and when she went to cross over, her feet got tangled together and she pitched to the side.

Strong arms caught her before she fell and set her back on her feet. She knew it was Squatch by the zing of electricity that rocketed through her abdomen. "It's okay, darlin'. You give me the shivers too."

He blended back into his line of dancers like nothing had happened.

Hope was still staring at the yeti, who effortlessly followed the steps of the dance, when the music ended, and Trip announced a break.

"I brought you a bottled water." Aiden said from behind her.

She'd forgotten he was there. "That's so thoughtful, thank you." She faced Aiden and noticed a sheen of sweat across his brow. Maybe it really was hot in the studio, and it wasn't just the yeti effect.

"I assumed we'd be dancing to some hick song, but this is kind of fun." He drained most of his bottle of water.

Hope rolled the cool bottle across her brow. "I didn't know what to expect. It's a lot to remember, but I really like the beat."

Aiden's features scrunched together. "You've never heard 'Shivers' before?"

She shook her head, fidgeting with the label on the bottle of water. "No, my parents didn't like it when I listened to secular music."

"But you did anyway, right?" He winked at her.

Honor your father and mother. It wasn't a suggestion, it was a commandment. But how many commandments had they broken? Was she still supposed to honor them after everything they'd done? "Not really, but one time a boy from school brought a video to a birthday party and we all tried to learn the 'Thriller' dance."

"Doesn't get much more secular than Michael Jackson." Aiden laughed, then downed the rest of his water. "If you need an introduction to current musical trends, I'll share my Spotify with you."

She didn't have a clue what a Spotify was, but she was already embarrassed about her lack of pop culture knowledge, so she just smiled and nodded. "Excuse me, I need to find a restroom." She started across the room to ask Ada where the bathroom was, but something tall and hairy stepped into her path.

"What do you think about line dancing so far?"

"It's a lot to remember and I'm so uncoordinated." She slid her fingers along the tie of her shirt, trying to focus on something besides the electricity emanating off Sharkey's massive frame.

He reached out, tucking a lock of her hair behind her ear, leaving a trail of fire where he touched. "Don't worry, no one is more uncoordinated than Riley."

Riley was such a strong, confident woman, just a few years older than Hope. "It seems like everyone picks on Riley. About cooking, about dancing…"

"Trust me, Riley is the first to admit her limitations. She's always a good sport and often rags on herself. She faces everything head on and is damn good at most things she attempts. That's why it's fun to tease her when she fails so epically. Have you tasted her cinnamon rolls yet?'

Chapter Twenty-One

Before now, he'd only seen her in oversized clothes. Hope Seaton in tight-fitting jeans with her shirt tied at her waist was a revelation. Who knew she'd have such a knock-out little body under those baggy overalls?

His blood had been pumping all night watching her perfect ass bop in a circle. Why had he requested this song, this dance? Just to torture himself? It took every ounce of restraint not to grab her by the waist and line his body up with hers. When she almost tipped over, he cheered inside, because it was a valid excuse to put his hands on her.

Ponytail really shot him daggers with his rescue move, but that guy was the least intimidating man in Eastport Beach, or Duke, or the state of North Carolina, for that matter. It was mildly entertaining to watch the scrawny academic drool over Hope. Sharkey knew when push came to shove, she'd never choose Book Boy.

It was like an electric current flowed between him and Tink. He hadn't felt this alive in decades. And the way she stared when she didn't think he was looking—he knew she felt it too.

Her and Riley had disappeared into the bathroom, and he was killing time studying the poster of basic ballet poses. His plan was to get her away from Aiden for the second half of the lesson and hopefully find a dozen new excuses to touch her. Although he would miss the view from behind.

"I teach Intro to Ballet on Wednesdays if you're interested." Ada tapped her finger against her cheek. "Although I'd probably need to special-order a tutu for you."

"Hilarious."

Trip joined them in the small hallway. It was getting pretty crowded with two men well over six feet tall and Ada right on their heels. "You know, Sharkey, some women find it creepy when men linger outside the bathroom." The couple exchanged a chuckle.

Sharkey pushed past Trip to extricate himself from the awkward situation. "You two should take your comedy act on the road. Jokes and Jives. I'll even let you steal the name." He slipped back into the studio where half of Eastport Beach milled about. Sharkey always ran hot, but between Tink's gyrations and the mass of people, it felt like he was marooned on the surface of the sun.

Two long strides got him out the door, escaping the clamor and heat.

Outside, Main Street pulsed with life despite it being a cool, winter weeknight. A group of teens were jumping off benches in the park, a couple walked hand in hand toward the pier, and the heavenly smell of Maude's famous pies wafted out the open door of The Spicy Mermaid. The diner wasn't normally open in the evenings, but the savvy owner had figured out pretty quickly that Easporters left the dance studio happy and hungry.

Sharkey tried to remember life in the sleepy town before Ada had brought the energy of music and movement to Eastport Beach. Festivals were common most of the year, but the winter months had always been quieter. Mad About Dancing had quickly become a favorite gathering place and it was waking their little town up.

Movement caught his eye outside the employee entrance to The Landing. Two people were canoodling in the shadows, further proof that cupid had been flitting around Eastport Beach. First Ben and Riley, then Ada and Trip. The couple separated and stepped into the light. Ah, Nic had snagged himself a candidate for the horizontal mambo.

Briefly, Sharkey wondered if he'd been hit by one of the love arrows. It wasn't like him to obsess over a woman. But ever since he'd snagged Hope off that picnic table, she'd invaded his heart and mind.

"Sharkey?"

Now he was imagining her voice. He really was far gone.

"Are you coming back inside?"

He spun around, realizing she wasn't a figment of his imagination. She was in the flesh, holding her hand out to him. Like a fricking wet dream. "Yeah, of course, just getting some air." He stuck one hand in his pocket, subtly adjusting his aching cock. This woman was imbedded so far under his skin, it would take an act of God to extract her.

Like a starving man, he took her tiny hand. She smiled up at him and his legs turned to jelly. So far gone.

Back inside, someone turned the music down, and Trip attempted to get everyone's attention. After fruitless shouting, he stuck his fingers in his mouth and let out a blistering whistle.

The crowd simmered down and reformed their lines. Hope pulled Sharkey to the front, where Book Boy stood, a pained smile painted on his hairless face. The beanpole probably couldn't grow a 'stach, let alone an exemplary beard.

"We're going to go over the steps one more time, so everyone can feel confident." Ada nodded at Trip to turn the song back on. "Let's start off facing the nine o'clock wall."

Everyone turned to their left, and Sharkey almost groaned out loud. Tink was bouncing on her feet, excited to begin the dance. The view was so distracting he missed the count. She was swirling her hips in a circle, and he hadn't moved yet.

"Uh, Sharkey, this is the part where you dance." Riley snickered from behind him.

He shot a glare over his shoulder and got ready to join the dance on the next eight count. Before Hope jumped to her left again and saw him ogling her like a schoolboy with a massive case of puppy love.

He was moving again when she shifted, so they were side by side. She stared, fixated on the woman in front of her now, desperately trying to follow the steps. And God help him, but when all the dancers turned to the three o'clock wall, Sharkey was ready to put on a little show for the sweet Tink.

As he rocked his hips in a circle, he could feel her eyes on him. He basked in the attention—a rarity for him—but with her, he wanted it all. He snuck a peek over this shoulder, hoping to catch her eye and give her a little wink. Instead, all he saw was Book Boy, staring at her rear, practically drooling. *Oh, hell no.*

A voice in his head accused him of doing the exact same thing not three minutes earlier. But logical Sharkey had left the building. Green-eyed-monster Sharkey had taken his place, and steam was building inside his brain.

By the time they faced the front again, the men were launching virtual firebombs at one another over Tink's head.

Ada must have felt the negativity in the air, because she turned and immediately accessed the situation. Frowning, she signaled to the men to cut it out with a slash across her throat. Hope was so fixated on following the teacher's steps, that she repeated the motion.

Disgusted with himself, Sharkey focused on getting through the dance and kept his eyes anywhere except Tink and the ponytail. As soon as the song ended, he thanked Trip and Ada and jetted for the door.

If he was going to act like a Neanderthal, he didn't deserve to be around Hope. So, he was taking his sorry ass home and putting it to bed.

***

Sharkey woke up in a foul mood. He'd berated himself until late in the night for his juvenile behavior at the dance studio. If he truly wanted a chance with Hope, he needed to get his act together and behave like a mature, enlightened adult. He was competing with a brainiac, so he had to up his game. Show her that Book Boy wasn't the only evolved man in the running.

But before he could turn over a new leaf, he had to get the bar rewired. The inspector was coming back in a few days and if he didn't have the work completed, his opening would be delayed even further.

He put on something that could be burned afterward and headed outside.

Once he gathered all his tools, he dropped to his knees and crawled under the container. A few more holes, and he should be able to complete the wiring to operate his tasting "room." Again. When he'd started this process, his vision of using an empty shipping container as a bar seemed genius. Reality had set in, and between doing the work himself and some idiot sabotaging him along the way, he found himself wishing he'd just hired a contractor to build the damn thing. Living in the cramped trailer and facing setbacks almost daily had worn his resolve down.

Then one day, a little blonde imp appeared, and he felt a spark of life he hadn't had in over fifteen years. He was feeling hopeful again.

A pinprick of light penetrated the darkness, and he squirmed to reach the last pilot hole he'd drilled. The corrugated metal on the underside of the container prevented him from doing this above ground. His drill wouldn't reach through the plywood floor and the layers of steel. Even from below, the thick metal required a special blade, which ground to a halt halfway through his last hole.

Cursing, he tried several more times, but either the blade or the drill was dead. He'd had to drive all the way to Myrtle Beach to get the first one.

He moved toward the hole in the sheeting, desperate to get out. His chest heaved as his pulse raced, which only slowed his progress, because it was a tight fit on a good day. Sweat dripped into his eyes as he wiggled his way back out into the open air. *Buck up, man. You are not claustrophobic. You are not claustrophobic.*

Sharkey had once believed in something bigger than himself, but after the betrayal of a lifetime, he'd hit rock bottom. Joining the military had been his turning point, and he'd slowly learned that if he worked hard enough, he could manage outcomes. When he worked, he didn't notice the emptiness as much.

Once out in the sunlight, he sucked in big breaths of fresh air, while his heart slowed down. He was lying there, staring up at the Carolina blue sky when he heard Hope talking to someone. His first instinct was to head to his camper and shower the cobwebs off. Instead, he army-crawled closer to the sound of her voice.

"I'm so glad you called me back. I'm freaking out."

Sharkey couldn't tell if it was excitement or nerves lacing her tone.

"I know it's early there, but I didn't know who else to talk to about this."

Was she speaking to someone in Uganda? But that didn't make sense, because it would be later there. He knew she had an aunt in Chicago, but that was only an hour different.

"...and he asked me on a date!"

Sharkey must have blacked out, because he missed most of what she said, but he distinctly heard the word "date." No way in hell was Book Boy taking his woman out on a date. He'd sooner go back under this metal box and have a death match with Stumpy.

"No, I haven't been on a date before. My parents didn't allow it, and besides, who would I have dated? It's just never been an issue, you know?"

As Hope shared her fears and trepidation about dating with whoever was on the other end of the line, Sharkey began to feel itchy all over—and it wasn't the arachnids likely hitching a ride. This was an intensely private conversation that he most definitely should not be listening to. He needed a plan. Because he'd rather every ounce of beer in his production facility go rancid than the nerd take Hope Seaton on her first date.

He hopped up, sprinted to his trailer, and raced for the shower. If he wanted a chance with Tink, he'd have to do a lot better than sweaty, spider-covered Sasquatch.

Bathing in his phone-booth-sized shower was hard enough, but shaving was out of the question, so he leaned over his thimble-sized sink trimming his beard into some semblance of containment. A bush hog would be more appropriate, but he didn't have time to get precious with his manscaping.

He slid into yet another pair of uncomfortable chinos and a collared shirt, but by the time he'd finished buttoning it, sweat ringed his pits. Tearing the damn thing off, he flung it across the trailer—all four feet of it—and pulled a Shark Bite Brewing Company tee over his head.

A plan slowly formed in his head as he dug through his cupboard (singular) and pulled fruit, deli meat and cheese from his fridge. Thank goodness he'd hit up Murrays yesterday. By the time he'd loaded everything into a cooler with a six-pack of cider and several bottles of water, his pants looked like they were part of an accordion.

He replaced the khakis with worn but clean jeans, feeling instantly more like himself. The plan solidified in his mind as he slipped down the tiny stairs. At this point, he didn't even care, because he was going to win Hope over, no matter what.

Shooting off a quick text, he dumped the cooler in the back of his truck and ran over to the production building to grab a couple promotional Shark Bite Brewing Company beach towels.

Chesnee texted back a thumbs up and Sharkey felt like maybe things were finally going his way.

He tossed the towels into the cab of the truck and slowly approached the picnic area, listening to see if Hope was still on the phone.

It was so quiet, he worried she'd left.

Rounding the corner, he found her back at the table, head bent over her notebook.

Not wanting to startle her, he stomped his feet a bit and cleared his throat.

When she turned to look at him, all his confidence whooshed out like a deflating balloon. He was pretty sure he even squeaked a little.

"Hey." Her lips quirked up on one side, and she dipped her head toward her shoulder. Her hazel eyes sparkled, and her cheeks glowed pink. She looked happy.

Had Book Boy made her happy? Was she excited about going on her first date with the nerd? Could he burst her bubble?

"Sleep okay last night? Hope you didn't get cold." She scrunched her perfect little nose. "Hey, are you okay?"

She expected him to speak. Like a normal human, not like a scared Bigfoot ready to run back to the safety of the forest. He cleared his throat again, this time to dislodge the boulder blocking it. "Yeah. Okay. Hot." *Sentences, dude.* "I mean, no. I didn't get cold." His feet weighed about a ton, but he managed to inch closer to her, try to seem halfway normal and not completely creepy. No one was going to agree to go on a date with a creep. Especially not Hope. She deserved a fucking knight in shining armor. He just hoped she'd settle for him.

Her phone beeped, and she glanced down at it before quickly turning it over.

Sharkey's hackles went up, restarting his resolve, and he strode confidently to the other side of the picnic table and sat on the bench. "Honestly, I didn't sleep well last night at all."

"No?" She straightened her body, so they were facing one another. Today she wore an oversized sweatshirt with a sea turtle on it. It was far too big for her, and she played with the too-long sleeves as she stared back at him.

He shook his head, holding her gaze until she looked away. "I might as well have been on fire." Part of him felt bad for the things he did to Hope in his mind while he released the tension that had been building since he'd laid eyes on her. Not enough that he didn't repeat it again this morning.

She glanced back up at him through long, pale eyelashes. He loved that she didn't cover her face with makeup. There were no improvements to be made. "I didn't sleep well either."

Was it because of excitement about her date with Book Boy? Or had their encounter on the porch rocked her world too? The only thing that had distracted him from obsessing over her lips was her shaking her hips last night. "Have you gotten a lot of writing done today?"

Straightening, she adjusted her notebook on the table, maybe a little off-balance from the sudden change of subject. "Yes, I have, actually."

"Good." He rose from the bench. "Then you can take the afternoon off."

She craned her neck back, looking up at him, her eyes wide and wondering. "Do you need me to leave?"

He chuckled, shaking his head. "No, but I'd like to take you somewhere." He held out his hand to her, holding his breath in anticipation of her decision. "Do you trust me?"

Chapter Twenty-Two

Hope wasn't sure she could trust anybody. Not her parents, not God. But without hesitating, she placed her small hand in his large one. Her nerves zinged, like shockwaves shooting through her entire body.

He pulled her to her feet, but her knees buckled, so she gripped the side of the picnic table with her free hand to steady herself.

"Should I bring my stuff?" His hand was rough and warm, and she didn't want to let go.

"Yeah. I wouldn't leave anything out here." He stood close while she gathered her things and shoved them into her bag.

Then the most magical thing happened. He took her hand again and pulled her to his truck.

The sparks lit up her skin this time, making her feel heated to the point of sweating in the giant hoodie on the cool winter day. When he opened the passenger door for her, she stepped back and jerked the bulky sweatshirt over her head.

Her undershirt rose up her torso a bit, and Sharkey swore under his breath. She didn't know much about these things—other than what she'd read in the last few weeks—but she thought maybe it was a good kind of swearing.

He helped her into the truck, his hand lingering on her arm, leaving a flaming patch of skin where he touched. She felt superheated, like the surface of the sun. Now she would be confined in the cab of a truck with this man that was all heat and muscle. It was possible she wouldn't survive it.

Sharkey closed the door, holding her gaze the entire time. His tongue peeked out from between his lips, and she stared, transfixed. Now the heat was inside her, too. He tapped the body of the truck before rounding it and sliding in on his side.

Breathing normally seemed impossible.

"Buckle up." His voice was low and throaty, even more so than usual. Maybe she wasn't the only one affected by their proximity.

If the romance books she'd devoured recently held any ounce of reality, maybe this giant, worldly man could like her. Maybe he could fall in love with her. The thought was simultaneously thrilling and terrifying.

In the course of a few hours, she'd gone from being asked on her first date to being whisked away by a man who made her insides boil. Her mother would think she'd become a wanton hussy overnight. Her cousin told her to live it up, have fun, and not get too serious. She was seriously wondering whose life this was.

The truck lumbered down a rough path cut through the woods, then Sharkey made the turn onto River Road heading toward town.

Hope had walked into Eastport Beach again that morning, before the small town came to life. The only business open at the time was a quaint coffee shop. She'd never liked the taste, or the jittering effect caffeine had on her. But she'd selected an orange cranberry muffin from the glass display case and savored the tug of sweet versus tart.

On her way back, the small market on the corner opened its doors, and more people filled the sidewalks. The town reminded her of a village outside Jinja, with an active fishing industry on Lake Victoria.

Sharkey pulled the truck into a parking lot next to the marina. "Ever been on a boat?"

She stared out the window at the boats bobbing up and down on the water. "Not on the ocean."

"Don't worry, we aren't going far." He jumped out of the truck and rushed to open her door.

Hope slung her backpack over her shoulder and slid off the seat, Sharkey catching her around the waist and setting her gently on her feet. When she looked up at him, he blocked most of the bright sun, but the remaining rays hovered around his head like a halo. Was Squatch the sign she'd been asking the Lord for? He finally released his grip on her midsection, and her lungs deflated as she released her held breath. She'd only read one historical romance so far, but standing in the marina parking lot, crushing hard on this man she barely knew, she felt like the duchess whose stable boy had supported her during a fainting spell. Within a few pages, the housemaid discovered them in a pile of hay in a compromising situation.

As Sharkey moved to the back of the truck, Hope fanned herself with her hand.

"You might want to grab your sweatshirt. It can get chilly out on the water." He hefted a cooler out of the bed of the truck, then grabbed a couple rolled-up towels.

She seriously doubted she'd ever be cold again, but she stuffed the hoodie in her bag anyway.

"Sharkey!" A good-looking older man with reddish brown hair waved from the deck of the restaurant that backed up to the marina. He jogged across the gravel and tossed something at the brewer. Squatch snagged the item with ease and waved as the man headed back inside.

Pocketing whatever it was, he hoisted the cooler and turned to Hope. "You ready?"

She snatched the towels off the lid of the cooler before they fell and nodded. "I guess."

"You guess?" He skidded to a stop in the sandy soil, an indignant scowl on his face. "Can I get a little more enthusiasm?"

His teasing tone made her smile, her chest loosening a little. Anxiety still battered her like the waves hitting the hulls of the nearby boats, but she realized she did trust him. She felt safe with Sharkey. "Let's go!" Throwing her fist up in a battle cry, she beamed up at the yeti, wondering why he'd chosen her for this adventure—and not someone more appropriate, like the deputy from the other day.

The smile he returned was blinding, and she decided not to question what was happening, but just enjoy it. Smiles rarely peeked out from behind all that fur on his face, so Hope felt honored to be on the receiving end of such a beautiful occurrence. He continued onto the decking, leading the way to the far end of the marina where a small boat sat moored to the dock. The boat didn't seem equipped to go up against ocean waves, but when Sharkey loaded the cooler and turned to offer his hand again, she didn't hesitate. No way would she pass up the opportunity to feel the bolt of lightning he produced every time he touched her.

As she stepped onto the side of the vessel, he moved his hands back to her waist, completely lifting her into the air and spinning around to set her down. Again, he didn't release his hold immediately. Her shirt had risen up slightly, and his thumb slipped underneath, twitching against her bare skin. Energy crackled between them as he stared at her mouth. She sucked her bottom lip in, chewing on it nervously, and his grip on her waist tightened.

Then, just like a scene from one of her books, he lowered his face toward hers.

"Shark Bite, wait up!"

Sharkey stepped back, dropping his hands and sending a mumbled curse skyward. Hope immediately missed his touch. Was he really about to kiss her?

It seemed unfathomable. She watched as the yeti stepped back onto the dock and intercepted a blond-haired man before he could reach the boat.

Was every man in Eastport Beach handsome? It was like something out of a movie.

The other man smiled and waved at her, but Sharkey used his big paw to push the blond further away from the boat. And Hope. Was he embarrassed to be seen with her?

The two men spoke for a few minutes, then Squatch patted the smaller man on the shoulder and headed back toward Hope. The blond waved again, flashing another brilliant smile at her. He seemed like the type that offered those pearly whites up regularly to anyone of the opposite sex.

The flower that blooms less often is that much sweeter.

Sharkey stepped back onto the boat, busying himself with the ropes that held it to the dock.

"Who was that?"

"A major pain in my ass," he mumbled.

"Did he want to come along?" She took the seat opposite the steering wheel and controls, tucking her bag at her feet.

Releasing the last rope, he pushed the boat away from the dock. "I'm sure that would have been his preference, but I asked to borrow the boat, not take him out on it."

"He seemed very friendly."

Squatch had the same stiff posture he'd had the other night, when he'd met Aiden. She still couldn't be certain, but she once again thought he might be jealous.

"Oh, Chesnee is *very* friendly." He turned the key, and the boat roared to life. "You should stay away from him."

A laugh bubbled out of her. "Because he's so friendly?"

"Exactly." He focused on steering the boat out of the marina and into open water.

Yup. Big, strong, green-eyed Squatch. Suddenly, Hope was a lot less nervous. She leaned back in her seat, raising her face to the midday sun, enjoying the breeze that ruffled her hair. They hadn't traveled far when another landmass appeared. Sharkey pointed out the lighthouse they called Old Baldy. From her vantage point, it looked like an old, tall rock. It was the oldest lighthouse still standing in North Carolina but wasn't a functional navigational tool any longer.

"If you want, we can go climb it sometime." He was squinting into the sun, focused on driving the boat.

Goosebumps broke out along her arms. He wanted to spend more time with her. Maybe this wouldn't be her last boat ride with the yeti. She grinned, imagining a real Bigfoot driving a boat, the wind blowing through his hair.

"Can I take that smile as a yes?"

Her thoughts had flitted away, and she'd failed to answer him. "Yes, that'd be fun. Do we have to take a boat over?"

"That or the ferry. Are you not enjoying the ride?" He slowed the boat, a distressed expression on his handsome face.

Without thinking, she reached over and gripped his forearm. It was thick and muscular. "No. I mean, yes. I mean, this is wonderful."

"Good." Relief washed over his face, and he set his large hand over hers.

Her cheeks heated, despite the cool wind blowing off the water. Every time this man touched her, she feared she'd combust.

He banked the boat to the left and headed upriver. He pointed out landmarks along the way. A small maritime museum run by a man named Captain Percy. Ben's sailboat. Heron House. When the shipping container came into sight, she immediately started searching the water for their reptilian friend. They continued a little further until he slowed the boat and bumped against the shore of a small island. It was on the opposite side of the river, and they could no longer see the brewery.

She was looking for a dock when Sharkey leapt out of the boat, splashing in the shallow water. He grabbed the front of the vessel and yanked it further up the small beach like he was pulling a wagon behind him. His biceps strained against his t-shirt, begging to be freed from their confines. Hope also wished they'd be set free. She'd seen him with his shirt off, and she'd very much like to see it again.

"Hope, throw me that rope at the front of the boat, just in case the tide comes in. We don't want to lose our ride home."

She scrambled out of her seat, grabbing the rope he pointed to and hefting it in his general direction. Catching it easily, he trekked up to a small grove of trees and looped the rope around several of them. He fought a little while tying it, because the trunks were small and the trees kept leaning under the pressure. Finally, he wound the rope in between the trunks, providing a more secure attachment. When he stepped back to assess his handiwork, he grabbed the hem of his shirt and wiped his brow with it.

Thank you, Lord. Regret immediately flooded her chest. While it wasn't exactly taking the Lord's name in vain, it didn't feel right to thank God for a glimpse of a taut, rippled stomach.

"You ready?" Sharkey was back at the bow of the boat, reaching his hand toward her.

Hope shoved the sound of her mother's condemnation out of her mind and allowed him to help her out of the boat. While she stood on a small beach, he heaved his massive body over the side of the boat and fetched the cooler and towels. She stared in awe as his arm muscles bunched with the effort. Desire rippled through her body. Foreign, and definitely against the teachings she'd had drilled into her head her whole life.

Back on shore, he hoisted the cooler while she grabbed the towels. "Follow me."

His broad shoulders led as they picked their way across the island. With one step, she'd admire his strong back. The next, she'd admonish herself for seeing him as an object. As they crested a small rise and stepped into denser foliage, her breath quickened when he shot a smile over his shoulder. Navigating down the other side, she recalled lectures about Proverbs 31 and staying chaste until marriage.

By the time they reached the postcard-perfect setting of a grove of palm trees on a private beach, she was hot, bothered and confused as hell.

Sharkey took the towels from her and stretched them across the sand. He buried each corner, a nifty little trick she'd have to remember if she ever got back to the beach. From the cooler, he pulled bottled water, a few cans, grapes, cheese, deli meat of some sort and a package of crackers. After arranging the feast on the cooler lid, he looked over at her, likely wondering what was wrong with the strange little girl. "Sit. We'll eat."

Hope stood stock still, taking in the beach, the towels, the food. The man waiting for her to join him. "It's a picnic."

"Yes." Squatch nodded slowly. "Do they not have those in Uganda?"

She furrowed her brow. This had all the elements of a date. And she was pretty certain he was teasing her. Flirting. No, that couldn't be right. He hadn't asked her on a date, had he? Maybe she missed that part when she was drooling over his physique?

"Hope, is something wrong? Do you want to go back?"

Emphatically, she shook her head. She didn't know what was happening here, but she wanted to stay with Sharkey. Wanted him to touch her again, her mother be damned. The woman was in prison for scamming people. What kind of moral authority did she possess? Excising the woman who lied to her for years from her thoughts, Hope took a seat on the towel opposite the confused Bigfoot.

He offered her a bottle of water, which she gratefully accepted. The cool water soothed her throat and her unease. "I'm sorry I'm acting so strange. This is really nice."

Squatch released a sigh that shook his entire frame. "Good. Great." He grabbed a can and bent the tab back. A fine spray of bubbles whooshed from the opening, reminding her of ginger ale. Her parents had only allowed soda on special occasions, like the end of the year, when they'd leave her a can of ginger ale and a note that said "Happy New Year's" while they jetted off to some glamorous locale. At the time, she thought they'd been helping starving children in India or Mongolia, but now she knew better.

Hope shook her head to chase the thoughts of *them* away. She was on a beach with a handsome man who made her insides feel like the bubbles escaping from that can.

"What is that?"

Sharkey held up the can for her to see. "It's one of my ciders. Do you want to try it?"

"Like apple cider?" She studied the graphic, which was a shark fin breaching a wave.

"Sort of, but alcoholic. This one is actually a pear cider. A little sweeter than apple." He offered it to her.

She'd rarely had soda—she'd never had alcohol. Not even holy wine. Their denomination was more the grape juice and crackers set. A war waged inside her. It had been building since her life flipped upside down. Did she keep doing what she'd been doing her whole life? Or did she accept change? Did she turn her back on everything she knew? Or forge ahead into this terrifying new world?

Hope shook her head. "No thanks. I don't drink." Dealing with these new feelings of lust was hard enough. She didn't need to add alcohol-reducing inhibitions to the mix.

He took a swig of the drink, then twisted it in the sand to carve out a little drink cocoon. "Well, eat something at least and tell me more about growing up in Uganda."

She popped a grape in her mouth, catching him staring. "Is this a date, Sharkey?"

Chapter Twenty-Three

The cracker he'd just shoved in his mouth flew out in a mist of crumbly spittle. He grabbed the can out of the sand, washing his shock and the remaining bits of cracker down his throat. The fizz of the cider hit the roof of his mouth, and the alcohol activated his brain. Did he come clean with her or play dumb? He wanted this to be a date, and he felt guilty as hell for basically tricking her into it. But he had to beat Book Boy to the punch, and he wasn't confident she would have agreed to a real, honest-to-goodness date with his hairy ass.

She grinned, whether at his surprise or at his inability to answer a simple question, he didn't know. When Hope smiled, it took his breath away.

For too many minutes, he just reveled in the glow of her radiance. He was such a goner. And it was only their first date. "Yes, I'd like this to be a date." He'd never been more sure of anything in his life.

Now it was Hope's turn to be shocked. Maybe she hadn't actually expected an answer. The color on her cheeks deepened to a rosy red. Her bottom lip disappeared into her mouth. She crossed her arms over her chest, suddenly finding the seam on her pants intensely interesting.

"Hey." He reached out, gently pulling her arms apart and taking her hands. They were tiny in his giant mitts, the skin so soft. He flicked his thumb back and forth, savoring the smoothness there. "Hope, look at me."

Slowly, she raised her head, her lip still tucked inside her mouth, her eyes wide like a fawn's.

"Is this okay?" He jerked his head toward their joined hands and held his breath, praying she wouldn't make him let go.

The nod was so subtle, he wondered if he imagined it. Willed it into happening. "I would never force you to do anything that made you feel uncomfortable." He kept his voice low, like they were having an intimate conversation, even though the only thing that might overhear them was a sandpiper darting in and out of the surf.

Her lip popped out, followed by her tongue, running over the surface to moisten it.

All the things he wouldn't force her to do came crashing into his mind. "Hope, would you please join me for a picnic?" Better late than never, right?

She nodded again, this time more emphatically.

"Good." He reluctantly dropped her hands, because the stress of waiting for her answers had caused beads of sweat to pop out along his hairline. Grabbing his cider, he gulped half the can down, trying to discreetly mop his brow. Maybe he should have stayed in his shorts, because it suddenly felt like they were on a deserted island located on the equator.

They ate in silence for a while, Sharkey worried that he'd done this all wrong and it couldn't be redeemed.

"Are you close to your parents?"

The question seemed out of left field, but he was just happy she was speaking to him again. "Not really." After Eve died, he was so angry. At God mostly. Why would he take such a young, amazing girl? A girl who loved Him more than anything. Up to the very end, she said she didn't blame God for her disease. She was excited to be with Him.

Well, Sharkey did blame Him. And he hadn't stepped foot in a church since the funeral.

His parents kicked him out after that. He went from a goodie-two-shoes youth group guy to stealing fruit from the produce stand to survive. The army saved him when God wouldn't.

"My life was pretty insulated, so it was just my parents and me most of the time. I can still hear their voices in my head, telling me what's right and wrong." She furrowed her brow, anger sparking in her eyes. "The truth according to them, I think now."

Sharkey remembered the crumbled-up page she'd thrown away. "They aren't who you thought they were." He still had trouble believing his parents had kicked him out. He was a kid. Grieving the loss of his best friend.

She nodded, her eyes glassy. "It's hard to know what to believe, but their voices are loud."

Riley had given him the *Entertainment Tonight* recap of the missionaries who fleeced their donors. Yet another reason to steer clear of church. "They definitely screwed over a lot of people, but they did one thing right as far as I can tell."

Hope leaned forward as if desperate to find one good thing her parents had done.

"You are amazing. In spite of them."

Her hand covered her mouth, but her eyes shone with something besides just tears. Hope.

He reached across the towel, ready to pull her closer to him when a clap of thunder sounded overhead, causing both Hope and the little sandpiper to jump back.

Fat black clouds rolled in, filling the sky within seconds. *What an idiot.* He'd been so focused on getting Hope alone, he hadn't checked the weather and now they were stuck on an uninhabited island in what could be a brief winter storm, or a full-blown nor'easter. He tamped down the anxiety that rose in his chest, keeping a neutral expression for Hope, who stared up at the sky as it transformed from clear Carolina blue to angry slashes of lightning against ominous dark clouds.

Chucking their picnic back into the cooler, he drained the can of cider, needing a little fortification for what came next. Did they try to make it back to the boat, which was basically a pleasure vessel with only a tiny bimini cover and nowhere to shelter below deck? They weren't far from his brewery and Heron House, but the boat was too large to tie up to Riley's dilapidated dock. Besides, even on the river, which was far more protected than open water, boating during a storm was a bad idea. A decent swell could overtake a vessel that size without any trouble.

They were better off sheltering on land and waiting for the storm to hopefully blow over quickly.

A deserted island had seemed like a flash of genius this morning when he wanted to whisk Hope away from all thoughts of her first date with Book Boy. Now it was looking more like a harebrained idea. This is what he got for being impulsive.

Sand began to swirl in small eddies as the wind picked up and the dune grasses bent until they touched the ground. The tiny sandpiper took off, heading for shelter of its own.

Grabbing the towels, he shook the sand out and stowed them in the cooler on top of the food, hoping to keep them dry for when they'd likely need them. He motioned for Hope to stay put as he trudged up a small rise to survey their options. The sand and scrub stretched north and south for what seemed like miles. The only break in the monotony of rolling dunes was the stand of palms nearby and the patch of small trees where he'd tied the boat off. Shit, what if they lost the boat? He pushed the fear down, deeper into his belly, past the anxiety. He didn't want to think about swimming across the massive Cape Fear River in the middle of winter. And he *refused* to think about Hope Seaton doing that.

The ocean waves were now slamming against the shore, the water choppy with thousands of whitecaps. On the other side, the river churned, dark and foreboding like the sky. Staying put was the only choice.

He ran down the slope back to Hope, who stood barely taller than an egret, her arms wrapped around herself as she shivered in the whipping wind. Bending close to her ear so she could hear him, he steadied her trembling with a hand on her waist. Chills ran up his arm to his chest, her trepidation transferring into his body. He'd take every ounce of her fear if he could.

"Can we get back to the marina in time?" Her words almost evaporated on the wind, but he didn't miss the panic lacing her words.

"No, we need to hunker down here. You go wait under those palms while I make sure the boat is secure. Don't want to lose our ride home." When he pulled back, he saw that his attempt at humor had not only fallen flat but had likely added another worry onto Hope's shoulders. He tucked a strand of hair behind her ear, his thumb stroking the soft skin of her cheek. "It'll be okay. I promise. I'll be right back."

She nodded but appeared on the verge of tears.

He dragged the cooler over to the copse of palms, tucking it in the most sheltered area and encouraged her to sit. It was pure torture to leave her there, clutching her backpack to her chest, looking like a little girl waiting alone for the bus on her first day of school. His survival instincts from his army days kicked in, and he knew he had to prioritize his actions. He could comfort her after the boat was secure, and he'd searched for additional supplies.

His trek back up the small rise in the middle of the island felt like scaling a mountain. His shoes sank into the shifting sand, and the wind was strong enough to battle his bulk the entire way. As he reached the top, he noticed the rope had come untied and was unwinding itself from the clump of shrubs. There was no time to waste.

He slid down the other side, scrambling to reach the rope before it worked its way completely free. A giant water droplet pinged off his shoulder. Then another. In slow motion, rain fell from the heavy clouds, drilling into the sand so hard it left nickel-sized holes. By the time Sharkey had the rope in his hands, water was coming down in sheets from the sky, plastering his clothes to his body.

Running toward the boat, he heaved it further up onto the land, praying the beach wouldn't wash out from under it in the storm. Once he'd pulled it up as far as possible, he secured the rope again, this time triple winding and knotting it. Finished, he launched himself over the side of the vessel, pausing briefly under the bimini top to wipe the water from his eyes. He wasn't usually a hat guy, but he'd proudly wear even a Yankees cap right now.

Time was slipping by, and he needed to get back to Hope. But he thought maybe he'd find something useful on the boat. Chunking seat cushions to the floor, he flung open the bench seats that lined the boat. There were several fancy lifejackets, but they were likely Chesnee's for watersports purposes and would be far too large for Tink's tiny frame. Digging under a pile of rope and bungees, he glimpsed a spot of fluorescent orange, hitting pay dirt. Down in the corner, covered in dust, was a standard life vest—the type that came free with the boat. He grabbed it and ducked back under the top to rake the rain out of his hair. Once he could see better, he realized there was a storage compartment along the back of the boat as well. Inside, a Carolina blue UNC Tarheels hat shined like a beacon. It was resting on top of a dirty brown tarp.

Praise Chesnee. The little punk had earned himself a beer when Sharkey got off this God-forsaken island.

He stuck the cap on his head—finally getting a little relief from the rain streaming into his eyes—then tucked the life vest inside the tarp and secured the bundle under his arm. Then he began the trek back to Hope, praying she was still okay. He surprised himself by pleading with God to keep them safe.

He climbed back up the rise, which had gotten a little easier from the rain compacting the loose sand. Once at the high point of the island, he could see waves crashing violently against the shore, just feet from where they'd had their picnic moments—or was it hours?—ago. Something flew into his face, and he batted it away with his free hand. The exposed skin above his beard burned, but he didn't have time to worry about himself.

His gaze scanned further to the right, and his heart stopped beating when he didn't see Hope under the palm trees. Fumbling down the side of the dune, he raced through the scrub, branches grabbing his pant legs and sand billowing around his feet. As he neared the grove of trees, he realized she was still there, but she'd pulled palm fronds down and built a cape of sorts to protect herself from the rain. It had effectively camouflaged her from a distance and through a curtain of water.

"Hope," he shouted, needing his voice to be heard over the wind and rain.

The shrouded figure didn't move.

Thunder boomed and lightning crackled against the angry clouds.

And Hope peeked out from her leafy hiding place.

Sharkey breathed again.

Inside the tiny shelter, rain streamed between the gaps in the leaves, reminiscent of the makeshift treehouse he'd built when he was fourteen. He and Eve would hide out there during storms, talking about their plans for the future—college, marriage, possibly the ministry. She'd been in remission then, and they were young and naïve about the real world.

Hope spread two of the fronds covering her face and stared up at him, her eyes wide and bright. Not scared, he was relieved to see. More excited. Like they were having a great adventure. He could work with that.

Unwrapping the life vest from the tarp, he thrust it in her direction. "Put this on."

"I thought you said we were staying on land until the storm passed."

"I did, but just in case." He didn't want her to know the scenarios racing through his head. They weren't adventures. They were disasters.

She quirked her mouth, like maybe she'd argue, but then started removing the leaves covering her and strapped the vest on.

He stepped out of the ring of palms, snapping open the tarp and hoisting it over the trees. It was a dollar store bandage on a massive head wound, but maybe it'd give them a little cover. He felt something tugging on the other side and when he investigated, he found Hope outside the shelter, stretching her side of the tarp tight and threading fronds through the grommets to secure it.

Smart, brave and feisty. Yeah, her parents may be charlatans, but they'd raised a hell of a woman.

He kicked himself for not grabbing an extra rope, but Hope's trick worked pretty well, and soon they had patched their holey roof.

They ducked back under the cover, Sharkey was one million percent aware of how soaked Tink was. Every nerve ending in his body sang out into the storm, screaming for rescue. Not from the island, but from the torture of wanting this woman he shouldn't have.

She laughed, throwing her head back and shaking the water from her hair.

He watched in awe as she rung her shirt out, then ran her hands down her legs to squeeze the excess water from her pants. His own shirt clung to his chest, and his jeans were tight from more than just the weight of the water they'd absorbed.

"Did you see that lightning? The sky looked like an etch-a-sketch." Her eyes sparked with life. He'd never seen her this carefree. This happy.

A bead of water ran over her temple, and without debating the merits of doing it, Sharkey reached out to catch the drop. She froze, her gaze darting up to his face, a gazelle assessing danger.

He held still, waiting to see what she decided. Was he a threat?

She gulped, her tongue darting out to moisten her lips—which hardly seemed necessary in this monsoon, but he was there for it. Then she took a step closer to him. Into his orbit.

Sharkey wasn't a genius, but he wasn't an idiot either. He slid his hand closer, cupping her cheek, then cradling the back of her head, until she was in the perfect position.

Their gazes locked, entire tomes being shared without a word, and Hope Seaton settled firmly into his soul. She gripped the sides of his shirt, edging even closer, never losing eye contact. He could see every breath she took, every shiver that whispered along her torso. It was only the two of them in the whole world, nature swirling around them, carrying them to this perfect moment.

Chapter Twenty-Four

They'd created a little bubble of protection from the storm—their own magical universe. Only the two of them. No parental voices admonishing, no indecision racking her consciousness. She wasn't afraid, she wasn't anxious. For the first time ever, Hope knew she was in exactly the right place and precisely the right moment. If someone had told her she'd have her first kiss on a deserted island with a yeti in the middle of a storm, she'd have laughed for days.

It was coming. She knew it with certainty. She didn't know what she'd be doing in three months, or a year, but she knew Squatch was going to kiss her. And she knew she wanted him to.

A few weeks ago, she'd never even read a romance novel. Now, she was on fire with anticipation for what she'd been reading about. That spark. That connection. Until she'd met Sharkey, the only thing she'd longed for was heaven. And the occasional pizza. She didn't know what physical longing was. But now, she'd done a little research—thank you, Harlequin—and she was ready to go into the field and practice what she'd learned.

His gaze bore into her very soul, and it felt like he was filling her, from her toes up, with adoration. She'd never felt so valued. As a person, and certainly not as a woman. No one would accuse Sharkey of being chatty, but his eyes were telling her everything she needed to know.

Then he was moving closer, bowing his head toward her. She lifted up onto her toes, stretching to her full height, grasping his shirt like she might blow away without him anchoring her. They met in the middle, his lips pressing against hers, his beard tickling the delicate skin around her mouth. His grip on her tightened, and he shifted her head slightly, so they pressed closer together.

She could feel the hard planes of his abdomen under her hands, and zings of electricity raced through her body like fireworks exploding inside her.

Just when she thought it couldn't get any better, she parted her lips at the same time as him, and they exchanged breath.

It was like life itself had been breathed into her. It was probably sacrilegious, but she swore she heard angels singing.

Before they parted, Squatch brushed his tongue across her bottom lip. Her knees buckled, but he caught her and crushed her into his chest.

All she could hear was the pounding inside her head and the thump, thump, thump of Sharkey's heart.

Best. Day. Of. Her. Life.

The rain slowed to a steady torrent, the wind no longer blowing it sideways.

Hope's arms stretched around his massive frame, her fingertips barely meeting at his lower back. Her front was plastered to his like her rain-soaked hair to her head. He was hard and soft at the same time, his body completely enveloping hers in a heavenly cocoon of comfort and desire. The skin of her palms tingled, like lightning had stuck her—and maybe it had.

Sharkey shifted on his feet, and she was afraid he would let go. She never wanted him to let go.

But instead, he lifted one hand, smoothing it over her hair and down her back, murmuring deep somethings. She didn't care what he said, as long as his hands were on her.

She pressed her cheek against his chest, relaxing her arms, but keeping a tight hold on the sides of his soaked shirt. His hand slipped lower, resting just above the waistband of her pants. Her heartrate picked up again, and she wondered if it'd be too forward of her to ask for another kiss. Like the ones she'd read about in Riley's books. In the end, she decided she'd had enough excitement for one day. She'd be floating on a cloud for days just from this embrace.

"Have you ever been in love?" She was so relaxed, the question slipped out before she could analyze it to death.

For a minute, she thought he hadn't heard, but then he cleared his throat and answered. "Once. A long time ago." Sadness laced his response.

She brought one of her hands up and placed it over his heart, hoping he'd know what she was feeling. "What happened?"

Sighing, he gripped her tighter. "She died."

Her heart ripped open for him. She wondered if he was still grieving her. If that's why he was single. "How long ago?"

"We were kids. Seventeen." He gathered the loose fabric of her shirt, crushing it in his hand as he pulled her even closer. "What about you? Have you been in love?"

She shook her head, her temple bumping into his chest. "No."

"Really? Not even a schoolgirl crush?" His tone was teasing, and she felt relieved that she hadn't made him sad thinking about his lost love.

"Homeschooled."

He chuckled and she relished the vibrations it produced. "That does limit the pool of candidates." He kissed the top of her head. "Childhood romances rarely work out, so you're probably better off."

If it meant Sharkey could be her first love, she was fine with missing out on teenage drama. It was hard to imagine anything feeling as special as this.

"Sometimes I wonder what else I missed out on." She'd never played sports, never performed a recital, never been to a dance.

"There's time." He placed his hand over hers on his chest, winding his fingers between hers.

The storm ebbed outside and still they remained.

***

Hope awoke slowly, not wanting the dream to be over. She kept her eyes shut tight, fighting against waking up to a reality where she hadn't just kissed Squatch.

Salty air tickled her nostrils and as she stirred, she realized she wasn't in bed. No, this surface was lumpy, firm.

Her eyelids fluttered open and the first thing she saw was sand. Holding her breath—praying it wasn't a dream—she widened her eyes, taking in long, jean-clad legs with thick, muscular thighs.

It was real.

Fully awake now, she soaked in the feel of Sharkey's arms cradling her as she slept on his lap. He was leaning against the cooler, managing to sleep while supporting them both. Carefully, she leaned back, taking in the sight of a sleeping yeti. The one who had kissed her. And now they had slept together.

If her mother were dead, she'd be rolling over in her grave. Maybe she rolled over on her prison cot.

Obviously, they hadn't *slept* together.

But they had slept together! To her, it meant more than sex. When you're asleep, you're vulnerable, and they trusted each other enough to curl up together and nap.

Plus, she had zero perspective as far as sex went.

Outside their palm-tree bubble, the rain had stopped, but the sky was still dark. She didn't know if it was due to storm clouds, or if the sun had set. All sense of time had evaporated the moment Sharkey's lips met hers.

He stirred, and she waited to see how he would react to waking up with a woman in his arms. For all she knew this was a normal occurrence for a handsome man like him. Would he disappointed that it was Hope?

Raking a hand over his beard, he yawned, his eyes popping open at the end. They were like emeralds, rich and warm as he stared down at her. The edges crinkled as his face lit up with a rare Sharkey smile. He pulled her close and kissed the top of her head again.

Not quite as nice as her lips, but she'd take what she could get.

"The storm over?"

"Looks like it."

Placing his finger under her chin, he tipped her head back. "I can't remember the last time I fell asleep during the day."

"Not a big napper, huh?" In her books, a man usually tipped a woman's chin up right before he kissed her. Her stomach somersaulted like an Olympic gymnast.

"I could become one with you around." He lowered his head, bending until his lips met hers again.

During their first kiss, she'd had to focus on not falling down, but this time, she was sitting on a very solid surface, so she took complete advantage. Winding her fingers through his hair, she pulled him closer. He chuckled, but reciprocated, turning her on his lap so she was straddling him.

Sensations overwhelmed her. His hands seemed to be everywhere all at once, like a blind man feeling his way. She felt exhilarated and naughty, but she tamped down the scolding voice in her head and reminded it that she was an adult.

When his tongue swiped across her lips this time, it pushed its way inside her mouth. Gentle at first, then as she responded by meeting his tongue with her own, the kiss deepened, and she nearly blacked out from the power of it. She felt lightheaded and heavy, all at the same time, like when she got malaria as a little girl and had fever dreams.

That's what this whole day felt like. A fever dream.

Maybe that's where the term lovesick came from.

Soon, she was getting the hang of this kissing thing, jousting, sliding, licking. Right before she backed away to catch her breath, she grabbed his bottom lip with her teeth, nipping at the subtle flesh.

She felt something twitch underneath her, and Sharkey moaned, just exactly the sound she'd expect a sasquatch to make.

Hope felt heady with the thrill of making this giant, strong man want her. And she was equally terrified. Pulling back, she covered her lips and looked everywhere but into Squatch's eyes. She started to scoot back, to put some distance between her and the beast she'd aroused from its slumber, but Sharkey grabbed her by the arms, holding her in place and forcing her to look at him.

"Hey, look at me. I'm sorry. I got carried away. Nothing you aren't ready for. Ever. Okay?"

She nodded, torn between wanting to kiss him more, but scared of everything else.

He kept one hand on her waist and dragged the other through his hair, which was sticking up like a porcupine after she'd nearly ripped it out of his head. "I can't believe you've never kissed anyone before." He caught her gaze again. "Because no one has ever kissed me like that."

Something burned in his eyes, and she guessed it might be the same thing happening in his pants. How could she have such an effect on this man? And why did it feel like her insides were on fire?

Chapter Twenty-Five

It was after ten by the time they pulled into the marina. Both Chesnee and Riley had called, one worried about his boat and the other worried about her houseguest.

That was the thing about staying at Heron House. It wasn't an impersonal hotel. It was an intimate home with a nosy hostess who needed all of her guests to be her best friends and drink her fresh-squeezed lemonade.

Sharkey assured them both that all was well and he'd have the boat and Hope back at a reasonable hour.

She'd been quiet on the ride back.

He'd screwed up big time kissing her again. He should have left it a sweet, chaste, meaningful kiss. All day he'd badgered himself about not taking advantage of her, about making it special for her. Her first date, her first kiss, maybe they'd hold hands.

But the hours they'd spent together on that island, in their tiny cocoon, she'd dug deeper into his heart. He told her about Eve, and he'd never told anyone about his first love. They'd talked about her life in Uganda and how he'd become interested in brewing beer. They'd freaking napped together.

She hadn't just scaled the walls around his heart, she'd shattered them like a mortar round through concrete.

Apparently, his heart and his dick were on speaking terms.

As he maneuvered into the slip, he watched her for signs she hated him, that he'd never have the chance to do it right. The boat bumped against the dock. He killed the engine and jumped onto the decking.

"Hand me that rope, please." It wasn't a word he used often, but he couldn't stomach the thought of ordering her around.

She grabbed the coiled rope and slung it over the side of the boat.

He snagged it on the first try. "Nice. I was afraid you'd throw like a girl." He had to know if there was any hope.

"Hey!" She perched her hands on her hips, indignant.

On the island, in the middle of a freak storm, she'd showed her fortitude. She'd shown just how tough she was. He winked. "Do it again." He pointed at the other rope.

She heaved the next one harder and it slammed into his chest. He roared with laughter, the sound echoing in the quiet marina. After he'd secured the boat, he reached his hand out to help her disembark. With a scowl, she handed him her backpack and stepped onto the side of the vessel and then the dock without accepting his assistance.

There was a lightness in his chest he hadn't felt in years. Like maybe something could grow there again.

He grabbed the back of her shirt and hauled her into his arms. "I'm truly sorry. Are we okay?" Resting his forehead against hers, he prayed she wouldn't push him away. Actually prayed. For the second time that day. He knew he wasn't worthy, but he asked anyway.

She stared up at him, her hazel eyes studying him, tunneling into his soul. Then the most magical thing happened. She pushed up on her toes and pressed her lips against his.

When he responded, he was almost certain she was the one moaning this time around.

***

They ran over to Bluffton and grabbed fast food since their island adventure had caused them to miss dinner. The restaurants in Eastport Beach had long since closed for the night. Watching Hope experience her first Big Mac was hilarious and slightly arousing. She could barely fit the burger in her mouth, which got Sharkey's mind headed in the wrong direction again.

As the truck bumped over the drive leading to Heron House, Sharkey deliberated how to handle saying goodbye to Tink. If Riley wasn't such a busybody, he'd take Hope back to his camper and just hold her close all night. But he knew it was too much too soon. Her reaction to his erection during their make-out session assured him of that. He had to pace himself. Not scare her away.

His mind understood it, but his body was driving a different train.

He couldn't kiss her goodbye at the door, because Riley would probably be peeking through the side lights and she'd never let him live it down. Sometimes he just wanted to live alone in the woods and be left alone. But most of the time, he loved having Ben and Riley as neighbors.

Pulling the truck to a stop just past the stairs, Sharkey took a steading breath. All in all, it'd been a good day. Sure, they'd been trapped on a deserted island for several hours, but he was pretty sure that had worked in his favor. Shutting the world out for a while helped them bond and explore their attraction in a safe and beautiful way. He'd be reliving that first kiss all night long.

"Thanks for hanging out with me today. Sorry about the storm." He turned the ignition off but made no move to get out of the truck.

She turned to him, and he could just barely make out her profile in the light from the porch. Of course, Riley left the light on for Hope. The better for her to spy on them. "It was fun, like *Robinson Crusoe*. Without the cannibalism." Her smile lit up his insides.

He pushed a strand of her hair behind her ear, leaning closer, breathing in her fresh scent. She smelled like salt and rain—and a little bit like him. He'd sleep well knowing that. "I hope I didn't make you miss anything." Like dinner plans with a certain Book Boy.

Shaking her head, she glanced toward the porch. "No, I didn't have any plans tonight."

The sound of tires bumping over gravel preceded headlights flashing over them.

Hope's eyes widened, almost panicked. "I must look like a rain-soaked goat." She grabbed her backpack, digging around and pulling her sweatshirt out.

"I think you look great." Who did she suddenly need to impress? "I wonder who'd be coming so late."

"It's probably just Aiden. He said he'd be late tonight." She pulled the hoodie over her head, smoothing her hair and looking everywhere except at Sharkey.

She couldn't possibly be attracted to that weenie. Not like the chemistry they had. And why does she know his schedule? Had he contacted her today? Hope didn't spend time on her phone like most people these days, but she could have checked her texts when he was driving the boat back to the marina.

Well, there was no longer a question. He was absolutely walking her to the door now. Before Ponytail turned his car off, Sharkey was out the door and on the passenger side of his truck, helping Hope step down, grabbing her backpack like a true gentleman. The way he gripped her waist was more like a cheetah marking his territory.

"You don't need to walk me in." Her eyes darted from Sharkey to Book Boy's car and back.

"It's no problem." He led her around the pompous prick's BMW and up the steps. "After a date, it's customary to see a lady to her door."

Hope audibly gulped.

Sharkey leaned close to her ear. "Best date I've had in years." He was bringing out the big guns, but he wasn't lying. It had been the most fun he'd had with a woman in decades. And they kept their clothes on the entire time.

"Hope! Are you just getting in?" Book Boy fumbled with a bag as he rushed out of his car and up the steps.

"Uh, dude, there's something falling out of your purse."

Tink turned her head into Sharkey's chest and snorted.

Book Boy's face turned ashen under his fake tan. "It's a messenger bag." He scooped up the papers that were strewn over the porch. "Where have you two been?"

"I took Hope out on the boat. Then to a fancy dinner."

She grinned up at him, their gazes locking, like the thesis-writing punk didn't exist.

"Uh, I thought, um," Book Boy sputtered.

"Gotta watch out for that. Studies show thinking too much can suck the fun right out of life." Sharkey yanked open the front door, startling Riley, who jumped back. "Hi, Ri. Lovely evening." He pulled Hope up the stairs with him, stopping only once they reached the door to her suite.

She bit her bottom lip, but her impish smile reached her eyes.

"I really did have a great time today. Thank you." He leaned down and kissed her gently, relishing in the salty taste of her lips from the fries. "Will I see you tomorrow?"

Tink nodded and Sharkey's world clicked into place.

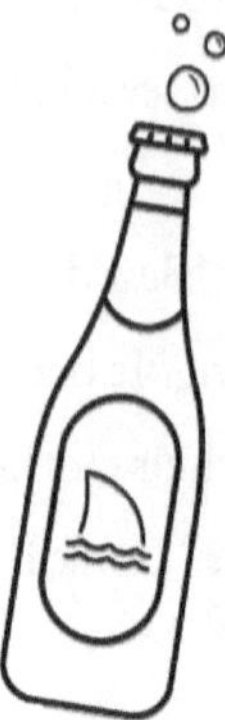

Chapter Twenty-Six

"Ohmygosh, ohmygosh, ohmygosh." Hope leaned against her closed door, letting out the anxiety that had been building since Aiden's car pulled in the driveway. Two men. Maybe she was a wanton hussy.

She dug her phone out of her bag to call her cousin, but a knock at her door stopped her. Maybe Squatch was back for some more of that dynamite kissing. Or Riley could tell she needed to talk to someone.

"Who is it?"

"It's Aiden."

Well, crap. She wasn't prepared to face man #2. But she could hardly put him off with him standing outside her suite. She cracked the door open. "Hey, what's up?" Her voice cracked like a teenage boy going through puberty.

He looked nice in a collared shirt with a Duke Blue Devil on the left chest and pressed slacks. If she had to guess, Sasquatches didn't iron. Aiden's hair was pulled back in its usual ponytail, and he smelled like some sort of spice—curry, maybe? "I'm just making sure we're still on for dinner tomorrow night." He kept shifting back and forth, bouncing on the balls of his feet.

Maybe they were both nervous. She wondered if he saw Sharkey kiss her goodnight. Her room was the first one near the stairs, so it's possible he could see from the foyer. Did she need to break her date because she'd kissed another man? Would Aiden consider it cheating? She didn't know all the rules. That's why she needed to call Bridget, pronto. "Yup, sure. Of course." *Awkward, much?*

He let out a whoosh of air. "Great. When I saw you with that brewer guy, I wasn't sure what to think."

Hope froze. She didn't want to lie to Aiden, but technically he hadn't asked her a question. How quickly she'd gone from following all the rules to justifying lies of omission. This dating thing was complicated. She didn't understand how people did it any younger. It was hard enough in her early twenties, but she guessed she wasn't a normal twenty-two-year-old, either. "What time should I be ready?"

"Six-thirty should be fine." He grinned, looking more relaxed now that their plans had been confirmed.

She had the distinct feeling Squatch wouldn't be as easy to pacify. "Well, night then."

"Yeah, good night." He leaned toward her, but she panicked and waved before shutting the door.

"Heckity Holy Heck. What have I gotten myself into?" Hope wound her body into the upholstered chair and called her cousin. Maybe she'd know what to do. Bridget had been dating since she was sixteen and probably never secretly crushed on Bigfoot.

The phone rang and rang. Hope checked the time again—it was still early on the west coast. Early enough that her cousin could be on a date of her own.

Bridget's bubbly voice told her to send a text, because who has time to listen to voicemails.

Hope typed out a message and said she'd be up for another hour or so. Her stomach flipped and flopped, like there was a scared frog stuck in her abdomen. She didn't know if it was nerves over this insane situation or the giant hamburger she'd had for a late dinner.

She'd had so many firsts since coming to Eastport Beach. Most of them with Sharkey. Heat rushed to her cheeks remembering their kisses. He made her excited, nervous, tingly, and somehow more comfortable than she'd ever been with another person.

Her brain buzzed with overload from her feelings, logic, what she'd learned from the Bible and her mother's warnings about impurity. Her cousin still hadn't returned her call, and she couldn't risk going to find Riley, lest she run into Aiden again, so she opened a fresh notebook and poured all her thoughts onto the page.

I know how Sharkey makes me feel, but are we compatible at all? Does he believe in God? Do I anymore? Maybe I shouldn't be thinking about men at all. I need to figure what I'm going to do with my life after this darn book. I always assumed I'd help people in Uganda, maybe marry a missionary who would enjoy that kind of work. Thanks to my parents' greed, I've lost everything. Most of all my identity. I should start there. Who is Hope Seaton? What do I want out of life? What does God want for my life?

Despite her crisis of identity and faith, questions about God always popped into her mind. He was still part of her, woven into her soul. Her parents hadn't completely severed that connection.

Figuring that out gave her a bit of peace. For the moment at least.

***

Sunlight streamed through the window, warming Hope's face and teasing her dreams. As she awoke, she stretched, trying to unkink her body. She'd fallen asleep in the chair, her notebook wedged uncomfortably between her and the arm. Her phone buzzed with a text. She grabbed it off the side table, noting the battery warning light. It wasn't yet second nature to charge the phone regularly. In Uganda, she'd had a wall phone with a curly cord that stretched halfway across the kitchen.

Squatch

Good Morning.

The palms of her hands tingled, her leg started to jiggle, and a smile slid up her face. Another message followed the first, but she had to switch out of Sharkey's text to see it. Maybe Bridget was finally getting back to her.

Aiden

Looking forward to dinner tonight.

Fully awake now, Hope shifted in her seat, wondering how to respond. To Sharkey. To Aiden. Apparently, sleeping had not brought any resolution.

She clicked out of Aiden's message and realized that her cousin had responded at some point during the night.

Bridget

It's like 2 there, so I'm not going to call you now. Can't wait to hear what's going on. You sound...happy? Confused? Dare I say, horny?

Heat rose up her neck and into her cheeks. *Hecka hippos. This is what horny feels like?* Hope couldn't decide if it was wonderful, like waiting for a banana split to arrive, or terrifying, like hearing the dentist's drill come closer.

Hope

Call me as soon as you wake up. It's an emergency!

She clicked over to Sharkey's message. Reading the words on the screen lit up her insides—knowing he had likely just woken up and thought immediately of her.

She typed three responses before settling on what she hoped sounded casual and maybe even funny.

Hope

Good morning. Any plans to be marooned today?

Squatch

Only if you're coming.

"Ohmygosh, ohmygosh, ohmygosh." She jumped up from the chair, pacing the room like a caged tiger. Sweat beaded on her forehead. Ripping her sweatshirt off, she quickly stripped down and turned the shower on.

She'd spent the night in an armchair, wearing damp clothes after she'd basically been a castaway. Throw in kissing Sharkey multiple times—it was no wonder she was out of sorts. Her body was short-circuiting. Her brain fried. Anyone in her shoes would be confused.

The water cooled her heated face, but as it coursed over her body, she flashed back to standing in the rain, to feeling Squatch's hands on her. And she was on fire again. If this was what being horny felt like, how did people function? Would she forever be this hot? This tingly?

If she showed up at the brewery today, would Sharkey kiss her again?

Was she allowed to kiss one man and then go to dinner with another in the same day? Without going straight to hell?

After her shower, Hope did something she'd rarely done in her life—she fussed over what to wear. At home, she'd just throw on her overalls and a tee shirt. The orphans didn't care how she looked. Now, she had all these outfits to choose from. Leggings, linen pants, dresses—why were there so many choices in America?

Sharkey with his gruff, raw manliness.

Aiden with his intellect and empathy.

Full body chills or quiet comfort?

She was tempted to get on a plane to escape all these hard decisions.

Finally settling on a soft cotton romper with a muted floral pattern, Hope smiled at herself in the mirror. Even she had to admit it was a huge step up from dirty dungarees and worn sneakers. She tucked her hair behind her ears, stuffed a couple notebooks in her bag and headed downstairs where the smell of cinnamon beckoned her from the kitchen.

"Morning!" Riley smiled from her perch on the counter and held her mug aloft in a greeting. "I've been waiting for you!" She hopped down and slipped into one of the chairs at the table. "Tell me everything."

Finally, someone to talk to about the emotional vortex swirling around in her head. "What is that amazing smell?"

"I've got cinnamon rolls in the oven. But we've got a few minutes before they're ready and maybe I was hallucinating, but I'm pretty sure Sharkey kissed you last night." She folded her hands under her chin and watched Hope as she poured a glass of milk.

"You didn't imagine it."

Riley squealed, clapping. "I knew there was something going on there. The way that man looks at you—" She froze, her gaze dropping, suddenly intently interested in her coffee.

"Are you guys talking about me?" Aiden asked from behind Hope.

Great balls of beezwax. Can I not catch a break?

He patted her on the shoulder before stepping over to the coffee maker. "Something smells delicious."

Riley's phone trilled, and she leapt from the table, grabbing a potholder shaped like a fish. "Homemade cinnamon rolls. Hot from the oven."

"What a treat." Aiden took the seat beside Hope, scooting his chair closer to her. "I don't want to overdo it though, we're having a nice dinner tonight." He winked at her.

She grinned back, praying he'd take his cinnamon roll and eat it somewhere else so she could finish talking to Riley.

Their hostess slid a plate in front of each of them.

Roll did not exactly describe the dish. It looked more like bread pudding, a little soggy and chunky. But how bad could a cinnamon roll be?

"Thanks a ton, Riley. You really go above and beyond." Aiden cut a huge chunk of the baked good off and shoved it in his mouth. He chewed a few times, then his face scrunched up, and he swallowed like someone was forcing him to eat poison.

Riley joined them at the table with her own plate. "What do you think? Moist, huh?"

He nodded and gave her a thumbs up. "Super moist."

Aiden hadn't fallen over dead, so Hope took a small bite of the "roll." She was not an expert, but something was wrong with the baked good. How could something be both soggy and dry at the same time? The bite stuck in her throat, so she took a huge swig of milk to push it down. Riley had an expectant puppy dog look on her face. Hope struggled to find something complimentary to say. She might be lustful, but she didn't want to add liar to her list of sins. "It's really different than anything I've had before." Suddenly she remembered Sharkey warning her about Riley's cinnamon rolls. Now she understood.

Her hostess grinned, shoveling bites of the roll down. "Yeah, I haven't perfected the shape just yet, but it's getting better with every batch."

Hope and Aiden exchanged a glance.

He grabbed his mug and plate and rose from the chair. "I've got a lot of writing to do, so I think I'll take this delightful breakfast upstairs with me. Hope, maybe we can write together this afternoon?"

She nodded, torn between following him and getting a chance to speak to her friend. Needing advice won out. She'd just have to force the pastry down.

After Aiden left, Riley pushed her empty plate aside. "Okay, dish."

"Dish?" Hope held out her plate, grateful her hostess was clearing the table.

Riley laughed and waved her hand. "No, it means spill the beans. Tell me what happened. I'm not taking your plate away."

"Oh," Hope laughed, embarrassed that there was so much she didn't know. About men, about slang, and apparently about Southern cuisine. "I'm so confused." Seeing her friend's face, she clarified. "Not about spilling the beans. About the beans."

For the next thirty minutes or so, Hope told Riley about Aiden asking her on a date, Sharkey taking her on a boat ride, the storm. The kiss. She laid out all her feelings, emotionally and some physically—even though it was mortifying. Throughout, she took tiny bites of cinnamon mush until it was mostly gone.

Riley sat enraptured the entire time, nodding and sipping her coffee.

"Do you think I'm a floozy?"

Her hostess laughed, covering her mouth with a napkin. Hope must have looked horrified, because Riley rushed to speak. "Of course not! The only reason I laughed is because I worried about the same thing right after I moved to Eastport Beach. I was recently divorced and the new girl in town. Ben and I connected pretty quickly, and I worried that the locals would see me as a loose woman who wanted to get her hooks in the widower."

"And they didn't?"

"Gosh, no. Eastporters are just about the least judgmental people you'll meet. Except for the prayer circle. Those ladies will condemn your soul for wearing white after Labor Day." She chuckled. "I'm kidding. Mostly."

Hope's chest tightened. She'd hoped to visit the local church, but not if they would judge her for her parents' sins. "I don't want anyone to think poorly of me."

Riley shook her head. "You are a good person, Hope. Don't doubt that. You've done absolutely nothing wrong. I had to give myself permission to fall in love with Ben. I'd failed at marriage and felt damaged. But we all deserve love. Especially if your family doesn't know how to give it freely."

Can she see inside my soul? Hope took a steadying breath. "Thanks, Riley. I really needed to talk about everything going on. I'm trying to take one day at a time, but things are happening so fast, the last twenty-fours feels like an eternity."

"You're in the love bubble."

"The what?"

Riley grinned. "The love bubble. It's the best. No one else matters, just you and him."

"So do I have two bubbles?" It was possible she was more confused than before.

"Oh no, you can only have one bubble at a time. But you don't have to decide who to let in your bubble right now." She rose from the table and rinsed her mug out. "Ben and I are still in the bubble. Best feeling ever."

Hope watched her hostess disappear into the not-so-secret passage that led to their private space. She felt slightly better about the whole dating thing, but things would be a lot easier if there were only one man in her life.

Chapter Twenty-Seven

She said she was coming. She'd kissed him goodnight in front of Riley *and* Book Boy. They'd had banter over text.

So, where the hell was the woman who'd dominated his dreams?

Sharkey was pacing in front of the container, checking his phone every five seconds like a lovesick fool, when a sheriff's car pulled in. Deputy Klein stepped out of the vehicle, straightening her utility belt and ducking back in to grab her notepad. He shot one last glance in the direction of Heron House before heading to meet the cop.

"Mr. McLaughlin, I need to ask you a few follow-up questions." Her posture rigid—like her sergeant had shown up for a spot inspection—she took in her surroundings subtly.

He wondered if she was also looking for the little blonde firecracker that was impossible to forget. "Only if you call me Sharkey." He almost added, *at ease, solider*, but he didn't know her well enough to joke around.

She nodded once, then flipped through her notepad. "Are you familiar with the property across the road?"

Now we're getting somewhere. "Somewhat. I considered purchasing it before this land became available." He waited to see where she was going before he revealed anymore of his hand.

"According to a local real estate agent, there have been many interested parties lately, particularly a corporation with ties to the area."

So she'd met Piper. "Brightside."

Her well-plucked eyebrow winged heavenward.

Looked like Nic's intel was solid. "You get a hit on the prints?"

"Yes. I've been tracking down that lead as I'm able."

In other works, Dirk "the dick" Morgan was throwing up roadblocks to her investigation. The county sheriff was of the "good-ol-boy" generation. Never met a rocking chair and beer he didn't like. Doing his job? Not so much. "It's a little different than New Hanover County, huh?"

Her pause was answer enough. "The suspect is familiar to law enforcement in my old jurisdiction. I hope to get up to Wilmington later this week."

"This suspect have a name?"

"I'm afraid I can't share that information. But since you brought up Brightside, have you had any dealings with them?"

Sharkey shook his head. "They don't bother with local brews. Strictly big names."

Klein pursed her lips and made a notation on her pad. "Have you seen anything unusual since the last time we spoke?"

"No, it's been quiet." And his attention had been firmly elsewhere. He'd even forgotten a critical step for a raspberry cider and had to throw the whole batch out. Hope was seriously fucking with his head. And his heart, which was even scarier.

"Good. Maybe this will blow over."

He doubted it. In his experience, bad people didn't stop doing bad things until someone made them. If Brightside bought that land, would his whole operation go up in smoke? He knew the locals would support him over the shiny new toy, but what else might the company pull if they felt threatened by his success? If they were coming after him from an hour away, how bad would it be from across the street?

He thanked the deputy and watched her drive away. He was glad she'd transferred when she did, because Sheriff Morgan couldn't be bothered to get off his ass and actually protect his citizens. But what if it was too little too late? And what if Sharkey was so distracted by Tink that he missed something crucial?

Shaking his head to clear it, he made a decision. He had to focus on his business. He couldn't afford to get into a courting challenge with a ponytail.

Sharkey turned his phone to silent and headed for the production facility, determined to get all his ducks in a row. Although seagulls would be more fitting, and they were way crazier than ducks.

***

A few hours later, he'd paid invoices, ordered supplies, and sealed the new batch of raspberry cider into the fermenter. The process had taken most of the day, but being in the production facility invigorated him. He much preferred this over construction—especially when someone was sabotaging him at every turn.

His phone blared his musical selection for the day—classic 80s rock—but as he washed his hands, he swore he heard a knock. Drying his hands, he turned the volume down and listened. Sure enough, another sharp rap echoed through the building. He guessed the fools who'd been messing around wouldn't bother to knock.

There were few windows in the steel building and none near the door. He opened the app on his phone and pulled up the camera feed. Hope looked even tinier from the angle of the camera. He'd stayed focused most of the day but had snuck several peeks at his phone to see if she'd texted. She hadn't.

But she was here now. Blood rushed through his body, his heart pumping faster. All from a grainy image on his phone.

He yanked open the door, desperate to put his eyes on her—in real life. And his hands. Oh yeah, lips, too. "Hey." Sweat beaded along his hairline. So much for playing it cool.

"Hey." She shifted from foot to foot on the steps, her gaze pinging around him.

"Come in." He stepped back to let her pass into his small vestibule.

Her bag was slung over one shoulder, pulling at her shirt, exposing the tender flesh near her neck. He wanted to lean down and nibble on her. Instead, he stepped to the glass-front fridge displaying cans of his product and a few bottles of water.

"Want a water?"

"Sure." She twisted her hands together, uncertainty clear in her body language.

Did she regret yesterday? Had she spent today with Book Boy? Now Sharkey was doubting everything between them too.

She took the water, gulped it, even dribbling a little down her chin—and Sharkey broke.

He grabbed her, pulling her close, settling her petite frame against his body, feeling at peace for the first time since he left her last night. Her arms stretched around him, and she rested her cheek on his chest, sighing contentedly. The connection healed most of his doubt. He kissed the top of her head, rubbing her back and squeezing her tighter.

When she pulled back and looked up at him, her hazel eyes shimmering with something—hope, maybe?—he bent forward, capturing her mouth and reclaiming the excitement of yesterday. She was exactly as sweet as he remembered. Like peaches and cream with a hint of cinnamon.

He pushed the hair back from her face, his lips straying from hers as he headed toward the hollow of her neck he'd noticed earlier. Planting kisses along the way, Hope mewled and adjusted her head to give him better access. She opened herself to him. Trusted him. The realization made him heady, like he'd drunk two cans of his 13% ABV beer. He pulled her delicate skin between his teeth, careful not to be rough, but wanting to taste her there. Her hands moved to his biceps, squeezing him, holding on for dear life.

His camper was steps away. But this was Tink. He couldn't take her there and ravish her, even if every cell in his body was screaming for release. So, he pulled back, secretly proud of the little spot he'd left on her neck. He'd bet anything it was her first hickey too.

"I waited for you at the picnic tables," she murmured breathlessly, her eyes half lidded.

So much for getting his head on straight—he couldn't very well protect her from inside this building. Further proof he didn't deserve to be her man. "I'm sorry. I had some stuff to do."

She straightened, her hand touching her neck where his mouth had been. "It's okay. I got some writing done. More organizing my thoughts, really."

"That's good." He glanced at his watch. "Maybe we can grab dinner?"

Her eyes widened, and she sucked her bottom lip in. "Um, I kind of have plans tonight."

Please let them be with Riley. Please tell me she's not keeping her date with the ponytail. Not after yesterday. Not after she burrowed her way into my heart.

"Okay." He tried to sound calm even as tornado sirens blasted in his head. "Tomorrow?" Pathetically, he held his breath.

"Sure, I'd like that."

If he made it to tomorrow without losing his mind obsessing over her possible date with Book Boy.

"Sharkey, can I ask you something?" She stood close but not touching—pure torture.

"Anything." Most people were lucky to get a grunt from him, but for Tink, he'd recite the entire book of Psalms.

"Have you kissed a lot of girls?"

The age difference hit him hard in that moment. He tried to tell himself it didn't matter, but eleven years was a big gap. Looking into her eyes, he pushed that doubt aside. "Only two that mattered."

He captured her mouth again, pouring his heart and soul into the kiss, hoping she understood how he felt. And making sure she'd be thinking about him tonight—even if a lesser man was buying her dinner.

After she left—a little unsteady on her feet, Sharkey noted proudly—he closed up the production facility for the night and wandered over to make sure the container was secure.

So much for focusing on Shark Bite. One smile from that beautiful woman and he was chucking his hat back in the ring, ready to go ten rounds with Mr. PhD. He wondered briefly if Eve would approve of Hope.

The night before she passed, when Sharkey was on his knees at her bedside, pleading his eternal love, Eve had taken his hand, using most of her strength to lift it to her lips. Sometimes, he could still feel her lips on his palm. She whispered, because he had snuck into her room, "You're gonna find someone more awesome than me. She shouldn't give you any slack or let you get away with stupid stuff. Sharkey, I'm your first love, not your only love. Don't give up."

He hadn't even considered another woman since that night.

Until Tink flitted into his life.

Now, it was painful to imagine his life without her in it. Hell, take this morning—he'd been distraught when she hadn't shown up after breakfast.

Eve had rolled into his life at an end-of-school pool party hosted by his church. She'd moved to town to see a specialist who hoped he could cure the disease that was killing her from the inside out. Sharkey had taken one look at her and decided she was the one. Despite needing a wheelchair most of the time, she'd laughed and cut up with the other teens and even taunted him into doing a cannonball off the diving board. That evening, they'd shared a pizza because out of nearly thirty kids, they were the only ones who'd eat the supreme.

Within a week, he'd asked her to be his girlfriend, and by the Fourth of July, he knew he would marry her.

She lived nearly a year after that. Three-hundred-seventy-seven days of Eve. That was all he got. Losing her broke him. He turned away from God, his parents turned him out, and he just barely graduated high school.

The Army stitched him back together—taught him how to function with the giant hole in his heart. Mentally, he moved on. Emotionally, he died with Eve.

Then Hope showed up, like a paramedic shocking him with a defibrillator—slowly reviving his heart.

For the past ten years, his whole world had been Shark Bite. Was there room for the business he lived for and someone to love?

Under one of the picnic tables, he spotted a wad of paper. Bending down, he smoothed it out and held it up in the fading light. He was getting used to finding Hope's rejects. He'd found two in the truck last night that must have fallen out of her backpack. To him, they were insightful and raw, along with her characteristic doodles. The collection in his drawer grew by the day. Little pieces of her heart. He felt honored to save them from garbage. She obviously didn't realize how impactful they were. How much he'd already gleaned from them.

Today's intended trash was just a few lines and a gorilla, maybe?

He took out his phone and shined the flashlight on the page.

Well, I'll be damned. It was Bigfoot. He chuckled, then read the text.

> *Scripture says to flee from sexual immorality. My parents told me I would remain pure until they determined a Godly partner for me. My body is betraying everything I've ever known. But my heart is telling me he is a good man. I've always done what's expected of me. Does following my heart make me a bad person?*

Sharkey pressed the paper against his chest, his eyes wet. He hadn't cried since Eve died. That couldn't be it. He was just tired. The weight of being with Hope pressed against his heart. It was too great a responsibility for someone who had turned away from the Lord, and love, almost two decades ago. She deserved someone who believed what she did. Someone who still had faith. Someone who could give his heart fully.

Why did he always fall for the girl he couldn't have? Eve had been sick when he met her. Logically, he knew she'd likely die from her illness, but his naive, young heart thought that love could cure anything—even a fatal disease.

Chapter Twenty-Eight

Hope checked her reflection. Cute outfit, check. New bracelet, check. Hair, check. She pushed her blonde locks behind her ears. *What the heck?* Leaning closer, she bent her head to the side. What was on her neck? A bruise?

She gasped. That was where Squatch had been kissing her. Where it had felt delicious and made the soles of her feet burn.

There was a knock on the door. *Crap!* She checked her phone, but it was still thirty minutes before she was supposed to meet Aiden.

"Hope? Can I come in?" Riley knocked again.

"Sure." She rubbed at the spot on her neck. Maybe she should change clothes. Find something that covered it up.

"Hey! I brought you a little surpris—." Her friend gasped. "Is that a hickey?"

Hope dropped her face into her hands. *A hickey?* Her mother would be mortified. Which made Hope secretly proud. If only she weren't going on a date with a different guy than the guy who gave her a hickey. "Is it really noticeable?"

"Uh, yeah." Riley wore an amused smile. "But we can put a little makeup on it. As long as no one gets too close, it should be fine."

She didn't intend on letting anyone else nibble on her neck today. "Do you have some?"

"Of course! I'll be right back." Riley darted out of the room and down the stairs.

Hope snapped a picture with her phone. First selfie. First hickey. Second first date. These were not milestones she'd imagined a month ago.

She sent the picture to her cousin with a plea for help.

Bridget

You go, girl!

Hope

I'm going to dinner with Aiden. I can't have this on my neck!

Bridget

Squatch gave you a hickey?!? Damn! I thought it was just kissing.

Hope

He was kissing my neck.

Bridget

Honey, that's more than just kissing. That yeti is marking his territory.

He is totally marking his territory!

"I've got concealer and pressed powder!" Riley tore into the room, triumphantly holding the makeup over her head.

"Shh! I don't want Aiden to hear." Hope peeked out into the hall, but luckily the coast was clear.

Riley waved her off. "He's not here." She grinned. "He may or may not have asked Ben where to buy flowers."

Flowers? Aww, that is so sweet. "I'm going to kill Sharkey. I mean, not really, but I'm so mad." Mad, and a little excited. Squatch was jealous. Over her.

"Hold still." Riley adjusted Hope's head so she could apply makeup to the small bruise. "I've only known Sharkey for about six months, but Ben said he's never seen him date anyone. He must really like you."

Her cheeks heated, turning them bright pink. In the mirror, she watched her friend try to cover up the spot. "I don't think it's working." Now she had a brown blob covering most of her neck, obvious against her pale skin.

Riley scrunched her face, appraising her work. "Yeah, I think the makeup's too dark, and your skin is too light. Time for Plan B." She reached in her pocket and unfurled a colorful scarf—like a magician performing a magic trick.

"Isn't it like sixty degrees today?"

"This was my uncle's. I think it's less for warmth and more for fashion." Riley shrugged.

What Hope knew about fashion could fit on the tip of a pencil, but the scarf was ugly.

Bridget

> Tell him you have girl problems. Guys are terrified of that.

She grabbed the scarf from Riley, wrapping it twice around her neck. "Is this right?" One end hung down to her belly button, and the other hovered near her chest.

The two faced the mirror. "Maybe wrap it again," Riley suggested.

"Your uncle really wore this?"

"I have no idea, but it was in his closet."

A headache was forming behind Hope's eyes.

Riley snapped her fingers. "Turtleneck!"

"I don't have any. It's always summer in Uganda." Hope unwound the scarf. "Do you have one I could borrow?"

"I haven't worn a turtleneck since I needed to cover up my own hickeys—back in high school." She made a face. "Larry was like a freaking Hoover."

Maybe if Hope had gone to a regular high school, she would be better prepared for this. She wouldn't be twenty-two and dealing with first dates, first kisses, and first inconvenient hickeys. "I don't feel well." She sat down on the bed.

Riley propped her hands on her hips. "You can't stand him up. He's buying flowers! The only time Larry got me flowers was after his grandma died, and he swiped one of the funeral arrangements. It literally said *RIP* on it."

"I'm assuming Larry is your ex." Riley's current boyfriend, Ben, seemed perfect as far as Hope could tell.

"Yeah, and he was my first love. Now I know I got jipped." She laughed. "Seriously, you deserve all the excitement, romance, and butterflies in your stomach."

Hope didn't think she should tell her she'd already had all that with Sharkey.

Riley pursed her lips. "What if we put makeup all over your neck and face? Make it match?"

"It's worth a shot, I guess." She really didn't want to wear the hideous scarf.

***

At half-past six, Hope was waiting on the porch, nauseous. Riley had assured her she looked great, but she had her doubts. Doubts about everything. Dinner. The makeup. Aiden. Sharkey. Writing the book.

The last time she'd felt secure in her life was before her parents were arrested. Before she found out that her entire world was a sham.

Was it better to be ignorant and happy or so aware that it felt like everything was crumbling around you?

Aiden's car pulled down the driveway, his headlights flashing over the fountain with the bronze heron on top. Apparently, Riley's uncle had been an artist, and the piece was his work. The bird appeared to be taking off, its wings outstretched, and its neck elongated. Hope wondered briefly what it would be like to fly, to escape everything weighing on her mind.

"Hi." Aiden had stopped the car and opened his door, stepping out with a bouquet of flowers. He rounded the front of the car and mounted the steps while she stood, frozen. "You look nice." His smile didn't fully reach his eyes. He extended the flowers to her.

She took the arrangement, drawing the blooms to her face, but they didn't smell like anything. Maybe they were fake. "Thank you, they're beautiful. I'll ask Riley for a vase." Escaping back into the house, Hope forced herself to breathe. *It's just dinner. A meal. And flowers. Crap, this is so a date.* It felt disingenuous to go out with Aiden when she couldn't stop thinking about Sharkey's mouth on her neck.

"Oo, those are gorgeous!" Riley rushed out of the parlor to meet her. If Hope had to guess, their hostess had been peeking out the leaded-glass windows.

Hope nodded, still arguing with herself in her mind. "Do you have a vase?"

"I'm sure Archie has something in the butler's pantry." She led the way to the kitchen and then to the pass-through that led to the owner's suite. "Aiden's starting off strong, huh?"

Hope sank into one of the chairs at the table. "I don't think I should go."

Riley reappeared with a crystal vase. "I promise, the makeup is hardly noticeable."

"It's not that." She dropped her head into her hands. "It feels wrong. Like I'm not being honest."

"Honest about what?"

She checked the hallway to make sure they were alone. "I don't think I like Aiden like I like Sharkey."

Riley sighed. "You don't want to lead him on."

"Yeah." Hope dropped her head to the table, letting the smooth surface cool her overheated skin. "Which is worse? Cancelling the date at the last minute or thinking about another man the whole time?"

Her usually chatty friend sat silent.

"I'm a horrible person."

Riley shook her head emphatically. "Not at all. You can't help the way you feel. But you haven't known either of them long, so maybe you should give Aiden a chance?"

Hope stuck the flowers in the vase. "Maybe."

"And if you don't feel anything by the end, just tell him you want to be friends."

"What if I do feel something?" *Besides the churning in my gut?*

Riley shrugged. "Then we might need wine."

"Does dating often drive people to drink?"

"All. The. Time." Riley scooped up the vase and took it to the sink. "I'll take care of these. You go have fun and don't take it too seriously. It's just a first date. You're not marrying the guy."

Okay, I can do this. She pushed up from the table. "Wish me luck."

"You've already gotten flowers. This date is already better than most."

"Was dating Ben hard in the beginning?"

Riley's face flushed. "God, no. Ben's perfect. It's actually the most annoying thing about him."

Neither Sharkey nor Aiden were perfect, but yesterday should have been a disaster, and it turned out to be one of the best days of her life. So maybe tonight wouldn't be so bad.

Chapter Twenty-Nine

Sharky pulled his arm back, bouncing on the balls of his feet, then let the punch fly. The bag wobbled, then swung back and forth. He was blasting hard rock, something raw with a lot of bass, trying to block out the image of Hope at dinner with the ponytail. He punched the bag again, totally not picturing Book Boy's face.

Sweat seeped through his tank top. He'd been at it for almost an hour, trying to wear himself out so he could collapse into bed and not be tempted to go back to Heron House and spy. Again.

His phone rang, interrupting the music and filling his chest with anticipation. Maybe she changed her mind. Maybe she dumped Book Boy and wanted to come over.

He ripped at the boxing gloves, anxious to get to the phone in time. Finally, one glove was off, and he swiped the screen without looking.

"Hello?"

"Sharkey. Nic here. We've got a situation."

Sighing, he wiped his face with the bottom of his shirt. The Landing had probably run out of beer. He'd warned the manager not to cut back just because it was winter. Eastporters got bored easily and partied more in the cooler months. "What can I do for you?"

The bartender dropped his voice, and the background noise dimmed like he'd stepped away from the bar. "I think someone messed with your kegs."

"What?" Nic had his full attention now. He yanked the other glove off and started gathering his things.

"All of your taps are bad. Only yours."

You've got to be shitting me. Now they're hitting a bar I supply? "These new or old?" It could be a warped gasket or something, but all his kegs at the same time?

"I put these on earlier in the week. They were fine last night. Tonight, first 33rd parallel I pour, it's got shit floating in the foam. Same with the pear cider. I changed out both kegs for a fresh one. Same thing."

"Let me see what I've got available. I'll be there in thirty." He hung up, a stream of profanity spewing from deep in his gut. These bastards were fighting the wrong guy. Seamus McLaughlin wouldn't just roll over and die.

He'd set up a corner of his production facility with some free weights and his bag, so it took no time to pull several kegs from his stock and load them in the truck. His reputation was on the line, so he couldn't show up at Eastport Beach's nicest restaurant sweaty and in workout gear. Jumping in the shower, he prayed the miscreants weren't hanging around ready to tamper with the kegs in his truck. He was clean and dressed within minutes.

The truck looked untouched, and when he jostled the kegs, they all seemed full, so he headed toward town. The Landing was located right on the water near the marina. He pulled into a loading zone and grabbed one of the kegs, entering through an employee entrance.

Nic was waiting for him. He shook the keg he held. "It's definitely light, but I just pulled it out of the back."

"Captain Dean may run a tight ship when he's out fishing, but this building is rarely locked down." He'd just walked through an employee's only entrance with no trouble.

The bartender nodded in agreement. "It wouldn't be hard to slip in the back undetected."

"You seen your friend sniffing around?"

"No, but he could've sent someone to do the dirty work." Nic switched canisters with Sharkey and headed back to the bar.

The brewer studied the keg, noticing tool marks on the coupler. By the time he'd lugged in all the replacements, his blood was boiling. He shot a quick text to Deputy Klein. She answered immediately, asking him to wait for him at the bar.

He was there, and it was dinnertime, so he gave Nic his order and then crossed to the main dining room to use the restroom. When he exited, he stopped dead in his tracks. For the winter, the restaurant had put plastic up around the deck and had industrial heaters to stave off the chilly temperatures. And that's where he saw Hope. Laughing at something Book Boy had said.

A knife sliced into his heart. He stared down at his arm, waiting for the tingling to start. This had to be a heart attack. He almost wished for it. Just end the torture.

But his heart continued to beat normally, and life went on around him. Diners chatted happily, sipping wine and eating tasty seafood.

He ducked back into the bathroom, staring at himself in the mirror over the sink. *Get a grip, man. It's one date. She's not marrying the guy.* He'd never felt this kind of animalistic jealousy before.

Because he hadn't allowed himself to get this attached to a woman since Eve.

Rinsing his face, he inhaled deeply and made a decision. He would be the man she deserved, so neither of them had any doubts. She'd forget about the ponytail, and they'd live happily ever after. *Yeah.* He patted his beard with a paper towel and smoothed out his shirt.

Resolved, he left the restroom and marched straight to the deck. Hope noticed him almost immediately, her eyes rounding to the size of silver dollars and her slight frame trying to melt into her chair. She looked beautiful—she always looked beautiful—but something was different, a little off. *Wait. Is she wearing makeup?* She put on makeup for the twerp?

Then he realized it wasn't just her face that was darker. It was her neck too. *Oh boy.* She wasn't trying to impress her date. She was trying to hide evidence of their earlier rendezvous. Puffing out his chest, he approached the table. "Hope, Austin. So good to see you."

Book Boy nearly choked on the bite of salmon he'd just put in his mouth. "What are you doing here?"

"You'll find that Eastport Beach is a small town. We're always running into each other." He winked at Hope, whose hand had shot up to her neck. *Yup. That's right where I marked you as mine.* A low growl slipped out unbidden.

"Huh, that's great." Mr. PhD gritted his teeth together. "Well, as you can see, we're having a nice dinner, so maybe we can run into you later." His laugh sounded like a hyena.

Sharkey turned his attention fully to Tink. "Hope, you look lovely, as always. Got a little sun today, I see."

The too-dark makeup couldn't hide the flush that crept up her neck and into her cheeks. She didn't answer but her eyes flared with indignation. His pixie was growing a little fire inside her.

He'd pay hell for it later, but something told him he'd enjoy the burn. "Have a nice meal." Sharkey headed back to the bar, feeling better than he had in weeks. His fried clams and Deputy Klein were waiting for him. His mood soured a little remembering the reason he was here.

Klein wasn't in uniform, and her hair hung in waves around her shoulders instead of the severe bun she typically wore. He could see how she would turn a man's head if he weren't already obsessed with a certain little imp. In fact, she and Nic were in such deep conversation that she didn't notice him claim the barstool next to her.

He dunked a few clams in cocktail sauce, waiting for the two to notice him. Nic, being the best bartender in Eastport Beach, had poured him a pint of 33rd parallel. Sharkey held it up to the light, and it looked perfect. Golden with a nice head. He took a swig, savoring the familiar flavor.

By the time the deputy swiveled toward him, his basket was empty, and he was draining the last of his beer. Nic was helping a new customer down the bar, likely the only reason the spell between the two had been broken.

"Mr. McLaughlin." She took a sip of water, furtively checking out Nic's ass.

Sharkey chuckled to himself. "Deputy Klein, I appreciate you coming out on your night off. And I appreciate you calling me Sharkey."

She laughed, her shoulders relaxing. "Maddy." She held out her hand—like they were meeting for the first time. "Nic was telling me about the tampering. Said there's not much security around here."

He nodded. "There's never been a need for it. Eastport Beach is a chill little town. Our crime is usually limited to indecent exposure, and Captain Percy is a landmark, so we all let it slide."

Her brow furrowed and he was surprised she didn't notate the offense in her notebook. "Do you mind showing me the damage?"

"Sure." He threw a couple bills on the table and waved at Nic.

The bartender winked at Maddy, and the deputy flushed like someone had turned the heat on high.

As they left the bar, Sharkey held the door open for her. "Nic's a good guy. He called as soon as he noticed the problem."

"No reason to suspect him, then?"

"God, no. My beer and his dimples make him a boatload of money."

She snickered, running her hand over her face. "Okay, so no motive then." She stopped short as his truck came into view. "You're parked in a loading zone."

And the deputy hat was back on. So much for loosening up a bit. "I was unloading my beer and loading the damaged kegs."

"And you inhaled a basket of clams."

She was more perceptive than he gave her credit for.

"Busted. You going to write me a parking ticket?"

Klein assessed him for a moment, then turned her attention to the kegs filling the bed of his truck. "All of these were tampered with?"

"As far as I can tell. There are tool marks." He shone the light from his phone onto one of the fittings. "If you disrupt the seal before it's attached to the tap, it compromises the beer. I'm not exactly sure what they did yet, but I can't trust any of these."

She nodded, moving her own light around the bed of the truck, checking every canister. "And you'll be able to analyze the contents?"

"There are a few tests I can do, but it could be just as simple as busting the seal and rendering them unusable."

"And someone who works with beer would know this?"

Like a certain GM of a brewery. "Yeah, anyone who's hooked up a keg would know."

"Can you reuse these containers?"

"Yeah, I can replace the fitting. The kegs themselves are fairly indestructible."

Klein tucked her notebook in her pocket. "I'd like to take one into evidence, but it seems fruitless to take them all."

He hadn't even considered that when he called the deputy. The equipment in the back of his truck represented a couple grand, not to mention the ruined beer. "That'd be great, thanks."

She pulled a pair of rubber gloves out of her back pocket and donned them, then grabbed a keg, whipping it out of the truck like it was a gallon of milk.

Impressive. No doubt Deputy Klein spent time in the gym. A full keg that size weighed over eighty pounds. He'd have to warn Nic she wasn't to be trifled with.

"I know the gloves are probably moot at this point, but just in case we can get something off it, can't hurt." She started to lift the keg again.

"I've got a handcart for that."

"Do you use it for one keg?"

He had to give her credit. "Not usually."

"Get that truck out of the loading zone, Sharkey."

"Goodnight, Deputy Klein." For the first time since all this started, he had hope the culprits might be brought to justice.

Chapter Thirty

"What's the deal with that guy?" Aiden had been strangely quiet since Squatch had appeared and spread his pheromones around the table. But apparently, his ire had been building.

"Deal?" Hope sipped her water, praying her flush had subsided. She knew Sharkey had zeroed in on the fact that she was wearing makeup—and he was smugly enjoying the reason for it.

"It's a colloquialism for problem."

"You think he has a problem?"

He narrowed his eyes at her, the first semi-rude thing he'd done since they'd met. Aiden might not be as dynamic and charismatic as Sharkey, but he was polite to a fault. "I can never tell if you're playing dumb or if you just aren't familiar with American linguistics because of your upbringing."

Either way, it felt like he was calling her stupid. "Sharkey's different, but that's what I like about him."

"Like him?" His voice rose unnaturally, and the couple at the next table stared.

She had zero dating experience, but something told her this wasn't going well. It went against her moral compass to lie, but she wasn't going to spell it out for Aiden either. "We're friends." *Friends who make out.*

"What could you possibly have in common with him?"

"Can we talk about something else?"

He picked up his utensils and cut his remaining salmon into equal pieces. "We were having a nice time until he showed up. Is he, like, stalking you?"

It was odd that he'd shown up during their date. But she doubted he would actually stoop to following her around. "Don't be silly. Now finish telling me about your semester in Italy."

Aiden shoved a bite of fish into his mouth and seemed to be considering his options while he chewed. He swallowed and then launched into a recap of every historical site he had visited.

Hope ate her crab cakes, nodding every few minutes, focusing on what her date was saying and not on the nagging feeling in the pit of her stomach. Was Sharkey showing up just a coincidence?

When Aiden slowed down to take a few more bites, she jumped into the conversation. "Did you visit Vatican City?"

He shook his head. "I don't buy into that religious mumbo-jumbo."

Mumbo-jumbo? Did he miss the part where I was raised by missionaries? Even if they were scam artists, they still believed and taught the word of God.

"Sorry." He wiped his mouth. "No offense."

Hope closed her mouth, dumbfounded. How did one not take offense at that? Her mind whirled. What to do now? End the date? Call Squatch for a ride back to Heron House? Feign illness? Never in a million years did she think she'd have to bail on her second first date.

Both their plates were mostly empty, so they'd be leaving soon. She just had to make it a few more minutes.

The waitress approached. "You two want some dessert?"

"Yes." "No." They answered at the same time.

Aiden looked shocked, but he cleared his throat and forced a smile. "I guess we'll just take the check."

The waitress left the bill and cleared their plates. An awkward silence hung between them for the first time since they'd met. Before he'd denigrated her entire worldview, Hope had thought he was interesting and intellectual. Now, she wished Heron House had more floors so she could change rooms and not risk meeting him in the hallway.

Reaching for her purse, she mentally calculated how much money she had in her bank account. She normally wouldn't splurge on an expensive meal, but it felt icky for Aiden to pay at this point. "How much is my part?"

Now *he* was the offended party if his audible gasp was any indication. "A gentleman always pays for the meal. Maybe the brewer doesn't follow that convention, but I most certainly do."

Part of her wanted to defend Squatch, but the bigger part didn't want to have to explain their time on the island, so she put her wallet away and kept that information to herself. "Thank you for dinner."

"At least the salmon was edible. Never know in these little hick towns."

"I need to use the powder room before we leave." Hope grabbed her purse and headed for the restroom before Aiden could reply. She'd never been so grateful to have a cell phone. She found Riley's contact and pressed it.

Please be there. Please be there. She paced the small bathroom while the phone rang.

"Hello? Is everything okay?" Riley sounded a little out of breath and a little panicky. Maybe she'd had to run for the phone.

"No, the date didn't go well, and I'm hoping you can be there when we get back. As a buffer."

"Does he know the date didn't go well?"

Hope sighed. "Honestly, I don't know, but it would just be easier if you were there to welcome us back."

"Of course I can do that." Riley paused. "But I'm going to need details."

"I may have to fill you in tomorrow, because as soon as Aiden goes upstairs, I'm going to Sharkey's."

***

The night had gone completely off the rails. Hope should have trusted her gut and cancelled the date. If she had, Squatch wouldn't have shown up, raising her blood pressure and making her date uncomfortable. Aiden wouldn't have discounted her entire identity. She would still be able to look at him with admiration—at least as a friend.

She blamed Sharkey and his wicked mouth. She blamed her lack of experience. Mostly, she blamed her parents for putting her in this insane situation in the first place.

Of course, then she never would have met Riley. She wouldn't have had her first magical kiss on an island in the rain. She wouldn't be falling in love with the most incorrigible yeti around.

If she were still in Uganda, she'd be preparing dinner for one, reading a book, and preparing to get up early to work at the orphanage. She wouldn't have been forced to grow.

Coming to America had stretched her in ways she'd never imagined. Being thrust into adulthood with no safety net had taught her that she could figure things out on her own. Visiting Eastport Beach had shown her what life outside her bubble could be.

As she stomped toward the brewery, she struggled to decipher the line between indignation and a different kind of fire. A flame no one had ever lit before.

The tasting area was quiet, everything closed up for the night. Sharkey had become diligent about securing everything in case someone came around to cause trouble. He'd probably be angry that she was out here alone in the dark.

She skirted the large silver container that would become a bar and, before she could talk herself out of it, mounted the stairs to his camper and pounded on the door.

The door opened, and Sharkey's very hairy chest greeted her. He was in only jeans, his broad shoulders making the camper door look like it belonged to a fun house. *Does he have to turn sideways to fit through it?*

She shook her head to stay on track. His sheer manliness was overpowering. "Did you follow us to the restaurant?" Hands on hips, she tried to appear confident, which was the exact opposite of how she felt at that moment. She probably should have stayed at Heron House. A voice nagged at the back of her mind—you shouldn't be alone with a man after dark. Especially a man you're intensely attracted to.

He reached out of the camper and grabbed her arm, hauling her up the rest of the stairs and closing the door behind her. "Did you walk here? In the dark?"

"Answer my question." It was claustrophobic inside the tiny living space. For a normal-sized person, it was probably fine, but Squatch had to lean over to keep from hitting his head on the ceiling and his giant body sucked up all the air in the room.

"Of course not." He sat in a swivel chair and gestured for her to take a seat on the small bench opposite him.

She was grateful to give her legs a break from the task of keeping her upright in the presence of his sheer manliness. "You just happened to be at the same restaurant as us?"

He dragged his hand across his beard. "I didn't plan on going anywhere tonight, but instead I got a call that a dozen of my kegs had been tampered with at The Landing."

"That's awful! Do you think it was someone who worked there?" Surely, a stranger couldn't just walk into a restaurant and cause trouble like that.

"I've known everyone there for years. But it's Eastport Beach. We aren't exactly Fort Knox. Anyone could have snuck in and done it."

Hope dragged her hand along her neck, suddenly feeling overheated. When she looked down at her fingers, the tips were dark. The reason for her visit overtook her empathy for his situation. "I'm sorry that happened, but it doesn't give you the right to harass Aiden while we were having dinner." Just because she never wanted to see his face again didn't give Sharkey license to be rude.

He growled, low and feral. "Trust me, I exhibited remarkable restraint."

"What's that supposed to mean?"

He barked out a laugh and leaned forward, filling the space between them. "You're kidding, right?"

Confused as usual, she shook her head. Why couldn't men just speak plainly?

"It killed me to see you there with him. On a date. Ripped my heart out."

"It did?" She worried if she breathed too deeply, she'd pass out. Seriously, was there no circulation in this metal box?

He dropped his head and his voice, to the point that she could barely make out his words.

Her heart raced, and her palms felt clammy. Surely, she'd misunderstood. "Can you repeat that?"

"You're supposed to be with me." This time he said it with conviction, eye contact and no mumbling. "I know I don't deserve you, but I'm going to do better. Be better. If you'll give me a chance."

This wasn't real. She'd fallen asleep reading one of her romance books, and this was all a dream.

"Hope, please say something."

She had questions about the last part, but for now, she clung to the first bit. Sharkey wanted to be with her. Her! "I want to be with you too."

"Thank God." He fell to his knees in front of her and pulled her into his chest.

Wrapping her arms around his neck, she pulled his head down to hers. Kissing Squatch was better than homemade peach ice cream, and that was her favorite thing in the world. Until now.

Chapter Thirty-One

Sharkey awoke from the most extraordinary dream—Hope had chosen him. He fought against opening his eyes, wanting to stay in the fantasy world.

A soft mewl emanated from the covers next to him. His eyes popped open in time to see a delicate hand reach across his chest. *Fuck. It was real.* Last night, he'd shot his shot and Hope had accepted.

He was waking up to a new reality, one where Tink was curled up against his torso, fitting neatly into the crook of his arm. She was still in the leggings and long-sleeved tee she'd shown up at his door in. He'd switched out his jeans for basketball shorts at some point. The night came rushing back in vivid color, complete with the morning reaction to waking up next to the girl you're into.

Angling the bottom half of his body away from the very innocent Hope, he pulled her up his chest, talking his dick off a very hard ledge. It was like telling a cow standing in a meadow not to eat grass.

They'd spent the night talking, making out, and cuddling. Just cuddling.

His heart and his head were completely on board with waiting until Hope was ready for more. His body had set out on its own path and was following a short cut that would lead straight to hell. He never wanted to make Hope feel uncomfortable.

Tink raised her head, blinking her big hazel eyes at the morning light streaming into the camper. The king-sized bed took up the entire back room, and Sharkey took up most of the mattress. There was exactly enough space left for a perfect little blonde imp. When she met his eyes, her cheeks flushed, whether over the realization that she'd spent the night with him or as memories started flooding in, he couldn't be sure. All he knew was that he didn't want her regretting a single thing.

"Morning." He leaned down and kissed her gently.

A shy smile graced her lips, even as her gaze darted around the room, almost as if she expected someone to catch them in bed together. "I've never spent the night with a man before."

"Me neither."

Her smile grew into a chuckle. "Well, I hope you haven't slept with a man."

"No, definitely haven't, but actually I meant that I've never spent the night with anyone." It was a hard and fast rule in Sharkey's extracurricular life. No sleepovers. No feelings.

He'd broken all his rules for Hope.

Her eyes grew wide. "Really? You're so," she sputtered, "handsome. You probably have women lining up at your door."

A lock of hair fell into her face. He tucked it behind her ear, stroking her cheek. "I'm not going to pretend that I'm a monk, but I haven't been serious enough about anyone to stay all night." He would have loved to have spent the night with Eve, but her parents would have killed them both, so it wasn't an option.

He could practically see Tink processing his admission, her expression going through a gambit of emotions. "So, let me get this straight. I'm your first?" The full grin lit up her face, making her even more beautiful.

Chucking, he nodded. "Yup, you're my first sleepover." Definitely the first time he'd stopped at kissing since Eve.

Satisfied, she snuggled down onto his chest, and he wrapped his arm around her, holding her close. His heart expanded, and he realized this feeling was better than an orgasm—although his cock wasn't entirely convinced.

They stayed in bed for several more hours, sleeping on and off, talking even more and munching on toaster pastries he found at the back of his tiny cupboard. He honestly couldn't remember buying the sweet breakfast treat.

He was content to stay in the little bubble they'd created, but by lunchtime, Riley was texting to make sure her guest hadn't been eaten by Stumpy. They couldn't avoid reality forever, so they finally crawled out of bed and made a game plan for the rest of the day.

His grand opening was quickly approaching, and the bar was nowhere near finished due to all the setbacks with the vandalism. Hope expressed her concern over finishing her book. Even though her official deadline was a few months out still, he got the impression she needed to have it finished sooner so she could get her final payment.

She was slowly opening up to him, giving him a peek behind her worried expression when she spoke about the future. He assured her that at twenty-two, he had zero clue what he would do with his life. He was stationed overseas then, but he knew he wasn't cut out for a life of military service. A lot of his buddies planned to go into law enforcement when they got out, but Sharkey knew he wanted to work for himself.

Hope would figure it out, and he would support her any way he could.

With a bit of reluctance, he kissed her goodbye and sent her back to Heron House to shower and change clothes. After that, she'd come back to write until he took her on a proper date that evening. One where they weren't stranded on an island in a storm—even though that had worked out pretty well in his opinion.

Sharkey needed to build shelving inside the container today, so he put off his shower until just before their date. He'd be sweaty within the hour anyway. When he stepped outside the camper, the sky was bright and clear and the temperature a mild sixty degrees. He hoped the weather continued to be pleasant, since his opening would obviously be in the elements. The entire tasting area was outside, after all.

In his state of contentment, he didn't notice anything wrong right away. He unlocked the container and swung the door wide. The entire floor was black. And it was moving. A stream of the palmetto bugs rushed the open door. Sharkey jumped back, trying to avoid the disgusting critters.

Anyone who lives near the water deals with the giant insects that resemble a cockroach on steroids, but he'd never seen this many in one place. They crawled up the walls, along the workbench he'd stored inside and were coming out of his tool bag. There was no way this was a natural occurrence. The bugs were attracted to moisture and food. The metal container was still bare walls and a few tools.

Someone had put these bugs here. While he and Hope slept a few yards away. *Fuck no.*

He was done tolerating this BS. He was going on the offensive, starting now.

First, he texted Hope that she needed to stay at Heron House today. As much as he wanted her nearby, he didn't want to subject her to the sight that would probably give him nightmares for a week.

A lot of the bugs had fled the container when he opened the door, but there were still hundreds of holdouts, who seemed content to hang out and keep him from working. So, he locked the container back up and drove over to Bluffville to get extermination supplies. He would mount a full-frontal attack against the palmettos, then he'd go after whoever put them there. Even if it meant staying up all night to catch them in the act.

He'd never reach opening day if this continued. And he refused to put Hope in danger if these miscreants decided to resort to violence.

Chapter Thirty-Two

Sharkey had been vague about why she shouldn't come back to the tasting area to write. Was he already tired of her? Had she done something wrong? Maybe she drooled in her sleep or had morning breath when he kissed her.

She finished dressing and studied herself in the mirror. Her clothes were different, but she was still the same. Limp, blonde hair, pale skin, freckles. Boring. No wonder Sharkey had sent her away. He could have any woman he wanted. She was just a skinny, blah kid.

Part of her wanted to curl up in the big chair in the corner of the room and cry the day away. But deep down another part of her roared to life. Being with Sharkey felt good—unlike anything she'd felt before. It was just for her. Selfish.

Fancy haircuts and makeup are for frivolous people. Her mother's voice echoed in her mind. *The poor don't care if your hair is curled.*

Hope clenched her fists. The whole time her parents were living lavishly in Paris and Rome. Wearing designer clothes and buying jewelry that cost more than their home in Uganda.

Maybe she deserved to be a little selfish for once.

Their "brand" of religion had cost her everything.

Finally, she'd found something she wanted. Someone. For only her.

She tossed her bag onto the bed and went downstairs to find Riley.

"I want to go to a salon."

Her hostess was at the sink, washing dishes. She turned, drying her hands on a bright orange towel. "Good afternoon. Did you have a nice night?" A sly smile teased at her lips.

Hope cringed. Just because she'd suddenly grown a backbone, she had no right to be rude. Besides, she was dying to talk to someone about what had happened last night. "Sorry, I got a little excited. Last night was amazing." She checked to make sure no one else was nearby and then leaned closer. "We slept together."

Riley's eyes looked like they might pop right out of her head.

"No, no! Not like that. Just sleeping." She shook her head emphatically. She hadn't considered how poorly staying over at Sharkey's would make her look. "Goodness, are people going to think that we had sex?" The last word came out as a whisper.

Clutching her chest, Riley sighed. "Whew. I mean, I never thought that you would, but Sharkey..."

"He was a perfect gentleman. Just held me and made me feel safe." *Whole.* She smiled, remembering the feeling. "We did kiss. A lot."

"Well, I'm glad he treated you well. I didn't mean to imply anything about him. He's a good man. Just a bit older, and more, um, experienced, than you."

Hope shifted from foot to foot. "I know. Which is why I think I need a makeover."

Riley tsked. "Hope, you're lovely. You don't need to change for a man."

"What if I want to change for me?" Her mother hadn't allowed her to wear nail polish, let alone lipstick. Now, she could make those decisions for herself. Last night, the only thing different was the makeup she'd worn to cover her hickey. And she'd ended up spending the night with Squatch. So, maybe he liked that stuff. Maybe if she took a little more care with her appearance, he'd want to spend more time with her.

"Well, if that's the case, then I will absolutely help. We'll go up to the mall in Wilmington. I'm sure we can get you a makeover and a haircut."

"We're going to dinner tonight." At least he hadn't called off their date yet.

"And a new outfit." Riley hung the dishtowel on the handle of the oven and clapped her hands. "My sister would be much better at this, but I'll do the best I can to help. We can always facetime her if we get in a pickle." She snapped her fingers. "Actually, maybe Ada can come. She's from New York City, she knows all about this stuff."

While Riley called the dancer, Hope did some quick mental math. She might have to eat noodles for the rest of her visit, but it'd be worth it if it meant Sharkey would invite her back to his bed. Back into the safety of his arms.

***

The three women visited the food court for ice cream after makeovers and manicures. They had a few minutes to kill before Hope's hair appointment.

"Riley, you have to let me pay you back for my nails. Really, it's too much." Hope took a bite of her salted caramel ice cream, rolling the flavor around her mouth.

Her friend shook her head. "Nope. My treat. Just mention Heron House in the acknowledgments of your book. That way, when it becomes a best seller, we'll be booked solid!"

Ada laughed as she sipped her smoothie. "I hope it's not too full. My dancers will need a place to stay for the competition."

"I've already blocked off that week, don't worry." Riley licked her cone. "Seriously, Hope, I'm happy to treat you. I've enjoyed having you around so much. And I think you'll be good for Sharkey. I worry he isolates himself too much."

Hope wiped her cold hands on a napkin. Her soft pink nails caught the light with a subtle shimmer. So pretty. "Well, then thank you. And I wouldn't be able to write this book without being here, so everyone will hear about Heron House from me." *If I ever finish the darn thing.*

"Riley told me you're writing a memoir. Trip has suggested I write about growing up with my mother, but I'm not really sure anyone would be interested."

"Ada's mom was a very famous artist," Riley added. "One of our suites is dedicated to her."

Hope pushed her half-eaten cup of ice cream away. "I wasn't sure anyone would care about my story, but my editor really seems to have confidence in me." So many people were counting on her, including herself. If she didn't complete the manuscript, she'd have to give back her advance. Where would she be then? "It's a little overwhelming at times. Digging up everything from the past."

Riley patted her hand. "If you ever need to talk something out, my lemonade and I are available."

Ada laughed. "That lemonade's like a truth serum, watch out."

"Hey now!" Riley acted affronted. "Sharkey's cider is the real truth serum. That stuff creeps up on you."

Now Hope was really glad she hadn't accepted his offer the other day. She probably would have done something crazy like blurted out how much she liked him. "Avoid the cider. Got it."

"And the beer," Ada agreed.

"You're so little, all it'd take is a sip and you'd be dancing on the picnic tables." Riley laughed.

"Well, I wasn't dancing. I was escaping an alligator."

"So, you've met Stumpy." Ada chuckled.

Hope relived that first moment when she'd fallen into Squatch's arms. "Yeah, he's not as bad as I thought." And neither was the alligator.

"Girl, wait 'til you see that hunk of a man sitting on top of him." Ada grinned.

Riley popped the last bite of her cone into her mouth and stood up. "Don't worry. We have it on video. Let's get to your hair appointment."

Bigfoot riding a three-legged gator? Life in Eastport Beach was never boring as far as Hope could tell. Maybe she'd stick around after the book was finished.

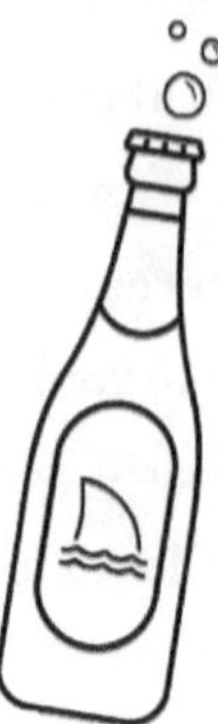

Chapter Thirty-Three

Something was different about her tonight. Not bad different, just not his normal sweet Tink.

She came down the steps slowly, gripping the banister and teetering on high heeled boots. Her hair was curled, and she was wearing more makeup than he preferred, but she was beautiful.

Damn, he'd missed her the six hours and forty-seven minutes they'd been apart. His phone chimed from his pocket. Normally, he'd leave the damn thing in the car, but the cameras he'd set up were motion activated and if someone showed up, he wanted to know about it. He slid it out of his khakis and tried to discreetly check out the screen. A snowy egret strutted in front of the camera. He returned his attention to Hope.

Her smile seemed forced as she hesitated on the bottom step—not her usual toothy grin beaming up at him. He wondered what she'd been doing while he secured the tasting area. Hopefully not hanging around with Book Boy. Surely after last night, she knew Sharkey's intentions—and they didn't include his girl associating with an over-educated ponytail.

"Hey, beautiful." He moved to the foot of the stairs, meeting her before she could step down. That step and the boots put her a little closer to his mouth, so he leaned down and captured hers—in front of God and a stunned Riley.

Ben chuckled at the shocked look on his girlfriend's face. Sharkey had once caught them half-naked on the front porch, so he knew Ri wasn't a prude. But she might think he would tarnish Hope's pure-as-driven-snow reputation. His Tink was innocent, but she was also a fully formed woman, and last night there had been some touching—more on her part than his because he was so hypersensitive about her lack of experience.

When he pulled back, her lips were still parted, the gloss now gone, and her real smile had returned. He trailed his thumb down her cheek and leaned close to her ear. "I missed you."

Hope sighed. "I missed you too. But I had a fun afternoon with Riley and Ada."

He raised his eyebrows. That explained the new hairdo and makeup. Riley was into jeans and tees, but Ada wore dresses and heels most of the time. She was a dancer, so it fit. He preferred his Tink in her baggy overalls and sneakers. "You look nice, but aren't those shoes uncomfortable?" The boots and tight leggings were hot as hell, but he wasn't into sharing his woman with the entire town of Eastport Beach.

She glanced over at Riley. "They're fine, I just need a little practice walking in heels."

Sharkey kissed her temple and whispered so their audience couldn't hear. "You don't need to wear stuff like that for me."

He hadn't known Hope for long, but he recognized the uncertainty in her eyes. And he felt it deep in his soul. Without a second thought, he hooked one arm under her legs and the other behind her back and swept her into his arms.

He was pretty sure he heard Riley audibly gasp as he carried Tink up the stairs and set her down in front of her door.

"What are you doing?" She whispered the question, her eyes darting to the door across the hall, where he assumed Book Boy was staying.

"Open the door." He crossed his arms over his chest, almost hoping the ponytail would show his face so he had something to pound on.

Her brow furrowed, uneasiness stalling her. "I don't under—"

"Please open the door so we can have this conversation in private." He could picture Riley standing under the stairs, straining to hear what they were saying. He loved his neighbor, but she was a busybody and expected all her guests to be her friends.

Anguish painted Hope's lovely features as she fumbled in her purse for a key. The purse was new too. As far as he was concerned, she didn't need to change a single thing.

As soon as the door closed behind them, he grabbed her and pulled her into his chest, cradling her head against his heart. He wondered if she could hear how fast it was racing. Riley and Ada were good people, and he wanted Hope to make friends, but she wasn't a doll for them to dress up and makeover. "You are perfect exactly the way you are. You don't have to be anyone else for me."

She shuddered in his embrace. He squeezed tighter. Her arms came around him, and she settled into his chest, sighing again. "I thought..." She trailed off, sniffling.

He pulled back, tilting her head up until their eyes met. "Perfect." Leaning down, he kissed her gently.

Her eyes fluttered closed and her tongue swiped across her lips like she was savoring his taste.

His pants were suddenly too tight.

"I thought you brought me up here to break up with me."

Sharkey roared loud enough for the entire house to hear. "Woman, you're crazy. I can't breathe without you."

One side of her mouth quirked up. "You called me a woman."

Her outfit tonight highlighted just how womanly she was, and he wanted to rip it off and show her exactly what she did to him. But this was Hope and little Sharkey was going to have to wait a while. "Don't let it go to your head. Now put on your regular clothes and let's get some dinner." If he stayed alone in this room with her and that big bed much longer, he couldn't be held liable for his actions.

When he stepped into the hall to give her some privacy, his phone chimed again. He swiped across the screen, his blood pressure spiking when he saw the box truck backing up to his container. *Fuck, no.*

He knocked on the door. "Hope, I need to take a raincheck. I'm sorry, but I've got to get back to the brewery."

She poked her head out the door, hiding her trim figure behind it. He could see just a hint of bare shoulder. He didn't have the luxury of lusting over his woman right now.

"Is something wrong?" The trepidation was back in her eyes, and he hated that he was causing her anxiety.

"Someone's up to no good, and I've got to handle it." He kissed her again, the fire in his gut growing. These jerks were keeping him away from Tink and they were going to pay for it. "I'll call you when it's safe."

Her worry morphed into fear before his eyes. "Is it dangerous? Maybe you should just call the police."

"Oh, I will, but I'm not going to sit back and let these creeps destroy my livelihood. I'll see you soon. Promise."

He jogged down the stairs. Ben and Riley had retreated to the kitchen once they couldn't eavesdrop any longer. "Ben. Someone's at the brewery. You mind giving me a little backup?"

"Sure thing."

It sounded like Riley mounted a counter argument, but Sharkey didn't stick around to hear it. As he flew to his truck, he dialed Deputy Klein. He didn't bother with pleasantries. "I'm sending you a video of the bastards at my place right now. I'm heading back over there, and I'm armed."

"Roger that. On my way."

Hopefully she'd leave the incompetent sheriff out of it.

The truck was running by the time Ben jumped into the passenger seat. Sharkey looked back at the porch before he pulled away. Riley and Hope stood side by side, matching worried expressions on their faces. Tink had changed into her overalls and sneakers. After this was finished, he'd find a way to make it up to her.

He backed the truck up and drove around the side of the house instead of to the main road. As long as he stayed away from the riverbank, he could maneuver between the trees back to the tasting area and hopefully get the jump on the bastards.

"I take it you got the cameras set up." Ben braced himself against the doorframe as the truck bumped over roots and pine straw.

Sharkey had called his friend on the way to Bluffville eariler and filled him in on the bug debacle and his plan of attack. "Yeah, I didn't think they'd be back so soon, but apparently they're ramping up their efforts." He thought he'd be able to have a nice dinner with his lady. Maybe a little more snuggling.

"Did you call the police?"

"Yeah, I called Deputy Klein's cell. She's on the way."

"Maybe we should hang back, just assess, until she arrives," Ben, ever the prudent attorney, suggested.

Sharkey grunted. *Depends on what the pricks are up to.*

The trees thinned out as they approached the tasting area. He pulled out of sight and turned the truck off. He could see the miscreants' vehicle, but everything appeared quiet on this side of the container. Pulling the camera app up on his phone, he held it so Ben could see. He switched the view to the camera he'd mounted on his trailer.

"You've got to be kidding me." He couldn't comprehend what he was seeing.

"Are they jacking the trailer up?"

Sure as shit, they had a massive hydraulic jack under one end of his bar. There were two guys, one a gym rat and the other with a beer gut. His bullets could penetrate muscle or flab if necessary.

Sharkey called the deputy back. "Maddy, how far out are you?"

"Maybe five. SITREP?" The woman was military to her core.

"I think they're planning a heist. They're jacking up my fucking bar."

She swore under her breath. "Not on my watch. Coming in lights and sirens. I'd like you to hang back."

He appreciated her asking instead of ordering. But he'd step in if necessary. "We're here for backup if needed. We're laying low south of the bar."

"How many?"

"Two friendlies, two hostiles."

"Good odds. Two minutes out."

Sharkey switched back to the camera. Thankfully, the work was slow going. Klein would have plenty of time to stop them in the act. "Let's approach from the water but hang back until she needs an assist."

Ben nodded and quietly slipped out of the truck.

Within seconds, the whoop of a siren blared, startling a heron from the reeds lining the river. It took off, its massive wingspan momentarily blocking out the light from the moon. They were now close enough to hear the commotion behind the container. The whoosh as the hydraulic jack released, swearing, and the truck's engine turning over. The punks actually thought they were getting away with a sheriff's vehicle coming down the drive.

The cameras continued to run as Maddy pulled her car behind the truck, blocking it off and exited the car, gun drawn. She shouted at the perps to get out with their hands in the air. Sharkey crept closer to the bar, ready to assist if the thugs decided to get squirrely. The driver got out of the truck, threw something on the ground and flattened himself over the hood, his hands raised. Sure, they were up to no good, but were they actually armed?

The passenger shot out of the truck, heading along the back of the container toward the river. Before Sharkey could change course, he saw Ben on the camera and within moments, his friend had the perp pinned with his arms behind his back. Who knew the congenial attorney was a bit of a bad ass?

Sharkey had to admit he was a bit disappointed that he hadn't gotten to shoot anyone, at least a small warning shot to show how pissed he was.

Maddy had the driver cuffed, so Sharkey rounded the truck and held the guy by the arm while she went to assist Ben. Another cruiser pulled up, lights flashing.

Deputy Scott got out, settling his hat on his head before approaching him. "What have we got here?"

Sharkey didn't know the man well, but from what he knew, he towed whatever line Sheriff Morgan threw out. "These guys were trying to jack my bar."

The deputy's beady eyes threatened to bug out of his head. "They were taking the whole trailer?"

"Seems like it." Vandalizing it repeatedly hadn't slowed Sharkey down, so apparently the next step was complete removal.

"Pretty ballsy."

"You gonna applaud their efforts or arrest them?" Sharkey would prefer a few hours alone in a room with them. These were clearly hired hands. He wanted to know who was behind this campaign to ruin Shark Bite Brewing.

The deputy glared at him but reached for the detainee. "Klein," he hollered, "I'm putting the suspect in the back of my car."

She waved at Scott as she pulled perp #2 to his feet. He had mud caked to one side of his face where Ben had ground his head into the dirt. Sharkey owed his friend a beer.

Scott was reading the driver his rights when Sharkey noticed something on the ground under the truck. With both deputies distracted, he bent down and pocketed the burner phone. Klein seemed okay, but if you wanted something done right...don't leave it to the local authorities.

With his luck, these bozos would be charged with trespassing and get a slap on the wrist. Hopefully, getting hauled down to jail would keep them from coming back, but if he didn't figure out who was orchestrating this siege, the hits would keep coming.

Klein loaded the runner into her car and then pulled Scott aside out of earshot.

Ben was brushing his pants off as he met Sharkey at the front of the box truck. "Get anything out of him?"

"Nah, Scott got here pretty fast. You?"

"He wasn't talking. Just a few colorful phrases as I tackled him." A hint of pride shone in his friend's eyes.

"Excellent takedown. Didn't know you had it in ya." Sharkey clapped him on the back.

Ben shrugged. "The only person I've ever tackled is Riley." He laughed. "But I just went for it."

His neighbor was one of the nicest people he knew, but Sharkey also knew Ben would have his back and tonight proved it. "I'm sure Riley is a formidable opponent." Ben's girlfriend was petite, but she was scrappy. He wasn't thrilled about the makeover, but Hope wouldn't find a more loyal friend.

One of the cruisers took off and Klein approached the two men. "The perps aren't talking. Yet. Hopefully a few hours in a cell will loosen their lips." She surveyed the scene. "I'm going to tape this area off and get my guys down here, but it may be morning."

Another delay. He would have to push his opening date back again. The bastards were getting exactly what they wanted.

"You got somewhere else to stay?"

Ben rested a hand on his shoulder. "He can stay with us."

"I appreciate the offer, but I need to stay here and keep an eye on things."

Klein shook her head. "It's a crime scene now. Get some sleep. Can't do anything until daylight anyway."

Sharkey sighed, giving in. At least he'd be able to see Hope. If she forgave him for running out on their date. "Okay, but I'll be back bright and early."

"Just don't mess with anything. I promise we'll handle it." She shook her head slightly. "I'll handle it."

"Thanks, Maddy. For coming when I called." No questions asked. Just showed up.

She chuckled. "Sharkey, if it weren't for this vendetta against you, I'd be questioning the Murray boy about shorting Ms. Windsor on her change."

"Well, I'm glad I'm keeping things interesting for you," he said dryly.

Maddy cringed. "Sorry. Didn't mean to revel in your misfortunate. Things are just a lot slower down here than I'm used to."

Sharkey forced a smile. He didn't mean to give her a hard time. She was the only one taking this situation seriously. "I really appreciate your help. This shit is starting to get to me."

"I'm not a fan either. The woman I love is on the other side of those trees." Ben gestured back toward Heron House. "We need to get to the bottom of this immediately. Before anyone gets hurt."

Klein straightened to her full height, adjusting her equipment belt. "Catching them in the act makes things a lot easier. Hard for Morgan to deny what's happening now."

"Thanks. Is it okay to grab some things out of my camper?" Sharkey couldn't get out of these damn khakis fast enough.

Maddy nodded. "Just stay clear of the container." She popped her trunk and pulled out a roll of crime scene tape.

The bright yellow tape brought the harsh reality to light. Sharkey's stomach grumbled. He couldn't tell if it was anxiety or hunger. What if he hadn't installed those cameras? What if he'd come back to an empty lot? *Fuck.* He wanted to go in his camper and hide out until morning. All his nerves endings tingled with rage. He was in no state to socialize. Maybe Ben would let him stay on the sailboat instead. It had even lower ceilings than his tin can on wheels, but he wouldn't have to play nice with the ponytail.

"Grab a bag and let's head back." Ben looked up from his phone. "Riley and Hope cooked us dinner, but I think they're pretty worried."

Now guilt piled on his emotional hoagie. He'd never want to cause Hope distress. Or Riley, for that matter. "Yeah, okay. Call me if anything else happens, Maddy. Any hour."

As she wound the tape around a live oak, she shot him a quick salute.

He had to leave his baby in her capable hands and pray that this stopped here.

Chapter Thirty-Four

No one would tell her what had happened at the brewery. Hope might as well be eating the lasagna she'd made at the kid's table.

Riley and Ben had disappeared into their bedroom when the guys got back, and Sharkey wouldn't meet her eyes as he helped cut up vegetables for the salad.

Now, they were all seated around the kitchen table talking about everything except why Sharkey had skipped out on their date.

"The house seems quiet. Are you expecting more guests this weekend, Riley?" Sharkey asked as he shoved a huge bite of pasta into his mouth.

"Yeah, we have two couples coming in on Friday, but until then it's just Hope. And you, I guess." Riley broke a piece of garlic bread in half and took a bite.

"I'll be out of your hair as soon as Klein says I can go back to my camper."

Riley nearly choked on the bread. "I didn't mean anything, Sharkey. You know you can stay as long as you need. You're always welcome in our home." She patted his arm.

Squatch ducked his head, clearly uncomfortable with the affection from his friend. "Thanks, Ri."

Wait, did she say it was just me? "Did Aiden leave?"

"Yeah, he checked out this afternoon. Said he needed to get back to school. Wouldn't even let me refund him for tonight."

Hope could feel Squatch's eyes on her. The hairs on the back of her neck were salsa dancing from the attention. "Huh, I'm surprised he didn't say goodbye."

Sharkey mumbled something under his breath. It sounded like, "He knew better."

She dug into her salad to avoid Squatch's invasive gaze. Clearly, things hadn't gone well with Aiden, but at least he'd treated her like an adult and respected her opinion. Even if he did think her faith was hogwash. It stung that he'd left without telling her. She was really bad at this dating thing.

"Hope, this lasagna is amazing." Ben loaded another piece onto his plate.

Riley shot her boyfriend a glare. "It's definitely better than mine."

Ben winced and Sharkey's eyes grew wide as he slid his chair further away from Riley.

"It's not better, Ri." Ben patted her leg. "It's just different than yours."

"I love you dearly hon, but you're a horrible liar." Riley kissed him on the cheek, then turned to address Hope. "They think it's some big secret that I can't cook."

Squatch shoveled another huge bite in his mouth, his gaze darting between the lovers.

Ben leaned over and whispered something in Riley's ear and then the two pressed their foreheads together in an intimate gesture.

Hope was envious of the easy affection between them and the way Riley felt comfortable expressing herself. Her mother's voice echoed in her mind. *A woman's place is to submit to her husband, never cause him any grief or embarrassment.* Hope clinched her fists under the table. *Turns out, swindling thousands of donors is pretty embarrassing, Mother.* She wondered if she'd ever have the courage to truly assert herself.

Everyone went back to eating, the couple across from her holding hands under the table. Riley chattered about Ada's upcoming dance competition and how many people would be staying at Heron House.

Hope's appetite waned the more she thought about the situation. She was a grown woman, dealing with very adult things—her parents' betrayal and fall from grace, finding a way to support herself in a new country, new feelings and sensations in her body every time she was around Squatch. She wasn't a delicate flower that needed to be protected. She'd been sheltered her entire life and look where it'd gotten her. Completely oblivious and floundering in the real world.

Her fork clattered to her plate as she rose from the table. Everyone stopped eating and stared. She planted her hands on her hips and stood as straight and tall as possible. Even though they were all seated, it could hardly be described as towering over them. She was tempted to climb up on the chair. Instead, she pointed a finger at Squatch, who swallowed the bite he was chewing with a gulp. "If you want me in your life, you need to tell me what happened down at the brewery tonight. And no sugar-coating it. I'm not a kid." Now she just had to keep from puking.

Sharkey sat like Bigfoot caught in the headlights while Riley and Ben exchanged a panicked glance.

"Hope, dinner was awesome, thanks so much," Ben said, sounding like the livestock auctioneer in their village. He rose from the table, grabbing his and Riley's plates. "Early morning. Sharkey, the Pop Art Room has clean sheets on the bed."

Riley echoed her boyfriend's accolades about dinner, and the two scurried away like mice into the pantry.

Silence settled over the kitchen like a damp fog rolling in from the hill country. Hope folded her hands in her lap, her appetite gone and acid churning in her gut. She felt bold and confident. And terrified and weak. But it was time to start standing up for herself and what she wanted and not let other people decide what she needed to know.

She really liked Squatch, but there was no point in their relationship proceeding without mutual respect.

But what if he decided life would be easier without the little virgin tagging along? What if he never kissed her again? What if no one did? It was one thing to go through life without that kind of affection, because she hadn't known what she was missing. Now that she knew how his lips, his touch, felt, life would feel empty without it. She'd have a giant Sasquatch-shaped hole in her heart.

Hope had known Sharkey for a couple weeks, and during that time, she'd figured out that he didn't say anything quickly. When he deemed it necessary to speak, he considered his words thoughtfully. But waiting for him to respond was pure torture. Was he trying to figure out how to let her down easy? So much for speaking her mind. She'd likely talked herself right out of a boyfriend.

Squatch rose from the table and grabbed both their plates. He scraped the half-eaten lasagna off her plate and loaded it in the dishwasher. Meticulously, he rinsed his plate and glass and rearranged the dirty silverware.

She kept her sanity reciting verses about patience to herself.

He finished clearing the table and wiped it clean with a wet rag, not saying a word, not making eye contact. Hope yearned for just a glance in her direction, some sign that he still cared.

Finally, after there was nothing left to clean, he looked at her. His eyes shimmered like their duck pond first thing in the morning. He really was going to end this. Before it even began. She wasn't strong enough. Not for this. Not on top of everything else. She didn't even know these feelings existed a few weeks ago and now she had to learn how to unfeel them. It was impossible.

"Will you please join me in the parlor?" Sharkey's voice was low, strained, like it took an incredible effort to utter the words.

Hope vacillated between fleeing to her room and being a grownup. Facing the music. Since part of her argument in the first place was that she wasn't a kid, running off seemed like the immature thing to do. *But, man, this is going to hurt.* She nodded and got her feet, which suddenly felt like concrete.

He waited for her to start down the hallway, then followed close behind. She could feel his presence like a warm blanket. When he ended it, would she ever be warm again? A chill raced up her spine, but she didn't know if it was dread or simply his nearness.

She sat on a velvet sofa, folding her hands in her lap, waiting for the hammer to fall. Sharkey joined her on the couch, his large frame crowding her. She welcomed the contact, savored the feel of his leg pressed against hers. Maybe she could take the ultimatum back. Rewind the clock to before she'd made the stupidest mistake of her young life.

He shifted so he could see her better and then grabbed her hands. Every time he'd touched her raced through her memory. She gripped his massive mitts like her life depended on it, tucking the feeling of holding his hands deep into her soul in case it was the last time.

"I messed up." His words were laced with anguish, like he was pulling razor blades out of his throat and each syllable cut his flesh.

This was it. The moment he told her everything was a mistake. Their closeness. The kiss. More kissing. Her opening up to him about her doubts for the future. Who could she turn to for comfort? *Do I have enough money left for a plane ticket to Bridget's?* The realization that she'd be all alone once again set off a chain reaction in her body. Her stomach cramped, her throat suddenly felt like the Sahara. Her eyes became heavy with moisture. She fought it with all her remaining might. *Do not cry in front of the sasquatch.*

"I promise you, I was not trying to keep you out. I was trying to protect you. But I was wrong. You are strong. You can handle the hard stuff." His thumb twitched over the back of her hand, sending sparks up her arm.

She nodded. He was right. She'd handle this like she'd handled everything in her life. On her own. All alone. "Are you done?" She'd hold it together until she was alone in her room. Just a few more minutes.

Sharkey's brow furrowed, creating a deep "v" between his eyes. He studied her for long, painful minutes, like he had x-ray vision and could see inside her mind. Inside her heart. "Done? I'll never be done with you."

Spots swam before her vision and the first tear leaked out. She really was wholly unprepared for all of this relationship stuff. Maybe she needed to read a few hundred more romance novels before she understood what was happening. In her delirious state, she thought he meant that he wanted to be with her forever.

"Don't cry, Tink." He swiped his meaty thumb under her eye, catching a tear as it fell.

"Tink?" Had she entered an alternate universe? Like Narnia? Where nothing made sense?

Sharkey leaned closer, kissing the dampness on her cheek. "You're my little imp. Like Tinkerbell."

All of her emotions exploded out of her in a heaving sob. Tears streaked down her face, her composure destroyed in the wake of his words. *He has a nickname for me?* Bigfoot and a fairy. Fitting, she supposed. *But why tell me this now?*

He pulled her into his chest, murmuring to her while he stroked her back. She didn't catch any of it over her ugly crying noises. She hadn't expected him to comfort her after ripping her heart out. Was this normal dating tradition? At this point, she didn't care. She was just happy to be in his arms and relieved to let out the pent-up emotion of the past few months.

"See how strong you are? I bet you haven't cried about your parents yet. About leaving your home and starting over. It's okay to cry. I'll keep you safe."

The realization interrupted her tears. Was he right? *Is this about him? Or partially about them?* She hadn't truly mourned everything that had happened. She hadn't wanted to look that closely. But how else could she write about what happened?

It didn't seem scary here in Squatch's arms. But when he was gone? Impossible.

Her sobs subsided, but she couldn't bring herself to let go of Sharkey, so she stayed right there, cradled in his embrace.

"There's a corporate brewery up in Wilmington. I think they're behind everything that's happened at Shark Bite. Tonight, two guys were trying to jack up the container and drive off with it. Don't worry, I stayed back and let Deputy Klein handle it." He chuckled, and she could feel the rumble inside her own chest. "Although Ben was pretty badass and took one of them down."

Hope wondered briefly how Riley would feel about her boyfriend taking a risk like that.

"I *want* to keep these pricks away from my business, but I *need* to keep you safe. You are my first priority."

She pulled back so fast, she nearly fell in the floor. "You aren't breaking up with me?" That priority thing seemed fairly clear, even to a dating novice like herself.

He steadied her and pulled her up into his lap, bracketing her face between his large hands. "God, no, Hope. I want to be with you as long as you'll have me."

"But you didn't speak for so long. And then you said you made a mistake." She was still confused, but when she looked into his eyes, the emotion there felt real.

"Oh, Tink." He brushed another tear off her cheek and lowered his forehead to hers. "I'm just a big, stupid oaf. It takes me too much damn time to figure out what I need to say. You aren't a mistake. Not telling you what's been going on is the mistake. Not letting you in." He pounded his chest like an ape. "I'm trying, but I'll try harder. I'll do better."

All she wanted to do was wipe the strife off his handsome face. The torture was plain as day. She leaned forward and placed a soft kiss against his lips, his beard tickling her cheeks. "I don't understand how all this works. I'm just a dumb fairy from a faraway land that doesn't understand the normal conventions here. I'll do better too."

He shook his head. "Tink, you're perfect just as you are. Don't ever doubt how I feel about you."

Heat surged up her body, propelling her forward. She wrapped her arms around his neck and pulled him close for another kiss. This one not the least bit chaste or soft.

Chapter Thirty-Five

Between all the talking in his head and Tink's lack of experience, he'd almost fucked this up. But right now, his sweet, innocent little imp was climbing him like a tree and kissing him like she'd been doing it for decades. He might be dense, but he wasn't stupid.

She was already basically straddling him, so he rose from the pint-sized couch, hooking his arm under her, never breaking the hottest kiss he'd ever experienced. Within minutes, he was up the stairs, standing outside her door, feeling like he was the luckiest man on the planet.

They had to stop kissing long enough for Hope to unlock the door, then she stood in the doorway—a delightful, sexy goddess with swollen lips and messed up hair—and crooked a finger at him. "Stay with me tonight, Squatch."

She didn't have to ask this yeti twice. He growled low and feral as he strode into the room after her, shutting and locking the door. Metal clanked as she unhooked one of her straps. Holy shit. Was sweet, little Hope Seaton taking off her clothes for him? *No way am I this lucky.* The second buckle released, and the baggy dungarees fell to the floor in a heap of denim.

Slender legs rose up from the discarded garment, and he took in every millimeter of supple, pale flesh. He wanted to soak it all in, to savor this moment and store it forever in his memory banks, because he knew all too well that it could be stolen at any moment. But then he remembered the scared Tink downstairs. The one who thought he was going to break up with her because he needed time to formulate his thoughts. *Nope.* He wouldn't let her suffer through uncertainty.

"You're so beautiful." Her shirt was just long enough to maintain a little modesty, but Sharkey was a solitary man who spent a lot of time living in his imagination. Not being able to see everything was somehow even hotter. Sweet anticipation. "You're little, but perfectly formed." He took one yeti-sized step toward her, eating up half the distance between them.

She was tugging on the hem of her shirt, her bottom lip tucked into her mouth. His sweet Tink. Experiencing all the firsts.

It was the old adage of a devil and an angel sitting on his shoulders, warring over what would happen next. But really, it was more a battle between his cock and his head. Thankfully, he was a man of remarkable consideration and patience. "We're going to communicate. Tonight. Tomorrow. Forever. Okay?" He waited for her to acknowledge with a nod. "We can curl up in that big bed and cuddle all night. We can kiss. I'm really banking on the kissing. It's spectacular." He was getting worked up, just thinking about her mouth. That's what this woman did to him. And that bed. The room was bigger than his entire camper. He might have a dance party later.

"Kissing is good." She stepped out of her pants and closer to him.

He could reach out and touch her. He could slide his hand under that shirt so easily. Devil Dick was making his case strongly. "We can just touch. Whatever you need. You're in control."

Hope licked her lips, and he almost came in his pants. It'd been too long. He couldn't remember when. He couldn't remember anything before her. DD urged him to throw her on the bed and ravish her like a true Sasquatch would.

But his heart remembered that teenage boy who loved the Lord and loved Eve, and how hard it was to break the promise he'd made to stay abstinent until marriage. Part of him blamed himself. Like Eve dying was a punishment for breaking that vow. The reality was that she wouldn't have made it long enough for them to marry. She was already at the end. It was her dying wish. The physical expression of their love for one another.

It took years for the guilt to lift. For him to appreciate that Eve was his first everything.

Suddenly, he saw it so clearly. He wasn't falling for this woman. He was already on the ground at her feet. She deserved for this to be perfect. To have no regrets.

"Hope," he closed the remaining distance between them, running his fingers lightly down one side of her face, "I love you." Saying the words out loud didn't scare him. Losing her scared him.

She rose up on her toes, cupping his face and drawing him closer. "I think I love you too."

He'd gladly be the first man she loved. He'd give up everything to be only one. Their lips crashed together, renewing the passion that had begun downstairs. But it was so much more than heat and desire. For the first time since Eve died, Sharkey's heart felt whole.

Tink gripped his shirt as she kissed him, trying to reach higher, so he scooped her up again, drawing her legs around his waist. Her shirt rose up and his forearm brushed against something satiny. He'd had her pegged to wear practical cotton briefs—what else was she hiding under those oversized clothes?

As she kissed him like she was practicing for the Olympics, he took a chance and slid his hand under her shirt and along the smooth skin of her back. She felt like velvet, if velvet could set your skin on fire.

It was too little and too much all at once.

The devil in his pants roared to life—he was a mere man, after all—as the kissing intensified.

Hope clung harder, rubbing herself against his hardness. When she moaned, Sharkey lost all restraint. He was a man, and she was a woman. The fact that they were falling in love made it that much clearer.

He pulled away from her mouth long enough to ask if he could take her shirt off.

She nodded and tugged at the hem of his shirt in turn.

It was a bit of a juggling act, but soon, they were skin to skin, with only a thin layer of green covering her chest.

Sharkey had never seen anyone so beautiful. He spread her out on the bed, taking in her smooth skin, gentle curves and the sexiest little grin. He unbuttoned his pants, watching her closely, in case she had second thoughts. Instead of doubt, he saw hunger in her eyes. His chest involuntarily puffed out with the knowledge that he was the first to make her feel this way. He would be the first to show her what love can feel like.

It'd been a long time since Sharkey believed in love. Hope had restored that for him.

"Squatch, please take your pants off and get in this bed with me."

A beautiful woman asking him to bed was one thing, but his Tink feeling bold enough to tell him what she needed was the most powerful aphrodisiac he'd ever encountered. He toed off his shoes and chucked his pants across the room. "Don't have to ask me twice."

Sliding into bed beside her, Sharkey's life clicked into place. They could burn his brewery to the ground. They could destroy his life's work. If he had Hope, he'd endure anything. He'd move heaven and earth to show her what love was, to take care of her, to help her realize every single dream in that giant heart of hers.

They laid on their sides, facing each other, the anticipation crackling in the air between them. He trailed his fingers down her arm, over her hand and continued to her hip. Her pale skin pebbled with goosebumps, her breathing quickened, and she licked her lips again.

"Please, Sharkey." She reached out and laid her palm against his wildly beating heart.

He hovered over her mouth, ready to taste those delicious lips again—because it had been too long—but stopped just shy of contact. "Tell me what you need."

Their eyes locked and they were the only two people on the planet. No saboteurs. No charlatan parents. No publishing houses with expectations. No annoying ponytails.

"I need you." She leaned closer, so their lips touched. "All of you."

How had he lived this long without her? The truth was he hadn't been living. He'd been existing. "You've got me."

As their kiss deepened, he slid his hand over her flat stomach and then upward. He brushed his fingertips under her breasts, toying with the lace trimming her bra. Part of him wanted to pull back and see her face when he touched her for the first time. Most of him never wanted to stop kissing Tink. It was like he'd fallen down a hole to Neverland, and he never wanted to find his way home.

Her petite hand slid down his arm and gripped his wrist. It was too much, too soon. She was going to tell him to stop. He'd fucked up the most perfect thing by moving too fast.

He was pulling back, ready to issue an apology and beg for a second chance, when she jerked his hand higher and positioned it over her breast. Relief flooded his system. He sank back into the kiss and lightly squeezed the mound that filled his palm. She was perfectly proportioned. Her direction emboldened him, and he slid his hand inside the lacy cup. Well, his fingers. No way his hand was fitting in there. Frustrated, he followed the lines of the bra to the back and fumbled with the clasp. *Stupid big, clumsy fingers.*

"Let me."

He missed the heat of her mouth but welcomed her intervention. With his luck, he'd rip the damn thing. But pausing the make out session had its own benefits. He got to watch as she unhooked the bra and pulled it off her shoulders, revealing the most perfect pair of breasts on this side of Heaven.

"Damn, Tink. You are so sexy."

Her cheeks reddened, the flush just making her even more stunning. He'd messed up her hair and her lips were swollen from their enthusiastic kissing.

He was done for. It'd kill him if she ever left, but he was determined to be with her until she kicked his hairy ass to the curb.

Lowering his mouth to her chest, he blew lightly over perfectly pink nipples, causing them to stand at attention. His tongue flicked out, tasting Hope here for the first time, memorizing the way she gasped, but held his head to her chest. The saltiness of her skin. The subtleness of her flesh.

Below the waist, Sharkey's blood was pumping with a frenzy. He tried to talk DD down. This was about Tink. Not about him. They'd have all the time in the world for that. First, he needed to show her how he felt. Show her how she could feel.

Encouraged by the sultry noises his sweet, innocent Hope was producing, he set up camp laving his attention on her chest, shoulders, neck, back to her chest, down to her stomach. She squirmed underneath him, pleading with him. He guessed she didn't even know what she was begging for—it was like she was in a trance. A pleasure trance, most likely. Overwhelmed by touch, hormones and emotion.

He missed her mouth, so he slid back up her body, supporting his weight so he didn't crush her. As he began kissing her again, he slid his hand down her stomach and settled it between her legs. She moaned and pressed up against him. His dick stood up, ready to be tagged into the action. *Soon.* But not yet.

Sharkey traced his fingers along the lines of her underwear, slipping his pinky just inside the elastic around her leg. Hope thrashed against him, wild with desire. It was sexy as hell. He gently pulled the last scrap of green fabric off her body, leaving her completely bare to him. Returning his hand to her mound, he could feel heat and dampness—she was ready.

It only took a few minutes to have her panting his name. He knew she was close, so he lightly pinched one of her nipples while his fingers strummed her clit with a perfect rhythm. When her back arched up, he captured her mouth just in time to swallow a scream of pleasure. They were the only two people on the second floor, so he doubted anyone would hear, but he selfishly wanted all that pleasure for himself.

Hope's legs clamped together over his hand, her body stiff from the orgasm. He stilled his fingers, but left them where they lay against her hot, wet center. A little piece of Heaven on earth.

She pulled her mouth from his, sinking back onto the pillow, her whole body relaxing at once. Her eyes were closed, her chest flushed red, and the most blissful smile clung to her lips.

He removed his hand, swiping the dampness across his boxer briefs, then pulled her close. She turned into him, resting her head on his chest and curling her body into a tight ball in the curve of his body.

"That was incredible." She didn't open her eyes but slid her arm around his waist.

His cock strained upward, like a tuning fork sensing water nearby. *Give her a moment to enjoy the orgasm, DD. We've got all night.*

Brushing damp hair off her forehead, Sharkey placed a kiss near her temple. "You're incredible."

He knew in that moment that he would be her first and she would be his last.

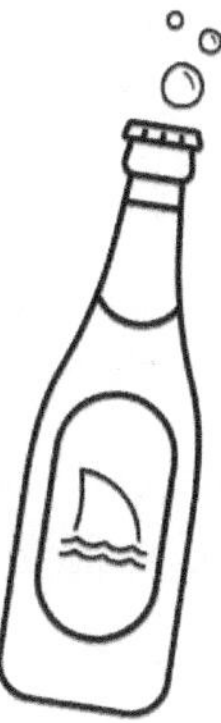

Chapter Thirty-Six

Her entire body vibrated with the aftershocks of the fire Sharkey had ignited inside her. Hope finally understood what the spicier romance books had alluded to. The pleasure, the release, the way her bones now felt like gelatin.

She'd had an orgasm.

Correction. Squatch had given her an orgasm.

It was like floating on a cloud, with rainbows and fireworks in the space around her. It was magical and surreal, yet she felt it in every inch of her flesh. Not just her flesh, but deep inside her. Was this the love bubble Riley had spoken of?

Her mother had taught her that sex was something to be endured to please your husband. She'd warned a young Hope of the dangers of letting a man touch her body.

Danger? Was her mother truly crazy?

All Hope felt right now was blissful happiness. She was laying in the strong embrace of the man she loved. He'd just given her this beautiful gift and asked for nothing in return.

She stiffened with the realization that maybe he expected her to return the favor.

His manhood was pressed against her stomach, big and hard. She was curious about it—she'd seen it before, albeit briefly—but now it felt much larger. Rationally, she understood what happens when a man gets excited. But she was wholly unprepared to make him feel as good as she felt.

Her pleasure started to wane as anxiety crept in. Maybe she could sneak into the bathroom and look up a how-to on her phone. But she was pretty sure she shouldn't be googling about sex. It seemed wrong on many levels. So how did one learn? How could she show Squatch that she loved him?

Her arm was laying across his stomach, her hand splayed against his back. He felt so strong under her fingers. Strong, but also tender. As big as he was, he'd been so gentle with her. Not rushing, checking in to make sure she was comfortable. Attuned to her pleasure—something she'd never managed on her own. By herself, guilt weighed heavily. Her mother's voice chiding her. With Sharkey, she was protected, honored, loved. Another thing her mother had been so wrong about.

As she edged her arm lower, toward the band of his underwear, she prayed she'd be able to please him. Maybe it was wrong to include God in this intimate moment. Or maybe it was exactly the right thing to do. How could something that felt so good be so wrong? They loved each other. Was that enough?

When she could feel his waistband against her forearm, she glanced down in time to see his penis twitch. The steady rhythm of his breath ceased, his chest solid under her head. He was waiting. Watching, if the hairs tingling along the back of her neck were any indication.

She wanted to touch him. But she didn't want to mess up. Just as she swept her hand toward the tent in his pants, an alarm sounded from across the room where he'd flung his pants.

"Shit." His grip on her tightened. "Damn, Tink. I don't want to leave." The blaring noise continued from his pants. "It's the alarm system at the production facility."

"It's okay, go. I'm okay." She lifted her face to his, kissing him. Letting him know she understood. It was his business. He'd worked his tail off to build his company and someone was trying to destroy it. "Just be careful."

He kissed her again, obviously reluctant to leave. "I promise I'll be back as soon as I can."

She rolled off him, and he climbed out of the bed and retrieved his phone. His handsome face morphed into a scowl and his neck flamed red. It had to be bad. Dialing, he held the phone between his ear and his shoulder while he quickly dressed.

"The alarm triggered at the production facility. All I can see is the open door with an axe in it." He listened for a moment, his expression somewhere between scorn and anguish. "On my way."

He pocketed the phone, then leaned back over the bed. "I will call you as soon as I know something. I promise." With a quick kiss he was gone.

Hope vacillated between fear, relief and lingering pleasure. There was no chance of sleeping tonight. She quickly dressed and headed up to the third floor. Maybe she could at least do a little research, so she was ready when he came back to her bed.

She chose a book with a bare-chested man on the cover and curled up in the chair. Within a few pages, she knew it was a fruitless endeavor. All she could think about was Sharkey, possibly in danger, or his business destroyed. Out the window, the lawn of Heron House was highlighted under the full moon. She could see the gazebo and a small rowboat knocking against the dock. Maybe the light would help the police catch the men who were attacking Shark Bite.

Bowing her head, she prayed for the safety of those involved. She prayed for the perpetrators to be caught, and justice served. While she was at it, she asked the Lord to lead her down this new path—her budding relationship with Sharkey, finishing the book and figuring out her purpose in life. She ended her prayer by asking that her parents admit their wrongdoing and repent. From her perspective, they were even more lost than she was.

"Hope?" Riley's voice was muted, like she was calling from the floor below.

Like a big dummy, she hadn't grabbed her phone. She just couldn't get used to toting that thing around. "Coming!" Sticking the unread book back on the shelf, she turned out the light in the library and headed down the stairs. Maybe Riley had news about the brewery.

The two women met on the second floor.

"Sharkey called me because he couldn't get you on the phone." Riley's hair was in a messy bun, and she wore an oversized Tarheels sweatshirt over plaid sleep pants.

"I'm sorry if he woke you." The last thing Hope wanted was to inconvenience her hostess, who had become a great friend.

Riley shook her head. "I was awake. He took Ben with him again, so I've been wearing a hole in the rug pacing the parlor. I didn't hear you so I thought you might be asleep."

Heat crept up Hope's cheeks as she recalled what they had been doing when the alarm went off. She shook her head and lowered her gaze, focusing on her friend's fuzzy slippers. "We hadn't gone to sleep yet."

The normally chatty Riley simply raised her eyebrows and wore an amused grin. "I'm guessing I won't need to change the sheets in the Pop Art room tomorrow."

Hope teetered between mortification and desperation. Could she ask Riley the burning questions she had about pleasing a man? Could she admit that Sharkey had given her an orgasm? Were these normal things that women talked about? She really had no idea. "What did Sharkey say?"

"Everything is under control. There was no one inside the production facility when they arrived and he's assessing the damage. But he wants you to call him."

"Damage?" Anguish for Sharkey seized her heart.

Riley nodded somberly. "Look, call him, and then come find me. I'll be in the parlor refluffing the rug."

Hope ducked into her room and grabbed her phone. Her call went straight to voicemail. "Hey, it's me. Sorry I didn't have my phone. You can call me back whenever. I'll be waiting for you." She hesitated. Should she say that she loved him? They'd said it once, did that mean that they said it every time now? Seriously, there should be a guidebook on how to do this.

A beep ended the message and stole her opportunity. She stared down at the screen like it might hold some answers. A text from Sharkey popped up.

Squatch: With the police. Will be back soon. Keep the bed warm for me.

Heat rushed up her neck. Would that happen every time she even thought about what had happened tonight? She'd never be able to go into public again. Not as long as Sharkey was around.

She sent back the thumb's up emoji, then immediately wondered if she should have sent a heart instead. Would she eventually get to a point where she didn't second guess every single thing?

As she headed downstairs, she decided that knowledge was worth a little humiliation. Riley and Ben lived together. When they were together, they almost always touched—even if it was just a quick brush of their shoulders as they prepared a meal. Hope was certain Riley would have some advice for her.

She found her hostess in the parlor, a book in her lap, fast asleep. Poor thing, dragged out of bed in the middle of the night. Hope couldn't bear to wake her. But maybe Bridget would still be up. It'd be easier to talk about s-e-x without having to look her in the eye, anyway.

While the phone rang, Hope wandered into the kitchen and filled the tea kettle with water. There was an assortment of teas and cocoa in a basket on the counter. She chose a raspberry hot chocolate and a mug with an alligator on it while the water heated up.

"What are you doing up so late?" Bridget didn't bother with hello.

"Um, couldn't sleep." Hope didn't know how to answer that question without launching into a full rundown of the entire situation.

Bridget squealed. "Something happened! Something more than kissing. I want details."

She didn't know how her cousin could deduce all that from three little words. "A lot has happened."

"With Aiden or Sharkey? Nevermind. Of course it's Squatch. Did he profess his love? Whisk you off to bed?"

Hope was dumbfounded. Was it really that obvious?

"Oh my God. You slept with him? Bravo. I didn't think you had it in you. I was afraid Aunt Martha had completely brainwashed you."

"We spent the night together last night. After my disastrous date with Aiden. Who left town, by the way. But we didn't do anything other than kissing. Last night."

"But tonight? Is he in your bed right now? Naked Sasquatch?" Bridget was giddy.

Hope scanned the kitchen to make sure she was still alone. Of course she was. The house was empty until tomorrow. Riley was asleep. The guys weren't back from the brewery yet. But she lowered her voice anyway. "He gave me a...a..." It was so hard to say the word out loud.

"Another hickey? A present? Oh! An orgasm! He gave you an orgasm! How do you feel? Isn't it amazing? How did he do it? His fingers? His tongue? His big, hairy cock?"

"Bridget!" She looked around again, certain her cousin had said the "c" word loud enough to wake the dead—or at least Riley.

Her cousin snickered. "Sorry, got a little carried away. I'm guessing it was his hand since it's the first time. He does know it's your first time, right?"

First time for everything. "Yeah, he was really sweet. He told me he loved me."

Her cousin was so quiet, she thought the call had disconnected.

"Bridget? You still there?"

"Yeah, I'm here. Listen, sweetie, I don't want to rain on your sexual liberation parade, but be careful. Men rarely say those words—especially not this soon—unless they want in your pants. I'm all for you exploring and having fun but guard your heart. Don't get too attached."

Too late. Fear gripped her chest. Could Bridget be right? Was Sharkey just saying what he thought she wanted to hear so she'd sleep with him? Was she just a naive little girl? Was she completely wrong about him? He would be back soon. And he'd likely want to pick up where they left off.

"Aw, fuck. You're already in love with him, aren't you?"

Tears welled in her eyes. Had her mother been right? Could men not be trusted? "How do I know?"

Bridget sighed. "Which part?"

"All of it." A sob broke free from her throat. "I'm just a stupid, gullible virgin." The tea kettle whistled and she looked up. Sharkey stood in the doorway, his arms crossed over his wide chest, a scowl on his handsome face. "I've got to go, Bridget. I'll call you tomorrow." She was pretty sure she heard her cousin scream "wait" before she ended the call. Wiping her face, she got up and removed the kettle from the burner and turned off the stove, unable to face the angry Sasquatch.

"Who was that?" His voice was low, calm. He approached her slowly, staying a few feet back, but she could feel the effect he always had on her.

"My cousin." Her stomach was in knots, but she poured water into the mug anyway, just for something to do. A reason not to look at him yet.

"Well, I don't know your cousin. And she obviously doesn't know you. Or me, for that matter."

Hope stirred the drink, watching as the brown powder dissolved into the hot liquid.

He took a step closer. "Tink. Look at me. Please."

Was the kindness really an act? How did she know what to believe? She took a deep breath and turned her body to face him. But she didn't have the strength to lift her head.

He brought his fingers to her chin and tilted it up. He was blurry through her tears.

"I know you don't have much experience with relationships. Hell, I don't either. But this I can tell you. Ours is special. It's not typical. Because we aren't typical. Let me guess. Your cousin. She dates a lot?"

Hope nodded.

"Then how does she know what love feels like?" He used the pad of his thumb to wipe away her tears.

It was a good point. Logical. And he looked so sincere. She wanted to believe she was a good judge of character, but her parents were an awful example of just how ignorant she could be. She wanted to tell him she believed him. Trusted him. Loved him. But she couldn't form the words. Could barely breathe.

"Aw, Tink." He pulled her into his chest and wrapped his arms around her. "It's okay to have doubts. I don't care. I'll just spend the rest of my life proving it to you. But don't ever call yourself stupid or gullible. You are strong and brave. And I do love you." He kissed the top of her head.

Now she was more confused than ever.

They were still standing that way when Riley and Ben walked through the kitchen saying their good nights.

They stood that way long enough for her hot chocolate to go cold.

Chapter Thirty-Seven

Sharkey was running on maybe two hours of sleep and a half a gallon of coffee. Yesterday had been a complete rollercoaster of emotions. For a man who normally avoided emotions, it was a rough ride.

Leaving Tink this morning had been pure torture, but she was finally sleeping, and he couldn't bear to wake her. They'd spent most of the night talking about her doubts—or more accurately, her cousin's doubts—and the mayhem at the production facility. He held to his promise. He didn't sugarcoat a damn thing. So, she knew that some bastard had broken in and fucked with the electrical panel, essentially ruining every ounce of beer and cider he had in progress. It was a quick and incredibly painful job.

The perpetrator was long gone by the time he arrived. Maddy got there a few minutes later, and together they watched the video of a man in a hoodie breaking into his building. The cameras had likely alerted Sharkey before the alarm went off, but he had been distracted by a mostly naked Hope.

The exhilarating part of the ride.

But damn if that drop off didn't hurt like a mofo.

In a matter of minutes, Shark Bite Brewing Company had lost all of its stock in production. His declaration of prioritizing his relationship with Hope over his business seemed prophetic now. He had to admit, she wasn't the only one with doubts.

It was a stark reminder of how love can fuck with your life.

Maddy had been there most of the morning with her crime scene tech from Wilmington. Now Sharkey's job was to empty all the spoiled beer and start over. An electrician was coming later to replace the breaker box, and his insurance adjuster had already shown up to take pictures and get a copy of the police report.

Tires crunched over gravel. Sharkey closed the tap he was draining and headed to the door. He was no longer on high alert. There wasn't much else they could do to him at this point.

Instead of a work truck, Chesnee's sporty convertible pulled down the gravel road, followed by a car Sharkey didn't recognize. Pretty soon, several men gathered, most wearing work gloves and boots.

The calvary had arrived—led by a somber Chesnee.

"Shark Bite, you've always had our back. Now it's time that we had yours. Tell us how we can help." The normally goofy guy was nowhere to be seen.

"Guys, I really appreciate it." Sharkey recognized several men who had patronized his booth at local events.

Trip and Ben appeared from the direction of Heron House. "We're here to help too."

He'd always considered himself a loner, but this outpouring of support proved otherwise. This community took care of its own. Another car pulled in, and Nic and Maddy joined the work crew. Meeting Hope had kickstarted his dead heart, but standing there surrounded by his friends, Sharkey's heart grew two sizes that day.

Soon, everyone was working together, emptying tanks, cleaning and disinfecting every piece of equipment and tossing around threats about whoever had pulled this stunt.

Nic pulled Sharkey outside. "I can't believe these creeps were so brazen. After the first two get arrested, they send someone else. On the same night."

"Yeah, I thought we'd had our share of drama for one night. Let my guard down." He was still kicking himself for not camping out at the site.

"Maddy said both the perps have ties to Wilmington." The bartender scanned the immediate area and seeing they were still alone, continued. "I say we take a little trip up there and rattle some cages."

The idea had appeal. It was better than sitting around waiting for the other steel-toed boot to drop. "Do they connect back to Brightside?" Last thing he wanted was to go off half-cocked without assurances that it was the right evil bastards.

Nic shook his head. "Not directly, but I think I can get the truth out of Craig. I bet he's following orders and might squeal on the higher ups."

Sharkey clinched his fists. What exactly had he done to become the target of these lowlifes? He just brewed great beer and minded his own business. "When are you free?"

"I've got a shift tonight, but we can go after. Catch him as he's closing up." Nic straightened, his gaze fixed over Sharkey's shoulder.

A quick glance confirmed that Maddy had spotted them talking. She was in civilian clothes, but her face was 100% no nonsense. "I'll pick you up at eleven."

Nic nodded, then broke into a smile as the deputy joined them.

"Sharkey, I just got a call from a friend at my old department. We've got a line on who paid the bozos who tried to haul away your trailer. I'm heading up there now to run it down." She narrowed her eyes at Nic. "I assume you're going to stick around here and help until your shift?"

"Yeah. I can catch a ride."

Sharkey felt awkward as hell as the two made eyes at each other. It was a combination of sexual tension and suspicion. He'd have to get the lowdown on the drive up the coast. "Thanks, Maddy."

"Just doing my job."

He knew full well that she was going above and beyond—and she'd likely get crap about it from the Sheriff. "Well, either way, count on a lifetime supply of beer."

She nodded with a slight grin and headed to her car.

"She's eating, sleeping and breathing this case." Nic watched as the car disappeared down the gravel road.

"Interesting that you know that," Sharkey commented.

"I'm the best bartender in Eastport Beach. I know everything."

He didn't have time to drill Nic about his relationship with the new sheriff's deputy, because he spotted Riley and Tink in the clearing near the tasting trailer. "Eleven o'clock." He didn't wait for a response but slapped the bartender on the shoulder as he passed him on the way to meet the women.

Riley carried a basket, and Hope had a reusable grocery bag over each shoulder.

"Hey Sharkey! Ben told me everyone was here helping, so we made sandwiches." Riley hoisted the basket a little higher.

His nerves were shot—a combination of excessive caffeine, sleep deprivation and fuckers ruining his business—but just the sight of sweet Tink soothed his soul. He grabbed the bags from her and set them on the ground, then scooped her off her feet into a tight embrace. "Excuse us," he called out over his shoulder as he ducked inside the container and closed the door.

"Squatch, I can't breathe." She struggled in his embrace, but her tone hinted that she was amused.

He relaxed his hold but didn't release her.

She snaked her arms around his neck and stared up at him, concern lacing her hazel eyes. "Are you okay?"

"Better now." He leaned down and rubbed their noses together, his lips ghosting over hers. He had half a mind to take her to his truck and drive away. Start over somewhere else. But then he remembered all the people who were inside his production facility helping, out of the kindness of their hearts.

"You're a great businessman, Sharkey. I know you can rebuild."

He could. With her by his side. "I think you should stay in Eastport Beach."

Her eyes widened but she shook her head slightly. "I love it here, but I can't afford to stay for much longer."

"You can live with me." He blamed the outburst on his tired brain. It was a logical solution to him, but he knew Hope wouldn't shack up with a man she wasn't married to. Marriage. It was something he'd never considered after Eve died. If he asked Tink now, would it be for the right reasons?

"Your camper isn't even big enough for you, let alone two people." She wiggled out of his arms, stepping back.

The space between them felt like an insurmountable chasm. "The camper is temporary." He lifted his hand to cover her mouth before she could voice her next argument. "Just think about it."

She gave a quick nod, then shuffled her feet. "I need to help Riley hand out lunch."

He grabbed her shoulder as she turned to leave. "Hey." Leaning in for a quick kiss, he resisted the urge to get down on his knees and beg. Tink was the only good thing happening in his life right now and it felt like even that was dangling by a thread. "I love you."

"I love you, too." She covered her mouth with her hand as she went back outside.

Did she regret saying it back? Sharkey grabbed a nearby roll of paper towels and squeezed them until they looked like a smart car crushed between two semi-trucks. He had to figure out a way to prove to her that he was sincere. He'd already lost several months' worth of product. He couldn't lose her too.

Chapter Thirty-Eight

They'd ended up staying to help with the cleanup, so it was late when Hope and Riley made their way back to Heron House. Sharkey had asked her to stay for a little while, but she knew if she was alone in that camper with him again, she wouldn't want to leave. Maybe ever.

"I can't believe someone would do that to Sharkey. He's a good man. He works hard and he does a lot for the community." Riley shined her phone on the path to help them navigate around tree roots and bushes.

"Have you known him long?" Hope carried the now empty basket. The volunteers had demolished the sandwiches the women had made.

"Ever since I moved here last summer. He bought the land from me pretty soon after, so we've spent some time socializing. But Ben's known him for years."

Her gut told her he was sincere. Riley was vouching for him. And look at all the people who'd shown up to help him. Bridget had to be wrong about Sharkey.

"My cousin warned me that men might say things they don't really mean to get a woman to sleep with them."

Riley stopped short, the beam of light jumping as she spun toward Hope. "Yes. There are absolutely men who will lie to get into a woman's pants." She placed a hand on Hope's shoulder. "But Sharkey isn't one of them. I've seen women approach him at festivals. If he just wanted sex, he'd have no problem finding a willing participant."

"He is very handsome." The idea of women hitting on Squatch made her stomach flip. *Who's jealous now?*

"He's very manly. A protector." Riley started walking toward the house again.

Hope followed along, thinking about the way he'd taken care of her—rescuing her from Stumpy, defending her when that sheriff's deputy drew a taser on her, keeping her safe during the storm. And he had said that he'd spend the rest of his life proving that he loved her. Did he really mean forever? "I don't trust myself to make a good decision. Look at my parents. I'm obviously a horrible judge of character to have not seen what they were doing."

Riley stopped again, just short of the porch steps. "Hope, you can't blame yourself for what your parents did. You were isolated and lied to. But you did take care of yourself, and you've grown into a strong, young woman despite them."

"How did you know you were in love with Ben?"

"It was once I felt completely comfortable with him. When I knew I could be myself and that was enough."

She never felt more comfortable with another person. Otherwise, last night would have never happened. Memories of his hands on her, his mouth on her, rushed heat to her face. Was lust clouding her judgement? "He asked me to move in with him."

Riley laughed. "In that tiny camper? He barely fits in there."

"That's what I said. But he said it was temporary."

"Yeah, he used to have a place closer to Bluffville, but he wanted to stay on site until the brewery was finished."

Hope shifted on her feet, the empty basket suddenly feeling very heavy. "It feels really fast."

Riley nodded. "It is. Which is why I think he has real feelings for you. He's not the type to date a lot." She laughed. "Or at all."

Her life the past few months had been a blur. She'd gone from a slow-paced, humble existence to a world she didn't recognize. Coming to Heron House was supposed to be a way to catch her breath. Reflect. Write her story. Figure out a future. Falling in love had not been part of the plan. "I wish I had more time."

"Hope, you're twenty-two. You have all the time in the world."

She shook her head. "After my stay here ends, I have to go back to my aunt's house in Chicago. She'll let me live there for free until I figure things out."

The light from the porch revealed a grin on Riley's face. "If it's about money, I can help with that."

"No, you've already been generous enough. As it is, you feed me half the time." Riley had also given her a reduced rate for her extended stay.

"I mean a job, Hope. You know I'm a disaster in the kitchen, and don't tell Ben, but I haven't had a proper lunch since Trip moved out. I've got rooms on the third floor. You can stay there and work off your rent with a little cleaning and some cooking." Riley took the basket from her. "You'd be doing me a favor, honestly."

Staying in Eastport Beach sure beat going back to Chicago in the dead of winter. "Are you sure?"

Riley nodded enthusiastically. "Yes! And you'll have plenty of time to see where this thing goes with Sharkey."

Time. Deadlines. Crap. "I need to finish the book."

"Of course, I'm only talking about a few hours a day, but you're paid up through the end of the month, so you can stay in your suite until then."

Yes, that could work. If she buckled down, she could finish the book by then. She needed to anyway, so she'd get the rest of her advance. "But I'm happy to make you lunch."

Riley laughed and hooked her arm in Hope's, pulling her up the stairs. "And maybe the occasional breakfast. That French toast casserole was amazing."

As they walked through the front door, Hope realized it felt a little bit like home.

Chapter Thirty-Nine

When he pulled up to The Landing, it was dark, locked up tight for the night. Nic appeared out of the shadows, wearing all black and carrying a backpack.

"I didn't get a memo about the ninja dress code. I thought we were just going to talk to the guy." Sharkey was at the end of his rope with this onslaught of mayhem, but he wasn't willing to break the law.

"Yeah, yeah. We'll just talk." The bartender rooted around in his bag before pulling a long tube out. "Jerky?"

Sharkey shook his head and did a quick U-turn on Main Street. "You heard from Maddy?"

Nic bit off a hunk of meat and glanced at his phone. "Just a text earlier warning me not to get involved."

"Involved with her? Or with the case?"

"Har har. What can I say? I'm a hot-blooded, American man and she's a smokin' hot veteran. If you weren't into the little blonde, you'd probably be vying for her attention."

Sharkey grunted as he turned north. "So, what did she mean?"

Nic shrugged. "I may have mentioned that something needed to be done to cut this thing off at the balls. She said to leave it to the professionals."

"If we left it to Morgan, I might as well sign the deed over to the bastards. At least Maddy's doing something. Maybe we should hang back and see what she shakes out." Sharkey's doubts about this plan grew with every mile.

"Maddy's solid. But she's a cop. No way Craig will tell her anything." Nic balled up his empty wrapper and stuffed it into his bag. "We're just two dudes having a beer and catching up with an old acquaintance."

The whole plan would implode if this Craig fella knew what Sharkey looked like. "Maybe you should talk to him alone. What if he recognizes me?"

"If he does, then his reaction will tell us everything. I worked with this guy for years—hell, I played poker with him—I'll know if he's involved." Nic dug around in his bag some more and then drained a mini bottle of liquor.

From the smell, Sharkey was guessing rum. He wasn't sure drinking before they went to grab a beer was the best strategy, but Nic was a grown man, and Sharkey wasn't about to tell him how to live his life.

It was nearing midnight by the time they reached the outskirts of Wilmington. Sharkey was wired on coffee and very little sleep, so the inevitable crash was looming. The plan worried him as it was, but he was operating on fumes, so his confidence in this endeavor was somewhere around ten percent.

The second bottle of booze Nic downed as they headed toward downtown didn't lessen Sharkey's anxiety. He should have stayed in Eastport Beach cozied up with Hope in that big bed at Heron House. That could also get him into trouble, but at least it'd be the fun kind. There were too many ways this could go bad.

Nic was giving him directions to Brightside when his phone rang. "Hey, Maddy." He listened for a few minutes, replying with one syllable answers, and banging his leg with his fist. "Yeah, okay." After tapping his screen, he held the phone between the two men.

"Sharkey? You there?" Maddy's voice sounded tinny coming from the speaker.

"Yeah."

"Hopefully I've reached you before the two of you did something incredibly stupid."

The men shared a panicked glance.

"I just got back from Wilmington, and surprise surprise, neither of you were home."

They might be foolhardy, but they weren't dumb enough to lie to her.

"A friend of mine in WPD did a little digging and found some interesting financial transactions between the perps we have in lock up and one Craig Miller, the general manager at Brightside Brewing Company. So, as an officer of the law, I headed up there and had a little talk with Mr. Miller."

There may as well have been blue lights behind them at this point. Sharkey got the message loud and clear and pulled into an empty parking lot.

"Luckily, I caught him off-guard, and he apparently doesn't think fast on his feet. He gave me some BS about Tweedle Dee and Tweedle Dum doing reno work for him. Weird, since the place looked fairly new."

Nic muted the phone. "Maybe we should head back."

"You think?" Sharkey pulled a U-turn as Maddy continued.

"As long as you boneheads don't interfere in my investigation, I should have this wrapped up in a few days. I'm waiting on phone records, and some bigshot at corporate to call me back."

Nic unmuted the phone. "Aren't you concerned he'll run?"

Maddy laughed. "Gosh, I hadn't thought of that. Good thing I've got a friend up there with nothing better to do than sit on his ass until I get my t's crossed and my i's dotted."

"See, Sharkey. I told you she had this under control."

He glanced away from the road long enough to shoot Nic an icy glare. "We'll be back soon, Maddy. Thanks for the hard work."

"Drive safe. And go ahead and drop Nic off at *his* house." She disconnected the call without saying goodbye.

Sharkey whistled. "I hope you weren't really into her, because that horse might be dead before it even made it around the first bend."

The bartender rolled his eyes. "I'm the one who gave her Craig's name. She owes me."

"Somehow, I doubt she'll see it that way."

"Easy come, easy go. I wasn't looking for anything serious. You know me, confirmed bachelor."

"That's what I thought, too." Funny how things sneak up on you when you least expect it.

***

Sharkey woke up unnerved. He'd gone to bed alone, exhausted, and praying he could convince Hope he was sincere about his feelings for her. Actually praying. To God.

He didn't expect to dream about Eve. For the longest time, she was the only woman he dreamed about. She was an adult, but it was clearly her. They were walking through the woods by her house, which she'd been unable to do in life. He'd pushed her chair down that path a hundred times, but in this dream, she was walking on her own—grown up and beautiful.

"Sharkey, it's time. Time to let go of me. Time to let go of your resentment toward God. If you want to be good enough for her, you know what you need to do."

He reached for her hand, but it was just out of reach. "It's been too long."

"It's never too long to come back to Him." She turned to face him, the setting sun creating a halo of light around her. "I'm the lucky one. I'm whole now. You won't be whole until you let go of the anger."

"I'm not angry anymore. Mostly I'm numb. Well, I was until—"

"Until you met Hope." Eve smiled. "Don't you get it? I sent her. He sent her. To put you back on the path. Bring you back to life."

Sharkey shook his head. "I love her, but I don't want to forget you."

"Read it again, Sharkey. Remember." She started to fade, until he could see straight through her.

"Eve, come back. I'm not ready," he pleaded with the retreating form. "How can I be sure I won't lose her too?"

"Read it." The words echoed into bright light, and she was gone.

Awake now, Sharkey pulled a pair of shorts on, then went to his built-in dresser and opened the top drawer.

Inside were several sheets of crumbled paper. Words of doubt, of conviction, of faith. Hope had thrown these sentiments away, seeing them as trash. But Sharkey knew better. They were pieces of her. Beautiful snippets of how she felt.

Beneath Hope's discarded scribbles, and several pairs of underwear, was another sheet of paper. The letter he'd found after Eve passed. She had hidden it in the back pocket of his backpack, with a handful of root beer barrels—the only kind of beer he'd had up until that point. He'd read it daily for the first year. Then it had traveled halfway around the world with him to boot camp and deployments. When things got really rough, he'd dig it out of this foot locker and read it again. The creases were worn, the ink faded. But the glitter still sparkled, just like Eve.

My sweet, strong Seamus,

Meeting you has made this one of the best years of my life. You treated me like a normal person and never minded the limitations of my illness. There are so many things you gave up to spend time with me and I'm so grateful for that. For your love.

Now, we will both get our freedom. I get to go be with my Heavenly Father in paradise and get a new, healthy body. I'll never feel pain again. You get to go out into the world and experience everything life has to offer. You can share your heart of service. I don't want you to be sad. Or mad at God. This is His plan, and I trust that He has a good reason for it. Someday, you'll meet someone who fits perfectly inside your giant heart. Don't worry, there'll be room enough for both of us. I pray you'll remember me fondly, but don't use me as an excuse not to love again. You deserve all the happiness in this world (and the next), so continue to love God, love people and love the woman He sends you. (And love sharks!)

Don't be scared to open your heart again. Wasn't our love worth it? No matter how short the time we had together? I certainly think so.

Forever yours, Eve

He couldn't remember the last time he'd read the letter. If someone had asked him, he'd have said he could recite it from memory. Boy, was he wrong. There was so much he'd forgotten. It felt like a betrayal. She had asked so little of him, and instead of honoring her last wishes, he'd selfishly clung to his resentment. To his misery. He'd convinced himself that he was fine in his own little bubble. Fine on his own. Fine without the Lord in his life.

How could someone so young be so wise? Eve knew him inside and out, and she knew he needed his faith to make it through. It was so obvious now.

It'd been creeping in the last few weeks—since Hope appeared in his life—slowly rooting back into his soul. Faith. Belief. Purpose.

He'd isolated himself. Insulated his heart. No feelings, no pain.

Instead, there was a giant gaping hole in his soul.

A God-shaped hole.

Then, clear as day, he realized the truth.

The only way to properly love Hope was to get right with the Lord. He couldn't be good enough on his own, but with Jesus in his heart, he had a fighting chance.

Invigorated, he returned the note to its spot, knowing it would always be there if he got off track, and jumped in the shower. Or more-accurately, turned sideways and wedged himself into the tight space.

While he bathed, he dug deep into his mind, trying to find the verses he used to store there. As a pre-teen, he'd won a prize (a large pizza, if he remembered correctly) for memorizing the most Bible verses at church camp. Had any of them stuck?

Something niggled in the back of his mind. Jeremiah. Prosper. Plans. Hope.

He rinsed, turned off the water, and dripping wet, stood over the minuscule kitchen counter, searching for the verse on his phone. When it came up, he read it over and over again, soaking it in, hearing it echo in his head. Something told him he wouldn't forget it again, because it brought instant peace.

Sharkey wasn't in charge. What a relief. God had a plan. All he had to do was trust it. So simple, yet extraordinarily hard. He'd been fighting it for half his life.

There it was in black and white. The Lord had sent him Hope.

Sinking down on the four-foot-wide cushion that masqueraded as a couch, he stopped fighting it. He was tired of doing it on his own. He was tired of his walls. Seamus McLaughlin was ready to let someone else in. First God, and then Hope, if she'd have him.

Chapter Forty

Hope was deep in a chapter about the time her parents had lied about visiting an orphanage in Sri Lanka when her phone rang. She didn't recognize the number, but she only had a dozen or so contacts in her phone.

"Hello?"

"Oh honey! It's so good to hear your voice."

She'd know that sweet, Southern accent anywhere. Her heart swelled. "Merry?" Meredith Cantor ran Clean Feet, a non-profit based in her village in Uganda. Hope had assumed she'd never hear from her again.

"Of course it's me! I've been trying to track you down for weeks."

"Really?" She thought Merry had abandoned her like everyone else back home after her parents were arrested.

"How are you? Where are you?"

Hope doodled a row of footsteps running up the side of the page, similar to the logo for Clean Feet. "You aren't mad at me?"

Meredith tsked. "Why on earth would I be mad at you? I've been worried sick about you. I was overseas when you left, and no one in town had a way to reach you. Glad you finally entered the 21st century and got a cellphone." Her melodic laugh echoed through the phone.

How she had missed her friend's laugh. "I'm in the States. North Carolina to be exact. I'm doing okay, I guess. Just a lot of adjustments." *That might be the understatement of the year.*

"Girl, you're in spittin' distance of my old stompin' ground. I thought you had family on the west coast."

"Yes, my dad's sister and my cousin. My mom's sister is in Chicago, but it was so awkward staying there. I don't really know any of them well."

Excited chatter echoed in the background. Meredith's house was always full of children from the nearby orphanage. "Did you throw a dart at a map?"

Hope laughed, her heart light upon discovering she wasn't a complete pariah. "I'm staying at a sort of retreat center. My agent suggested it."

"Yes, I heard you're writing a book. That's actually how I tracked you down. I saw the article and called in some favors. Your agent plays pickleball with my fundraising chair's sister-in-law." Meredith was the kind of person who saw a problem, then did everything in her power to find a solution. "I hope you don't mind."

"No, of course not. I'm thrilled to hear from you. I thought..." Hope didn't want to get Kelly, the assistant director, in trouble. "I had to leave quickly. They froze my parents' assets, and without a job, I had no way to maintain the property in Uganda."

Merry sighed. "I'm so sorry I wasn't there. I would have moved you in with me." She paused, long enough for Hope to wonder if the call had dropped. "Kelly's no longer with the organization. She had no right to say you weren't welcome."

Hope cringed. Was she responsible for Kelly getting let go? "I'm sorry. I know she was a big help to your organization."

"You have nothing to apologize for. That was just the final thing that showed me we didn't have the same values. Honey, what your parents did was dishonest and unethical. But anyone who knows you, knows you are not those things. You are good and kind and have a huge heart for helping others. You should not be judged for your parents' sins."

"Thank you for saying that. This whole thing has been really confusing. Writing the book is really forcing me to look at everything I used to believe." She'd been making progress, but it was gut-wrenching.

"That's great. I'm really proud of you for doing the hard work. Most people would just move on instead of digging deep and really understanding where things went wrong. Hold on." Meredith spoke to someone, but it was muffled like her hand was covering the phone. "Sorry, I've got to run. But listen. You aren't the only person they fooled. They lied to all of us and all their donors. For years. Don't be too hard on yourself. And I am always available if you want to hash something out. I hope I can see you soon. I want to give you a major hug."

She closed her eyes, imagining it. "I'd love to see you too. Thank you so much for calling."

"Love ya, honey."

"Love you too, Merry." Hope ended the call, then held the phone to her chest. Speaking to Meredith was like applying a healing salve to a wound. It felt like it stitched her heart back together a little bit.

Renewed, she got back to work, finishing the Sri Lanka chapter. As she considered what came next, she colored in the footprints she'd drawn. Clean Feet had been a huge part of her life, with Meredith serving as a mentor to Hope. She was one of the few Americans nearby, and her story was inspirational.

Starting a fresh chapter, she wrote about when Merry had arrived in Uganda to start her ministry. Hope had been a teenager, left alone constantly now that she was old enough to take care of herself. The new woman in the village had seemed so brave—moving to a foreign land with passion and a purpose—and little else.

Most of the people where they lived spoke at least some English, but Hope stepped in to help translate when Meredith traveled to small, more remote villages to teach the locals about jiggers and the importance of washing their feet and wearing shoes. Clean Feet had partnered with another ministry called Sole Hope, which made shoes for the orphans of Uganda.

Hope got to watch both ministries grow from the ground up, led by strong, spiritual women. Now, looking back, she realized how valuable that was. Her parents may be horrible role models, but she was lucky enough to have seen real ministry in action.

By the time she finished the new chapter, the sun had set, and she realized she'd missed several texts.

One of them was from her aunt in Chicago. It was odd, because she had never texted Hope before. She wanted to know when she'd be coming back and asked how the book was going.

When Hope flew down to North Carolina, she hadn't told her aunt when, or if, she'd return. She barely knew the woman and had been uncomfortable the entire time she'd stayed in her dark and stuffy home. Once the book was complete, she'd have enough money to get settled somewhere. Chicago was way down the list of places she might want to live.

Eastport Beach was a serious contender at this point.

Flying out to the west coast was another possibility, but she didn't want to impose on Bridget. They'd been pen pals for years, but they'd never actually met in person.

Now, after speaking to Merry, she wondered if moving back to Uganda was an option. She didn't know about the legalities of passports and visas—her parents had always handled those particulars.

The last two texts were both about dinner. One, an invitation from Riley to go eat Mexican with her and Ben, and the other from Sharkey, saying he still owed her a "real" date. The texts were over an hour old. Normal people would have had dinner by now.

Feeling emotionally drained, she answered all three texts by saying she was going to bed early and would talk to them tomorrow.

She found a pack of peanut butter crackers in her bag, so she munched on those while she got into her pajamas and washed her face.

Her phone chimed as she was brushing her hair.

Chapter Forty-One

Maddy texted first thing to let him know they were arresting Craig Miller for hiring the two goons who'd tried to make off with his bar.

Sharkey crawled out of bed, feeling energized. Maybe now he could finally get the tasting area up and running. He'd spent weeks in defensive mode, just reacting to all the terror that a-hole had inflicted on Shark Bite Brewing.

He rushed through his morning routine, anxious to get to work—and to see Hope. It was a bright new day.

His phone chimed again as he was walking out the door. Glancing down, he saw a link and a picture of a cross. Skidding to a stop, he backtracked and took a seat at the tiny table. One day in, and he was already forgetting.

Thankfully, he had signed up for text alerts for a daily devotional. Determined to start every day in the Word, he clicked through to the link and took his time reading the scripture and short passage that accompanied it. His Bible was packed up in storage, having collected dust since Eve passed. For now, his phone would have to do.

The topic was especially timely, reminding him about spending time daily in prayer and scripture. Maybe this is what they threw at all the new subscribers on their first day. Whether intentional, or inspired, Sharkey felt grateful. He prayed, focusing on what he needed to do instead of what the Lord could do for him.

Now, as he left the camper, he felt peace in his heart and hope for the future.

He hurried around the container, anxious to see Tink after being apart for more than twenty-four hours. It was hard to believe that a few weeks ago, he thought being alone was fine. Thought he didn't need anyone else in his life. That he shouldn't love again.

His heart was bursting as he stepped into the picnic area, ready to gather her in his arms and not let go.

But the tables were all empty. He checked the time and his messages. Normally, she'd be here by now. Scribbling away in one of her notebooks. Focused on getting words down. Looking adorable in her too big overalls.

Shooting off a text, he tried not to overreact. It was fine. Maybe a miscommunication about when she was coming. Or she got caught up with Riley. She overslept.

To distract himself, Sharkey got to work, opening the container, and making a game plan for all the final fixes he needed to make. Mentally, he calculated how long he needed for sufficient product. Losing most of his stock had really set him back. He didn't know much about the law, but he wanted them to throw the book at Craig for all the time, money and energy Sharkey had lost.

He was hanging a dry erase board for daily specials when he heard tires crunching on the gravel driveway.

The sound was followed by three quick horn blasts.

No way! It was too early. His cousin wasn't supposed to arrive for several more weeks.

But sure enough, as he rounded the corner of the container, he saw Mav's giant white truck and the Nacho Average Taco trailer pulling to a stop near Sharkey's camper.

It'd been months since he'd seen his cousin—basically the only person in his family who still associated with Sharkey. He and Maverick had been best friends growing up and then spent several years vending together at festivals while getting their respective businesses off the ground.

"What's up, old man?" Maverick jumped out of the truck and approached Sharkey with open arms.

The two men embraced, slapping one another on the back. "I'm so happy to see you, I won't even rag you about that sad excuse for a beard."

"Sorry I couldn't keep up with my manscaping while driving for three days straight to get here."

"Aren't you supposed to be in Texas?"

Maverick's eyes bugged out. "Have you been living under a rock? They had some freak flooding down there. Completely took out the fairgrounds, so festival cancelled."

Sharkey stroked his superior beard. "I don't have tv in that little cracker jack box and I've been a little preoccupied with assholes trying to ruin my business." He led his cousin to the door of his camper. "Speaking of that, they're arresting the guy behind all of it."

"Seriously? That's great. I hope he has to pay restitution for all that wasted beer. Such a shame."

"And emotional trauma for the thousands of bugs."

Mav sprawled on the bench that passed for a sofa. He was a couple inches shorter and about forty pounds lighter than Sharkey, but that had never stopped the cousins from epic wrestling matches as kids. "Remember that event in the Mojave?"

Sharkey cringed. "I had nightmares about scorpions for months after that. At least palmetto bugs don't sting."

"Yeah, but scorpions don't fly, so you get a pass."

"You want a water or something?"

Maverick shook his head. "Is it too early for a 33rd Parallel? I've been craving one for months."

Sharkey sighed. "You'll have to wait until The Landing opens for lunch. I lost all of my stock here."

"Rat bastards. Hang 'em."

"We've got a couple hours before the restaurant opens. Why don't you put on some work clothes, and you can help me install these cabinets?" He'd planned on asking Ben and Chesnee to help, but he didn't have any beer to lure them with.

"Throwing me right into the fray, huh?"

Sharkey shrugged. "A lot to do."

Maverick rose, nearly hitting his head on the upper cabinet over the bench. "I don't know how you've managed here. My trailer is bigger than this and I have a huge cooktop and a full-sized refrigerator."

"Now that the perp's been pinched, I shouldn't have to stay much longer." Besides, he needed a place for two people now. "You're just trying to get me out so you can move in."

"You know how hard it is to entertain a woman in the cab of a truck? I'd kill for an actual bed."

Sharkey laughed. "That's the only thing remotely my size. But I have to perform acrobatics to get out of it in the morning."

"You think your neighbor's got room for me on short notice?"

"Worse comes to worse, you can bunk in her staff quarters."

Mav stopped on his way out the door and glanced back at his cousin. "Will she expect me to work?"

"Make her dinner once a week and she'll name a suite after you."

"She single?" He wiggled his eyebrows

Sharkey shook his head. "Not even a little bit."

***

By the time they were done hanging the cabinets, the sun was high in the sky and the temperature unseasonably warm for January.

"You said they arrested the guys responsible, right?"

Sharkey used the hem of his shirt to wipe sweat off his forehead. "Yeah."

Maverick grabbed a bottle of water from the cooler. "Then why do you keep looking over your shoulder? I've never seen you this antsy."

He hadn't mentioned Hope to his cousin. Sharkey thought he had another couple weeks before Mav showed up. No doubt he'd give him hell about it. *Might as well get it over with.* "There's this girl…"

"A girl?" Mav's voice reached an octave only dogs could hear.

Tink would have his ass for the slipup. "I mean, woman."

"Is it the neighbor? Is that why she's not single? I can't believe you kept this from me." Maverick paced between the picnic tables, throwing his hands up in the air. "I can't believe you're actually dating someone!"

"Have you always been this dramatic?"

"Dramatic? You haven't had a second date since…" He trailed off as he realized he'd stepped in it.

Sharkey ran his hand through his hair. "It's okay. You can say it."

Eve's name hung in the air between them.

"I need a beer."

Slapping his cousin on the back, Sharkey pushed him toward his truck. "You've earned it. Let's grab some lunch, and I'll tell you about Hope."

"She has a name. Does she have a sister?"

It was like having another Chesnee around, except Sharkey knew all of Maverick's skeletons and where they were buried. *A little blackmail goes a long way.* "You've got some competition for town heartthrob. But wait until spring break. There'll be more than enough to go around."

"I don't know. Since I'll be putting down anchor, maybe I need to look into one of those second dates. Apparently, hell has frozen over or rhinos are flying."

"Pretty sure the expression is pigs."

"Pretty sure a rhino is harder to get off the ground." He gestured at his towering cousin.

Sharkey grunted.

Maverick's phone rang, but he sent the call to voicemail without checking the screen. "Invite your lady friend to lunch."

"Hell, no." He wasn't about to overwhelm Hope with his larger-than-life, and often inappropriate cousin. "We'll have to ease into that."

"I'm delightful."

Sharkey hit him with an incredulous glower. "Since when?"

"Since always. You were too busy hermiting to notice."

"Pretty sure that's not a word."

"Good thing we aren't playing Scrabble."

Groaning, Sharkey started the truck. "I've missed you, Mav."

"Right back at you."

Chapter Forty-Two

Skipping dinner had been a mistake. An empty stomach kept Hope from falling asleep, so around midnight, she'd finally crept downstairs to make a sandwich. By the time she finished eating, she was wide awake and thinking about the time she'd taught children at the orphanage how to make sandwiches. Merry had gotten a huge donation with boxes of peanut butter and jelly. They'd baked bread and introduced the kids to the tasty American treat.

She'd stayed up until three writing that chapter.

Now, she woke up to full sun streaming in the window and realized she'd missed the entire morning.

While she was freshening up, her phone rang. She finished brushing her teeth and combed her hair. She'd call back whoever it was. It could be her agent or editor checking on her progress. She needed to type up everything she'd written and see how much she had.

When she glanced at her phone, the missed number was one she didn't recognize. She gathered her laptop and notebooks and stuffed them in her bag then headed downstairs. A missed meal had already screwed up her schedule and now it was almost lunchtime.

She shot Sharkey a quick text so he wouldn't worry.

Hope

> I slept late today. Would it be okay if I came over after lunch?

Squatch

> Not there right now. Will text you when I'm on my way back. Can't wait to see you.

Warmth spread throughout her body. She pressed her hands to her chest, like they could hold in her rapidly beating heart. She wanted to be wrapped up in his arms again. He made her feel alive—every nerve ending tingled with anticipation. Maybe tonight they could pick up where they'd left off the other night.

"Hey, Hope. You feeling okay?" Riley buttered two slices of bread and set a frying pan on the stovetop.

Her hand flew to her cheek and she felt the heat there. "Yes, I'm fine. Why do you ask?" *Is it really that obvious?*

"You've been holed up in your room and missing meals. And you're all flushed." She gestured toward Hope's face with a spatula. "Are you sick?"

"No, no. I've just been working on the book. Maybe got a little overheated." She set her bag in one of the chairs. "I came down to get some lunch."

Riley's face transformed from concern to happiness. "Great, let me make you a sandwich."

Hope knew about her hostess's limits in the kitchen. "That's okay, I can make something."

"Even I can't screw up grilled cheese."

It did seem like a safe option. "That'd be great, thanks. I'll cut up a couple oranges to go with it."

"Good idea. While you're doing that, you can tell me how things are going with a certain brooding brewer."

Hope grabbed a cutting board and knife. A fruit bowl in the center of the kitchen table held apples, oranges and bananas. She selected a couple oranges and started slicing them. "There's not much to tell. I've been writing a ton and haven't seen him since we were over there helping with the cleanup."

The pan sizzled as Riley placed a slice of bread in the melted butter. "You haven't heard from him at all?"

"He asked me to dinner last night, but I didn't see the text until later."

Riley laughed. "Good to know we weren't the only invitation you blew off."

She cringed. "I'm so sorry. I didn't mean to be rude, I was just on a streak and didn't notice the texts come in."

"Hope, I'm just teasing you. It's fine. I'm glad you're making progress on the book." Riley flipped the sandwich over, revealing a golden brown toasted slice of bread.

It was so hard to figure out the nuances of speech here in America. Somehow it was like she didn't really speak the language, even though she'd been speaking English her whole life. Reading was helping a little, but she needed more help learning all the idioms and turns of phrase common in every day life in the States. "I've had a revelation about the book that has really helped me get the words down on paper."

Riley opened another slice of cheese for the second sandwich. She gestured with her hand for Hope to continue.

"I've been struggling to write a book about my parents and what they did. Then it occurred to me, I can't write that book. I can't step into their shoes and see it through their eyes. I don't even feel like I know them anymore. But I can write a book about my life and how my parents' actions affected me. And it finally clicked that it wasn't all bad. I had a beautiful life of service in Uganda. I owe a lot of that to them, even if their intentions weren't pure. It's complicated, but the story makes more sense in my head now."

Smoke rose from the pan. "Fudge brownie!" Riley grabbed her spatula and rescued the half-burnt sandwich from the skillet. "Turns out I can screw up something as simple as a grilled cheese. Thank goodness you're sticking around, or we might all starve."

"I won't let that happen. Why don't you have a seat, and I'll take over." As Hope grabbed two more slices of bread from the bag, she realized how good it felt to have purpose—even if it was as simple as preparing lunch. Cooking Riley lunch probably wouldn't turn into a career, but at least she had landed in a place where she was appreciated. And loved.

***

After lunch, Hope settled at the large dining table to transcribe her mess of thoughts into something resembling a story. Her editor had been asking for the first three chapters for several weeks now. It was time to buckle down.

She'd just started typing when her phone rang. Maybe it was Sharkey saying she could come over. She swiped to answer the call, before belatedly realizing it was the same unknown number from earlier.

"Hope? Baby? Is that you?"

Her excitement crashed to the bottom of her gut, causing her entire abdomen to clinch in shock. Bile rose in her throat. She'd been trying to exile her mother's voice from her mind for weeks and now it was in her ear, clear as day.

Martha Seaton cleared her throat. "It says in the Word to honor your mother and father." Gone was the cheerful greeting. This was the tone Hope recognized. Dreaded.

"Hello, Mother." Panic clawed at her throat. *Was she out of prison? Does she know where I am?*

"Honey, I've missed you so much. Why haven't you visited me?" The saccharine tone was back, laced with the guilt she'd perfected over the years.

Visited? That implied she was still locked up. Hope breathed a little easier. "I'm not in Chicago."

"I can't very well hop on a plane to visit you. You need to make a little effort to maintain a relationship with your father and me."

Emotions warred for her attention. Fear, surprise, remorse. "I'm sorry, Mother. As soon as I get back up there, I'll be sure to come see you."

"And your father." It was a directive, not a request.

"Yes, and Father." She didn't mention the part about never wanting to return to Chicago.

"In the meantime, you can help me out by sending me some money. You wouldn't believe how awful it is in here. I've run out of my face cream, they don't have milk substitutes for my coffee, and my hair is an absolute disaster. But if you add money to my account, I can at least set up a color appointment."

Hope looked around the room. Was this a joke? Was someone pranking her? It sounded like her mother, but was she in prison or a three-star resort? There were no cameras, no one jumping from behind the curtains yelling, "Gotcha!".

"I'm sorry. Do you have something more important to do than speak to your mother? Have you lost all your manners in the short period of time you've been back in the states?" Her mother's use of the phrase "I'm sorry" had never been used as an apology. It was always as an accusation.

"I'm just surprised to hear from you, is all. I'd love to help you out, but I don't have any money." Did she conveniently forget that they'd left their daughter penniless?

Martha tsked. "That's funny, because I heard you are taking the devil's money to write a tell-all about your own parents."

Hope jumped up from her chair, slammed her laptop closed and gathered all her notebooks. This wasn't happening. They were supposed to be locked up.

Away from polite society and especially her. Somewhere they couldn't continue to betray their daughter.

She ran from the room, her arms full, her mother yelling from the other end of the phone. She ran like someone was chasing her.

"Hope Harriet Seaton, you disappoint me. You are disappointing the Lord."

Throwing the front door open, Hope ran out onto the porch, with no plan other than to get away.

A familiar truck rounded the heron fountain in front of the house.

Hope collapsed onto the top step, her books and computer sliding across the floor of the porch. She was still clutching the phone in her hand, her mother hurling scripture over the line.

Sharkey jumped out of the cab of the truck, racing toward her. "What is it? Are you okay?"

She held the phone out, mute. Her entire body shook.

"You will obey your mother, Hope. Or else you will feel my wrath," her mother screamed.

Sharkey's eyes widened, then immediately reversed into a scowl. He took the phone from her and tapped the screen, then chucked the device into the fountain "It's okay. She's gone. We'll change your number. Hell, change your name. I'm here." He wrapped his big, strong arms around her and pulled her close. His familiar scent soothed her, calmed her rapidly beating heart.

As far as she was concerned, this was the only place she might be safe. In his arms.

Chapter Forty-Three

"She knows. She knows about the book." Hope sat at the kitchen table, her hands around a mug of hot cocoa. She was paler than usual, with a haunted look in her eyes. Scared.

It took every ounce of restraint he possessed to not call that number back and show that woman his wrath. It helped that the phone was toast after taking a swim. He pulled his chair closer to her, his arm across her shoulders, praying his presence gave her some peace. "She can't hurt you. She's locked up."

Her eyes cut up to him, searching. "She has a phone. In prison."

Sharkey didn't want to tell her about where white-collar criminals were held in this country. How it was basically a spa with a barbed wire fence. "We'll get your number changed."

"My aunt will just give her the new one."

"Then don't give it to your aunt."

Her face transformed from disbelief to consideration.

He leaned closer. "Blood doesn't make family." It certainly didn't make people love unconditionally. His parents were proof of that.

"I don't know what to do."

"You keep doing what you're doing. You're remarkable, Hope. Don't let her make you think any different."

She sighed, her whole body slumping like the air had been let out of a tire. "I'm scared," she whispered.

They were hardly alone, with Riley next door in her study and Maverick waiting in the parlor, but Sharkey didn't care. He pulled Tink into his lap, cradling her against his body, hoping to infuse strength into her through osmosis. "I got you."

"You don't know my mother. She always gets her way. Even in prison, apparently."

"I can be fairly stubborn myself." And he would move heaven and earth to keep Tink safe.

She chuckled, and the sound soothed some of his ire.

He wasn't sure how long they sat that way, but eventually her trembling ceased and her breathing evened out. As he carried her upstairs, he signaled to his cousin that he'd be right back. Depositing her on the bed in her suite, he covered her with a throw and left a quick note on her latest notebook—a black and purple tie dye design.

With a quick kiss to her forehead, he slipped quietly out the door and downstairs. His blood boiled with rage at her mother for continuing to distress her. How could anyone speak like that to someone as sweet and good as Hope?

"Whose ass do we need to kick?" Maverick jumped up from one of the armchairs, ready for action.

Mav had always had Sharkey's back, whether it was a sneak attack on a couple older kids giving Sharkey hell for having a beard in middle school, or hiding him in the attic after his parents had kicked him out, or getting him a coveted vending spot at a popular festival in the desert when Shark Bite Brewing was less than a year old.

"Turns out my parents aren't the only ones out there giving Christians a bad name." He held the front door open. "I'll drive you back to the camper and give you the condensed version. Guess you'll be getting that big bed sooner than you hoped for." Sharkey would grab some clothes and stay at Heron House. No way he'd leave Hope alone after that.

***

The next day, Sharkey and Hope drove to Myrtle Beach and he got her a new phone. He programmed the important numbers—his, Riley, Ben—and enabled a setting that prevented unknown numbers from calling. She protested briefly when he pulled out his wallet, but he insisted on replacing it, since he'd been the one to destroy it.

Now, they were on their way back to Eastport Beach, and he was praying.

It was like someone had dimmed her light. No, not someone. Her own flesh and blood.

Sharkey hadn't spoken to his parents in sixteen years. Almost half his life. Hope's wound was fresh, and raw. She was huddled against the passenger door, folded in on herself, staring blankly ahead.

Gone was the bright, toothy grin. The twinkle in her eyes. Her spirit was broken.

The pain in his chest was physical. Stabbing. His heart had just barely come back to life, and now it ached for her.

He'd been praying a lot since he met Hope. It started to feel almost second nature. Old Sharkey would have accused, cursed, turned away from God. This Sharkey understood that this evil was free will. Greed. Selfishness. God was the remedy, not the cause. Eve had helped him see that.

He knew from Hopes's discarded writings that she struggled with the same doubts. He knew from experience how a parents' betrayal could test one's faith. A test Sharkey had failed. He'd been alone in the world when everything fell apart. No one told him to hold tight. That the Lord had a plan. But Hope had him. And he wouldn't let her make his mistakes.

He'd find the light inside her and turn it as bright as it could go.

Making a last-minute decision, he veered off the main road, winding through a marshy area, past a small subdivision and into a thicket of live oaks. When they emerged on the other side, the Atlantic stretched out before them, meeting the horizon in the distance.

It was enough to make her sit up. Focus on the waving dune grass. Speak. "Where are we?"

"Come on, I'll show you." He pulled into the driveway of a summer place. The owners were bicoastal and often held parties at the large beach house. Shark Bite Brewing had a regular gig for their annual Memorial Day party, and that's how he knew they weren't in town.

Turning the truck off, he rounded the bed and opened the passenger door. "Is this your house?" Hope's eyes nearly bugged out of her head as she stared up at the mansion.

He chuckled, and it occurred to him how often he'd laughed since Tink had flitted into his life. "No, I need to find something now that the brewery will be opening." He wanted to say "we," but he held back. Taking her hand, he pulled her toward the dunes, where a wooden walkway led to the ocean. "I've worked a few parties here. They're in California now, but they've told me I could use their beach access."

"So you come here a lot?" The wind off the ocean blew her hair into her face. She pushed it back behind her ears, and a smile emerged. The first one he'd seen all day.

"I've never taken them up on it before." He grabbed her hand and pulled her toward the sand. They stopped at the rack line, taking in the vast ocean—waves lapping against the sand, wind blowing salty spray their way.

She stood, mesmerized by it.

Sharkey stood, mesmerized by her.

"I grew up in the mountains. We weren't a beach family. Honestly, we rarely took a vacation at all. Six Flags one year. Camping near Pigeon Forge." He didn't like to talk about the past, about his parents, about the grief of losing everything in the blink of an eye.

Hope tugged on his hand and plopped down in the sand. He followed and pulled her close. The feel of her against him, her steady gaze, emboldened him. She needed to know all of him, even the ugly bits. And he hoped it would help her.

"The first time I saw the ocean, I was seventeen. When Eve passed, my world ended. I was a naive kid. I couldn't comprehend how a loving God would take someone so young. She'd lived her life for Him, and that's how He repaid her?" He wiped the moisture from his face. Just spray from the waves.

Tink pressed her hand against his knee, and it anchored him to the present.

"I turned away from God. Refused to go to church. And that wasn't acceptable to my parents. They told me I was no longer welcome under their roof." The massive lump in his throat made it hard to speak. To breathe. "Parents are supposed to love their kids unconditionally." He slipped his hand over hers and squeezed. "But sometimes they don't."

She bit her bottom lip, and her eyes went glassy.

"I left that day and just drove. I didn't stop until I reached the ocean. It felt like the end of the world. The end of my world. All I had with me was my backpack, and I thought maybe I had some gum, or trail mix, or something, but instead I found a letter from Eve. And a handful of candy." He laughed, but it morphed into more of a sob. "I read that letter for the first time, sitting like this, staring out at the ocean. It gave me just enough strength to make a plan. Eve and the ocean. I moved in with my cousin, finished school, and enlisted. And I promised myself I'd end up here, where I could see the ocean every day." His throat was dry from all the talking.

"Have you seen them? Since they kicked you out?" Her voice quivered, almost like she was dreading the answer.

Sharkey shook his head. "I wrote them letters when I was in the service, but I never got a response. Maverick assures me they are alive and well, but the few times he's seen them, they've never asked about me."

"Were you close before that?" She spoke so quietly, it was hard to hear her over the waves.

He leaned closer. "Yeah. We were a normal family. Pizza on Monday night, games on Fridays, church on Sunday and Wednesday."

"Oh, Sharkey, I'm so sorry you lost your family." Hope wrapped her arms around him and buried her face in his neck. He could feel the dampness from her tears.

"I'm sorry you lost yours." He scooped her into his lap and held on tight. "But you know what I've realized?"

"What?" The question came out muffled.

He pulled back so he could see her lovely face. "We can make our own family. Ben and Riley are my family. Maverick is more like a brother than a cousin. Trip, Ada, hell, even Chesnee." He tucked her hair behind her ear. "You. I want you to be my family."

Fat tears rolled down her cheeks, emotion choking her. She nodded fervently, pulling him close again, her cries morphing into delighted laughter.

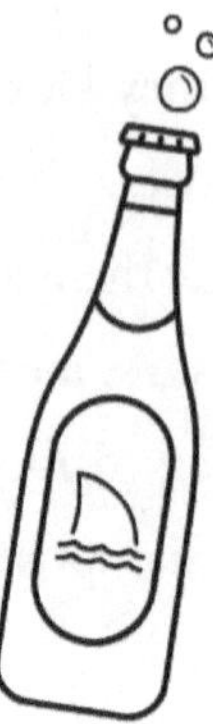

Chapter Forty-Four

Emotions crashed inside her chest like the waves slamming into the jetty. Excitement and love for Sharkey. Sadness about the way his parents treated him. Anger at her own mother and father for their greed and lack of remorse.

He held her tight to his chest, his steady heartbeat comforting her. Since her parents' arrest, it'd felt like her life was in limbo. Here, holding tight to this man, listening to the waves ebb and flow, she could feel solid ground underneath her. Stability. A future. Hope.

Eventually, she ran out of tears. She'd tried hard not to feel after the phone call from her mother. Had spent the night numb, unresponsive, closing her eyes, but barely sleeping. It wasn't like her to avoid hard things. She'd learned how to construct a cistern and collect rainwater. Installed solar panels by herself. Grew sunflowers in soil that shouldn't produce anything.

Realizing just how narcissistic and cruel her mother was, forced Hope into a cocoon of denial and shame. She couldn't face it. Needed to protect her heart. It was easier to ignore it than really examine it.

After Sharkey shared his story, she realized there was a chance her parents would never repent. Never apologize. Never do good in the world around them. Until now, she'd been living under the assumption that this was all temporary. That one day her parents would return to the virtuous path. Would miss their daughter. Would try to mend their relationship.

It was beyond scary to release them from her life. Completely. Maybe if she'd been able to stay in Uganda. If the locals hadn't condemned her too. If she had the support network she'd grown up with. Maybe then it wouldn't seem so scary.

But they'd basically abandoned her. Let her penniless, floundering, and questioning everything she'd ever known. She was angry and hurt. Disillusioned and confused. Scared and weak.

Sharkey shifted, tightening his grip on her.

That's when light shone in. This strong man wanted to be with her. To love her. Had been watching out for her since she arrived in Eastport Beach. He'd shown her so many things. Made her feel things she'd never imagined. Introduced her to romantic love. Physical pleasure. Emotional connection.

He could be her family.

"Sharkey?" She sniffled, swiping her forearm under her nose.

"Yeah?"

Her heart raced. What if she was reading too much into his words? She kept her head buried in his chest, too scared to look at him. "When you say you want to be my family, do you mean like a protective older brother?"

His chest rumbled with laughter. "No. Not even a little bit. Although I will always keep you safe."

She felt a little bit better, but uncertainty still lingered. All this was so new to her. "Like an uncle?"

He growled, pulling her away from his chest so she was forced to look at his handsome face. His emerald eyes glowed with intensity. "No." He leaned closer, until their lips were almost touching. "Like a husband."

The kiss was more intense than any they'd shared. It was fire and ice. Hot and chill-inducing at the same time. It left no doubt.

This moment would be forever imprinted in her mind. The salty air, the gentle spray of ocean water, the silky sand underneath them. Sun beating down on her shoulders like a warm blanket, safety in Sharkey's embrace. Her nerve-endings lighting up like fireworks on the Fourth of July.

Briefly, she considered stripping down right there on the beach, offering all of herself to this man she loved. But it was still winter and who was she kidding? Her first time wouldn't be outdoors where a stranger could just walk by.

She was pretty worked up, breath coming fast, desperate for another mind-blowing orgasm when something occurred to her. "Are we engaged?"

Sharkey pulled back, catching her chin in his big mitt. "Darlin', you'll know when I propose to you."

It almost sounded like a promise.

Chapter Forty-Five

If they stayed on the beach making out much longer, they were going to end up with sand in some uncomfortable places. Besides, he'd already told DD he'd have to wait until their wedding night. Hope deserved that.

Hand in hand, they walked back to the truck, a beautiful smile on Hope's face. Mission accomplished.

"Are you hungry?" She'd been like a zombie all morning and hadn't eaten breakfast.

"Yes!"

He opened the passenger door and she climbed in. *Damn, she's beautiful.* "Okay, lunch is our next stop." They were still about twenty minutes from Eastport Beach and there were more options in Bluffville, so he started the truck and headed that way. He wasn't even to the main road when his phone rang. "Sharkey here."

"I've been trying to reach you." Maddy sounded more like a panicked friend and less like a neutral sheriff's deputy.

Bile churned in his empty gut. If Tink didn't eat, neither did Squatch. "Sorry, left my phone in the car. What's up?" He tried to keep his voice light for Hope's sake.

"Miller's been released."

An epic Irish curse word slipped out before he could stop it. "Seriously?"

"He's got some bigshot from Raleigh representing him, and the DA said there wasn't enough to hold him."

Brightside was likely paying for his attorney. "Surely he's not dumb enough to keep coming after me." Getting hauled off to jail would be enough for a normal person to stop their bad behavior.

"I spent over an hour with him in the car. I wouldn't put it past him."

Sharkey grunted. He needed to get back to the brewery ASAP. He glanced over at Hope who was paying close attention to his side of the conversation, a concerned crease between her brows. Nope. He had to feed his lady first. And reassure her that everything would be okay. "Thanks for the heads up, Maddy." His phone beeped. "I've got another call. I'll touch base with you later." He switched to the other caller. "Yeah?"

"Did you become a dealer in the six months since I saw you last?" Maverick asked without saying hello.

There was way too much going on for his cousin's nonsensical theoreticals. "On what planet?" Sharkey wanted to give Mav a heads up about Miller, but he didn't want to unnecessarily worry Hope.

"Your burner phone has been lighting up like a winning slot machine."

"My what?"

"Often a second phone without registration that criminals use to keep from incriminating themselves. Also, it usually doesn't support Candy Crush." Mav often did this bit where it sounded like he was reading from a dictionary. If he hadn't gone into the food truck biz, he probably would have been a stand-up comedian. Only problem is, he's not particularly funny.

Criminals. Burner. Sharkey had forgotten all about the phone he'd swiped from the crime scene of the attempted heist. That particular thief was still in custody as far as he knew, so who was blowing up his phone? "Mav, we're grabbing some food, then we'll be back. Why don't we meet up at Heron House? The camper's a little tight."

"I haven't had decent fried chicken in months. The southwest just doesn't understand Southern cuisine."

"Sounds good. See you in thirty at the House." Silently, Sharkey willed his cousin to listen to him for once, without questioning. He glanced down at the speedometer and depressed the petal a bit harder. Hopefully, the highway patrol was sticking to the Interstate today.

"What's going on? Is something happening at the brewery?" Hope pounced as soon as he ended the call.

He debated omitting the truth versus out-and-out lying. No, he'd promised her he wouldn't keep her in the dark. "The man they arrested for possibly orchestrating all this crap was released from jail. Maddy was calling to let us know."

She gripped his bicep. "And she thinks he's going to come after you?"

"No, he just gives the orders. He doesn't dirty his hands. Besides, getting arrested is sure to slow him down."

"Or maybe now he thinks he's invincible."

Despite her age and sheltered life, Hope was surprisingly shrewd. "I'm sure it's fine, but just in case, we can all stay at Heron House until they find more evidence." Like the burner phone of one of Miller's associates.

Sharkey whipped into the parking lot of Hortons. They had the best fried chicken in a three-state radius. The restaurant was located in an old bank, so he pulled up to the teller window, which they had converted into a drive thru. "I'll take a family meal with all the fixins."

The woman at the window hollered his order over her shoulder. "You want a pie, sweetie? It's only ten bucks if you add it to a meal. I've got apple and pecan." She pronounced it like a pot to piss in.

"What do you think, Tink? Apple or pecan?"

"Apple. But what are fixins?"

"Reginald, grab an apple!" She turned back to Sharkey. "That'll be $48 even."

He handed her three twenties. "You keep the rest."

The cashier fanned herself with the bills. "If I weren't in a semi-committed relationship with Reggie back there, whoo-wee. I'd be all over you, boy. I'm gonna throw in a gallon of sweet tea, even though you're already as sweet as they come."

Hope covered her mouth, but he could see the humor in her eyes. She was loving every minute of this true Southern experience. And she hadn't even tasted the chicken yet.

Six bags and a jug of tea later, they were heading back toward Eastport Beach when his phone rang again. "We'll be there in ten, and I've got enough chicken to feed a baseball team."

"Yeah, about that." Mav clicked his tongue. "You're gonna want to stop by the camper first."

A million disastrous scenarios flitted through his mind. "Why?"

"Your friend from Wilmington stopped by for a visit. We're having a nice chat, but I think you might want to call your friendly neighborhood cop."

"Mav, are you okay?"

"I'm fine, don't worry. I know where you keep the Skipper."

Leave it to Maverick to find Sharkey's gun in the Grapenuts box. "Is Barney Fife in your trailer?" He'd grab Mav's semi-automatic on his way in.

"Right where he likes to sleep."

"Out." Sharkey hung up and called Maddy back. "Miller's at the camper. My cousin might be holding him at gunpoint. I'm five minutes out."

"I was already heading that way just in case. Meet you there."

He reached for Hope's thigh and squeezed it. "I don't suppose you'd let me drop you off at Heron House first?"

"There's no time for that. We have to make sure Maverick's okay."

His sweet Hope. But if anything happened to her... "Will you at least stay locked in the truck?"

"Yes. I know you'll just worry about me, and you can't afford any distractions."

Seriously, how did she get so smart? It wasn't her parents. "I love you."

"I love you, too. We'll get through this. Together." She lifted his hand off her leg and to her lips.

The whisper of a kiss raced up his arm and exploded inside his chest. He wanted to propose right then. Fucking Craig Miller, ruining everything.

He pulled down the gravel road toward Shark Bite Brewing. He slotted his truck behind Mav's trailer, kissed Hope and locked her in. Slipping into Nacho Average Taco, he bent below the pass-thru window and found Maverick's gun velcroed to the underside. Either Barney Fife had gained a few pounds, or Mav had upgraded his protection. He hefted the piece, adjusting to its weight. This was no pea shooter.

Sharkey left the trailer and crept around the back of the camper to the kitchen window. He said a quick prayer for protection for Maverick and Hope, then leaned to peek in the window. His cousin sat casually in one of his swivel chairs, holding Sharkey's pistol on a man who was hogtied and laying facedown on the bench.

His phone buzzed in his pocket. He checked the screen, replying to Maddy's text that everything was under control. Leave it to Mav to take care of matters within a day of his arrival. Now if the authorities could just hold on to Miller this time.

Rounding the camper, he scaled the steps, keeping his hand on the gun in his waistband. Just in case.

"Sharkey! Thanks for joining us. Craig and I were just getting acquainted. Seems like he's been a busy fella."

Once inside, he had a better view of the detainee. His hands were bounded behind his back with furry, leopard-skin handcuffs, and his feet were tied with an old phone charger. "Do I need to worry about this? The deputy will be here in five." He gestured at Miller, who looked like he'd stumbled into a kinky sex game.

"Nah, we've got him dead to rights. The cameras caught him trying to set a fire that would have taken out more than the brewery. He's got enough fuel to burn down the Amazon. Plus, we have these." He held up two burner phones. "Lots of super incriminating messages on these puppies. I'm assuming this one isn't yours?"

"I found it when the other two stooges were trying to jack my container."

"That was what? A week ago?" Mav grabbed a towel off the counter and wiped both phones down. "Maybe your deputy should find it now." He chucked one of the phones at the man moaning on the bench and handed the towel and other phone to Sharkey.

Maverick had his back, as usual. Where Sharkey was deliberate and thoughtful, his cousin could think on the fly and vamp with the best of them. For the first time since he'd discovered the compromised kegs on New Year's Eve, Sharkey felt like he could breathe. He had Mav, his business, and Hope. Sending up a prayer of gratitude, he realized the most important thing. His relationship with the Lord had been restored. It was becoming second nature again.

When he exited the camper, he could hear Maddy's car on the gravel. He dropped the phone under the steps and tossed the towel back inside. "I'll be right back."

He hurried to his truck, anxious to put eyes on Hope. Rationally, he knew she was fine. But love was rarely rational.

She opened the door, meeting him halfway. "Everything okay?"

"Everything is perfect." He wrapped his arms around her, sweeping her off her feet.

She giggled, and the sound soothed his soul. It was all good stuff from here.

"Sorry to interrupt, but care to update me?" Maddy appeared, cutting their make-out session short.

He reluctantly set Hope on her feet but kept his arm tight around her. "The perp is in the camper, we've got footage of his latest attempt to take out Shark Bite Brewing, and my cousin is a bad ass."

The deputy gestured toward the trailer. "Taco truck?"

"He's also the best chef on wheels. Once you lock up Miller for good, I'll get back to opening my brewery, and you can eat tacos anytime you want."

"I'm not going to say no to tacos. I'll put the suspect in my car, and then you can show me this video footage."

"Okay, but first I've got to feed my lady. I promised her fried chicken and fried chicken she shall have."

Maverick leaned out the door of the camper. "Technically, you promised *me* fried chicken." His gaze slid over the deputy, and his jaw dropped. "Thank God the law has arrived. I'm going to need you to deputize me, ma'am."

A faint blush crept up the bad-ass deputy's cheeks. It looked like Nic might have a little competition for town Romeo.

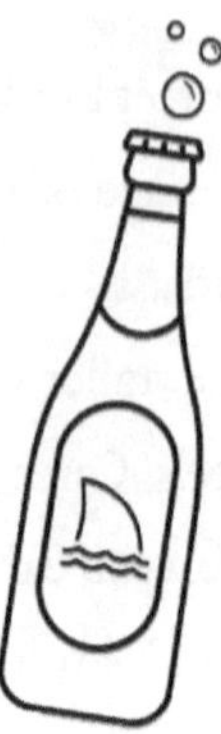

Chapter Forty-Six

Her cursor hovered over the send arrow. She scanned everything again. Address: check. Subject: check. Attachment: check. Oxygen: lacking. Composure: Zero.

"Not to rush you, but the oven timer went off like six minutes ago." Riley hovered over Hope's shoulder, likely checking that she wasn't sending her editor a video of dancing goats by mistake.

She was technologically deficient. Another thing she could blame her parents for. Clicking send, she slammed the laptop closed and snapped the rubber band on her wrist. It was getting better. She'd only thought about them three times so far today.

Pastor White said she wouldn't be able to move on until she forgave them, but she just wasn't there yet. During their weekly counseling sessions, he always told her two things. 1) Healing takes time. 2) Give yourself grace, because God does.

She'd settled happily into life in Eastport Beach. Cooking at Heron House, attending church services, spending time in the evenings with Sharkey. Writing. Editing. Rewriting. She had thought she was done when Squatch presented her with a sparkly purple box full of wrinkled pages. That sentimental yeti had collected all her throwaways and kept them. There were more than a few pearls in those discarded thoughts. His confidence in her had given her the strength to write a story filled with pain, truth, and grace. With the click of a button, it was gone. Out into the world.

Grabbing a pair of potholders, she pulled the sizzling casserole dish from the oven. The extra minutes had the cheese bubbling. Perfect.

"That smells amazing. I should probably go running with Ben tomorrow."

"Riley, I don't know what you're worried about. You look great."

Her host, turned best friend, grinned. "I know. But if I go running tomorrow, I can have seconds tonight."

Hope laughed. "You don't even know if you'll like it yet."

"You haven't made a single thing I haven't liked. Except for that banana thing."

"Matoke. And it's made with plantains. The only reason you didn't like it is because you thought it was mashed potatoes."

She shrugged. "I still say gravy would have helped."

"What is that delicious smell?" Sharkey shouted from the front door. Before Hope could run to greet him, his giant feet carried him to the kitchen. He grabbed her and spun her around the room.

"I hope you made plenty because we skipped lunch." Maverick followed his cousin, carrying a plastic container. "My secret salsa, madam." He bowed as he handed it to Hope.

She'd grown to love Mav like a brother, but he tended to be a tad dramatic. "Thank you! This will be the perfect complement to my enchilada casserole."

Riley set a pile of plates next to the steaming dish. "Are you going to tell them?"

"Tell us what?" Sharkey leaned down, settling a kiss behind her ear.

"Come on, or I'm going to burst. You know I will." Riley was practically vibrating.

Hope took a deep breath and faced Sharkey. "I sent it."

Everyone in the room shouted and converged on her, squishing her in the middle of a giant group hug. Their support over the few weeks had been invaluable. She owed all of them her eternal gratitude.

"What are we celebrating?" Ben's voice somehow managed to penetrate the noisy mass of bodies.

"She sent the final manuscript to her editor!" Riley broke free from the group hug to embrace her boyfriend.

"Congratulations, Hope!" Ben shouted over Riley's head.

Hope extracted herself from between Sharkey and Maverick and started dishing up plates. "I couldn't have done it without your encouragement." She made eye contact with each of them. "All of you."

"Just don't forget us when you're famous." Mav took a plate from her and sat at the kitchen table. "And plug Nacho Average Taco in all your interviews."

"Yeah, that should be really easy to slide in while she talks about helping people in Uganda, Mav." Sharkey deadpanned.

Ugh, she hadn't considered that she'd have to do interviews. That rubber band would be getting quite the workout. Her wrist may not survive the abuse.

While everyone was digging into their meal, Sharkey leaned close to Hope and whispered. "After dinner, I want to show you something. Okay?"

"Of course." The cousins had been working day and night to finish the brewery and with the grand opening just a week away, he probably wanted to show off their progress. It didn't really matter though. She'd follow him most anywhere.

Thirty minutes later, the casserole dish was empty, Riley insisted on doing the dishes, and Sharkey was dragging Hope out the front door. "You know, Squatch, they don't recommend vigorous activity so soon after a large meal." Normally, he was very aware of their height difference and kept a slower pace so she could keep up without running. But tonight, he was practically jogging toward the brewery.

"You're absolutely right, Tink. I wasn't thinking." He stopped, grabbed her by the waist, and hoisted her over his shoulder.

Hope squealed. The big yeti loved slinging her over his shoulder. Her struggling was mostly for show, because it was fun to see the world from his height, and the view of his backside was delightful indeed. They'd been sleeping side by side since the night Craig Miller tried to burn down the brewery. She fit perfectly inside his massive embrace, protected and loved by the man she'd never dared dream of.

That same night, he'd explained that he was exploring his faith again, trying to get right with God. He was reading the Word, praying non-stop, and attending services at the big white church on Main Street. They'd gone together the following Sunday and that's when she'd met Pastor White, who had become a mentor of sorts. He was a true man of God, and he was helping her see that her parents' sins didn't have to define her.

The other thing Sharkey shared that night was his intention to slow down their intimacy. Every day, he showed her his love in little and big ways and neither of them was in a hurry. They both had healing to do and snuggling up in his arms every night was the perfect remedy.

"Put me down, you big yeti!" She kicked her feet and flailed her arms, not so accidentally walloping him on his butt.

"We're almost there."

They passed the hammocks strung between live oak trees, past the spot where she'd seen that fine Bigfoot bottom for the first time, and into the clearing where the container sat, ready to serve the people of Eastport Beach. "Oh, you put up lights!" She was upside down, but she could see the twinkle of string lights as she craned her neck.

"Woman, stop wiggling, or I'm gonna drop you."

She loved it when he called her "woman," because that combined with his husky growl gave her chills all the way to her toes. With Squatch, she didn't feel like a naive, lost little girl. She felt empowered, cherished, sexy. "Oh, please, you could carry me all the way to Wilmington and back."

"I don't know how I feel about you picking up this Southern sass." He swung her so he was cradling her in his arms.

Lifting her face to his, she kissed him. "You love it."

"I love you. The sass I could live without." The twinkle in his eyes belied his words.

Right side up, the tasting area looked like something out of a fairy tale. The guys had strung old-fashioned lights in all the trees surrounding the clearing and across the front of the bar. The picnic tables had lanterns with flickering lights and piles of fresh blooms. "Where'd you get all the flowers? It's February. It's beautiful, but I'm not sure how practical it is."

Sharkey chuckled, his chest rumbling against her. "Tink, this is all for you. Not for a bunch of drunk Eastporters." He walked over to "her" picnic table and set her carefully on the top. For only the second time in their relationship, she towered over him.

"Are we expecting Stumpy?" She shimmied her hips a little.

He shook his head, and the most magnificent smile filled his face. "This is where you were the first time I saw you."

Hope giggled. "A lot has changed since then." She was no longer scared of the large, handsome stranger. And she rarely worried about the three-legged alligator.

"Yes, and I owe it all to you."

She could feel the flush creeping up her cheeks. She still wasn't entirely used to his compliments, or the way he'd scan her body like he was starving. It was kind of like that first meeting—intimidated but intrigued. "Mav helped a lot."

He scooped her off the table and set her on the ground, then got down on one knee.

"Ohmygosh, ohmygosh, ohmygosh." She rubbed her eyes, but when she pulled her hands away, he was still there, down on one knee, holding a purple velvet box. Then his image was swimming as the tears welled up.

"My sweet Tink. My Hope." He took one of her hands. "Before I met you, I wasn't living. I was merely existing. You showed me that my heart still had much to give. That there was a void there, and you fit perfectly. I love you from here to Neverland and I want to spend the rest of my days under your spell." He opened the box to reveal a sparkling pink stone. "Will you marry me?"

She flung her arms around his neck, falling against him, tears streaming down her cheeks. She'd spent the last year second-guessing everything she did or thought. But she'd found a lot of things in Eastport Beach. Confidence, gratitude, friendship, family. Love. "Yes," she screamed without an ounce of doubt or hesitation.

His arms came around her, then they were moving—up, up, up—and spinning around. "You've made me the happiest sasquatch in the world. No more living alone in the woods." He buried his face in her neck, and she felt moisture there.

She'd found the answer to the age-old question: If Bigfoot falls in love with a fairy, will they live happily ever after? Hell, yes.

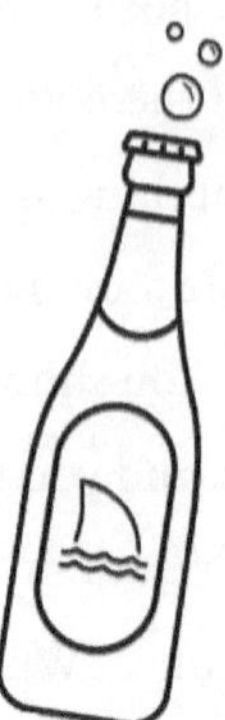

Epilogue

Shark Bite Brewing Grand Opening

It was a perfect day. Not as perfect as the day Hope said yes to his proposal, but pretty darn close. It was a mild sixty degrees with a cloudless, Carolina blue sky and the sparkling waters of the Cape Fear River lazily wandering by on its way to meet the ocean.

All of his friends—hell, they were his family—were here, eating sloppy joe tacos and buffalo chicken nachos courtesy of Nacho Average Taco and drinking the finest beer east of the Mississippi.

The band was rocking covers of all his favorite music, and so far, he'd only had to get Chesnee off the picnic tables one time.

The star of the day, the light of his life, milled through the crowd hugging people and making them feel welcome. His Tink, his perfect little imp, the woman he would spend forever with, sought him out, pulled him onto the makeshift dance floor and rolled her hips to "Shivers."

A familiar spark of desire raced through him, blocking out the rest of the world, and narrowing his vision to the woman who'd captured his heart. Who had healed him.

There was a commotion closer to the stage, drawing his attention away from Hope, who'd spent countless nights practicing until she'd gotten the dance down pat. Riley was squealing, and the crowd pressed toward the new arrivals. He saw a familiar flash of red hair and another woman wearing a sleek pantsuit. She definitely wasn't from around here.

Hope stopped dancing and stretched to her tiptoes. "What's going on?"

Poor little thing didn't have a chance of seeing anything over the crowd. Sharkey pulled her close. "Our friend Gina just showed up. Haven't seen her in months." He scanned the crowd, looking for Chesnee. The last thing he needed was a jealous, drunken scene. "This band played at the Heron House grand opening, and Gina hooked up with the bass player. She left Eastport Beach to be with him. Chesnee took it hard."

Concern etched Hope's beautiful face. "Oh, did they used to date?"

"Not since I've known them, but he's always carried a torch for her. I think there's a history there."

"Oh, how romantic. Like a second chance romance."

Hope had become an avid romance reader and now that her memoir was finished, she'd actually started writing her first novel. "I think it might be a little one-sided."

"How sad, unrequited love." She squeezed his side, molding herself closer to him.

"Don't worry about Chesnee. He's good at finding someone to take his mind off Gina."

The band stopped playing and Gina jumped up on the low stage, rushing to the bass player and kissing him. He wrapped his arm around her waist and stared down at her. Sharkey recognized that look. Devotion. Affection. Love.

The drummer counted out the next beat, and the bassist released Gina, popping her on the ass. She blew him a kiss as she hopped off the stage. The lead singer, Mack, was staring at the pantsuit woman and missed his cue. The guitar player whistled, grabbing Mack's attention, and he quickly found his way into the song.

Interesting. Before Sharkey had time to question the dynamics at play, Gina was standing in front of him, clutching pantsuit's arm. The woman appeared to be about his age and looked extremely uncomfortable. He wasn't sure if it was the brewery, the music, or the way Gina was yanking on her.

"Sharkey!!" Gina released the woman long enough to give him a hug.

"Gina, good to see you." He once again scanned the crowd but didn't see Chesnee's familiar blonde head.

"Is it true? Are you really engaged?"

Pride filled his chest. "Yes, this is Hope."

"It's so nice to meet you!"

Sharkey had never seen Gina this enthusiastic about anything. Except a musician.

"It's lovely to meet you too." Hope returned the hug. She'd grown comfortable letting the people of Eastport Beach into her trusted circle. Sharkey was so proud of the confident woman she'd become.

As soon as the women separated, Gina thrust her hand out. "I'm engaged too!"

Ah, shit. Chesnee was going to lose it. "Great. So happy for you."

Hope echoed his sentiments.

"So, I was just talking to Riley about having the wedding at Heron House. And of course, I need Shark Bite to cater!" This excited Gina was a lot to take.

"We'd be honored. And my cousin can do food if needed." He gestured toward the taco trailer.

Gina glanced at pantsuit. "Maybe. We haven't decided on a menu yet." She grabbed the woman's arm again. "This is my wedding planner, Georgia. She's Billy's sister."

He vaguely remembered the bassist's name was William. "When are you thinking?"

"We haven't chosen the exact date yet, but it will be this summer." From the rigid set of her jaw, Georgia was either constipated or stressed. "It's a tight timeline, but the band is going on tour in July, so it needs to happen before they leave." Definitely stressed.

"Well, you can count on us." He squeezed Hope's shoulder. *Us.* It still gave him chills. They'd be married by then. No reason to waste another day.

"When are you guys getting hitched?" Gina bounced excitedly on her heels.

Hope blushed, pink tinging her beautiful cheeks. "In three weeks. We're eloping. Very small, very intimate."

"When we get back, we'll have a reception here. We'd love for you to come. Both of you." He gestured at each woman. "And your fiancé, of course, Gina. Georgia, you're welcome to bring your significant other."

She chuckled nervously. "Unfortunately, I'm married to my job."

Gina squeezed Georgia's shoulders. "Always the event planner, never the bride!"

The wedding planner looked like she wanted the Earth to open up and swallow her whole. Sharkey wondered if a three-legged alligator would suffice as a distraction. Stumpy hadn't been around the last few weeks, but Hope was convinced he'd make an appearance today. The band announced a break. Within minutes, William was at Gina's side, his arm around her waist, pure worship in his eyes. Sharkey couldn't judge, because he looked at Hope the same way.

The lead singer also joined the group, his hands in his pockets, shoulders hunched. No longer the confident rock star who'd just been performing on stage. "Georgie." He nodded at the brunette, then stared at the ground.

She acknowledged him with a small smile, then turned to her brother. "William, you need to call our mother as soon as possible. She's freaking out because the invitations haven't gone out yet." She threw him a stern look, likely an older sister thing. "You need to explain that I've got everything ready, I'm just waiting on a date."

"Chill, Georgie. It'll be fine. We're staying here for a few days, so we'll iron out the details with Riley. And I'll call Mom later tonight. She needs to pay the deposit anyway."

Georgia sighed. "Sorry, we don't mean to bore you with our family drama. Sharkey, it was great to meet you. As soon as we confirm a date, I'll contact you about the details." She stepped away before he could reply.

"Are you going to play a little longer? I'm really enjoying the music." Hope directed the question to the lead singer, because William and Gina had their heads together whispering.

Mack didn't answer right away, because he was staring after Georgia, a wistful expression on his face.

"Can I get you fellas a couple beers before your next set?" They had a great turnout for the opening, and Sharkey knew if the band played a few more songs, he could sell a lot more beer.

The second question seemed to penetrate Mack's trance. "Yeah, that'd be great. We've got another thirty-minute set planned." He smiled at Hope before glancing back the direction Georgia had walked. She was gone.

"Come on, Tink. Let's get these guys a beer." He kept his arm around her, steering her toward the bar, but instead of going in the side door, he stepped around the backside and hemmed her in between his arms. "Have I told you how beautiful you look today?"

Hope's bright smile delivered a quick dopamine hit—straight to Sharkey's heart. Every single time. "A few times, actually."

He shook his head. "That won't do at all. A few isn't enough." He leaned down, hovering centimeters from her lips.

She grabbed his shirt, fisting her hands in it. "Just being here is enough."

Sharkey growled deep in his throat. The things this woman did to his cock, to his mind, to his heart. Three weeks couldn't come soon enough. "We should just get married tonight."

"We've got the chapel reserved." She kissed him lightly, but he wanted more. He wanted every inch of her.

Framing her face with his hands, he deepened the kiss until they were both moaning.

"We don't have to wait, Squatch," she whispered against his mouth.

It'd be so easy. The camper was still there until Mav found a place. But Hope deserved so much more than a frenzy in a camper. "I think Pastor White is still here. All our friends are here. Let's just do it now."

"It." She wrinkled her nose and snickered. His sweet, innocent Tink had developed quite the dirty mind since she'd been reading all that smut.

"Woman," he growled.

"Yours," she replied.

He closed his eyes, sending up a quick prayer that had become a mantra. *Lord, let me be worthy of her.* Kissing her again, he savored her sweetness and memorized how she felt in his arms. He never took a minute with her for granted. "Forever." He stepped back and straightened her top, so she didn't look like she'd just been kissed into next week. "People need beer."

Her grin was radiant. "Love you, Squatch."

"Three weeks, Tink. Not a day longer."

"Not a minute."

Bonus Epilogue
The Wedding Night

Want more of Squatch & Tink? Sign up for my newsletter to get the Bonus Epilogue – The Wedding Night.
Visit tararyanbooks.com to sign up now! Your bonus epilogue will be emailed to you.

Author's Note

While Hope's parents didn't have the purest intentions, there is an organization in Uganda, right now, doing amazing work every day. Sole Hope was started in 2010 by my good friend after she saw a video about jiggers and how the parasite impacted people, specifically children's daily lives in Uganda. She was so concerned about this issue that she developed a way to help orphans suffering from this ailment. It turns out closed-toed shoes can make a huge impact. So she started making shoes out of old jeans and tire inner tubes. Then she figured out that she could teach widows in Uganda to make the shoes for the vulnerable. So, she uprooted her family (including a brand-new baby) and moved to Africa.

Now, Sole Hope provides just that to thousands of people – HOPE. They offer footwashing, jigger removal, and medical care for those affected by jiggers, and then they provide them with shoes to prevent reinfection. They started out traveling to villages to treat those infected. Then they started adding staff. People would travel from all over to their compound for treatment. Now, there are sixty-two staff members on the ground and Hope Center is a place people can go to heal.

When the character Hope spoke to me, I didn't make the connection. I knew her parents were missionaries and that they were going to mess up, big time. I chose Uganda because I knew a little from my friend's journey and it was a great excuse to reach out when I had questions about life there. It wasn't until I dropped Sole Hope into the story that I realized why her name was Hope. (I guess

I can be a little dense sometimes.) I'm so proud of all the good this organization has done over the last 15 years and blessed to call Asher my friend. She truly has a heart of gold.

How you can help: Donations are always welcome. If you want something more hands-on, you can host a shoe cutting party – gather your friends and do a little good. You can volunteer or shop their store. You can also spread the word about the amazing things they do every day.

Visit SoleHope.org today.

About the author

Tara grew up with her nose buried in a book, and not much has changed. She's a serial entrepreneur – doggie daycare owner, quilt shop owner, maker and, of course, author. Currently, she lives in the mountains of North Carolina with her #1 love, a shichon named Agador Spartacus. Her whole family lives nearby, including her two grown sons, who are inspirations for the "cool" things young people say.

Stay up-to-date by visiting my website. www.tararyanbooks.com – you can even sign up for my newsletter!

If you enjoyed this book, please consider leaving a review on Goodreads or Amazon.com. Thanks!

Also by

Eastport Beach Romances

Book 1 Welcome to Heron House

Meet Riley and Ben as they are each starting over and learning to love after loss.

Book 2 A Heron House Affair

Trip and Ada will dance their way into your heart in this fake-dating romance.

Book 3 Something's Brewing at Heron House

Sharkey & Hope navigate an opposites-attract romance in a hilarious and moving way.

Book 4 Love Songs at Heron House (coming June 2026)

PREORDER on Amazon

Turn the page for an excerpt!

Standalones

Above Average Girl (2022)

This is a sweet romance about a plus-sized girl trying to find her way in the dating world with a little help from her friends.

The Things I Do For Her (2022)

Truly a story of friendship, this sweet romance is about growing up, finding love and moving on.

www.tararyanbooks.com

For signed paperback copies, visit www.dreamingoftheseafabrics.com.

Love Songs at Heron House
Chapter 1

Walking to work in New York City was not for the faint of heart. Georgia hobbled into her office and collapsed into her chair, kicking off her broken pump. Yanking open the bottom drawer of her desk, she pulled out her backup shoes. She was slipping them on when her boss stormed into her office.

Caitlin slammed the newspaper on the desk, like Georgia hadn't seen it at every single newsstand on her way into work.

The front-page picture of *the* Maurice Jacobs being rolled down the aisle on a stretcher. The bold headline. Groom Suffers Life-Threatening Emergency at Central Park Wedding.

In most cities, newspapers were dead. But New York wasn't most cities. The Manhattan elite were like American royalty. The wedding between the legendary philanthropist and the senator's daughter was the social event of the year. Which meant about a thousand prominent people witnessed the catastrophe firsthand. It was blowing up social media before the minister finished dialing 911.

"How was I supposed to know he had a deadly horse allergy? His fiancée didn't even know." Georgia didn't feel qualified to judge anyone's relationship because her last boyfriend checked out about six months before she even noticed he was missing. But if she had to guess, maybe the couple didn't know one another very well?

Her boss's lips thinned out—her Botoxed, collagenized version of a grimace. "It's your job to know."

It had practically taken an act of Congress to get permission for the bride to ride across the park to her waiting groom and a thousand of their closest kiss-asses. No one once mentioned equine anaphylaxis. Georgia would have made a note. She was a meticulous note taker.

Heat crept up her body. Thighs, stomach, chest. She could already feel the hives forming. The itching intensified with every tap of Caitlin's kitten heels. "I sent over an apology basket this morning." She had even popped for the cronuts. Mini muffins were so last year.

"An apology parade through the streets of Midtown wouldn't have sufficed." Caitlin leaned over Georgia's desk, that vein that hadn't disappeared with her last facelift throbbing. "Don't think just because your last name is on the front door that I won't fire you in a heartbeat. Your mother has made it perfectly clear there is to be no special treatment."

Georgia worked nights and weekends to prove that she was worthy of her position at Everett Enterprises. Lately, she'd been pushing extra hard, hoping to secure the soon-to-be vacant role of Director of Events. Caitlin's job. This horse incident was not helping her cause. "I'll take a full medical history for future clients."

"Whatever you need to do to keep your events running smoothly." She stood upright, straightening her skirt. "And I'd keep my head on a swivel if I were you.

Mommy dearest is going to have a front row seat at your next wedding. It could make or break you."

Her brother's wedding was in two weeks and there were still a million little details for Georgia to take care of. Eastport Beach was so small the closest airport was forty-five minutes away. It was a logistical nightmare. Not to mention the bride, her soon-to-be sister-in-law, changed her mind as often as most people changed their underwear. "It's under control."

Caitlin narrowed her eyes—well, as much as she could with all the toxin in her forehead. "I know you've got your eye on my job. Just know I didn't get here by sending grooms to the emergency room or releasing doves into a drone show."

Georgia cringed. Those poor birds never saw it coming. Neither did she. "I fly out tomorrow. It will be the most elegant wedding North Carolina has ever seen." She didn't mention the non-traditional taco truck or the fact that the bride had purchased a red dress despite repeated protestations.

"That might be your only saving grace. Even if a reporter cared enough to show up, they probably wouldn't be able to find the place."

She'd been to Eastport Beach twice now, and the town was idyllic and welcoming. As long as no one in the wedding party was allergic to Carolina Barbecue tacos, it'd be just fine.

***

By the time she turned her desk lamp off, it was after nine and the cleaners were vacuuming. It had taken the entire afternoon to wrap up various projects before she left town for two weeks. She'd still need to manage a few things remotely, but she was an excellent multi-tasker.

The allergy pill had taken effect, and the hives were nearly gone. She had one spot on her neck that was persistent, so she dabbed a little ointment on it as she walked to the elevator. Being away from Caitlin for two weeks was the best medicine she could ask for. That woman was a walking anxiety attack.

The doors slid open, and Georgia was shocked to find her mother inside.

"Darling, I'm so glad I caught you." Louise Everett looked like she'd just stepped out of a salon after having a full makeover.

Georgia felt like she'd been dragged behind a trash truck the day after the ball dropped. "Mother." She fruitlessly tried to brush the wrinkles from her pantsuit.

The women leaned their heads together, kissing the air, like they were acquaintances meeting on the streets of Paris instead of family.

"I expect you have everything under control for William's wedding, but there's a last-minute scheduling snafu." Louise checked her perfect makeup in a small, diamond-encrusted compact.

Fire crept up Georgia's torso, her skin betraying her just as her mother was. "I'm sure it won't be a problem." She'd been putting on a brave front for her mother since kindergarten, when she was the only kid whose parents didn't show up for the Christmas pageant.

Snapping the compact shut, her mother smiled. "Oh, I know you can handle anything, dear. That whole horse thing was overblown. He was fine after a couple shots."

She made a mental note to add an epipen to her emergency kit. "Caitlin was pretty worked up over it."

"There will be something new for Caitlin to worry about tomorrow." The elevator reached the bottom floor and the women stepped out. "I've got a late dinner with your father and the mayor, dear." She started toward the front door.

"Mom? The snafu?"

Louise threw her head back laughing, somehow managing to still look regal despite the tiny snort at the end. "This is why you'll be perfect as the Director of Events. So good at keeping everyone on track." She tucked Georgia's straight brown hair behind one of her ears, channeling a real mom for just a second. "Your father and I need to pop over to Wales, so we won't be back in the States until Friday next."

Friday next? Who even talks like that? "As in the day of the rehearsal dinner?" She tried to keep the panic out of her voice, but her heart was racing and her neck felt like it was the color of a beet.

"We'll be there in plenty of time for dinner. Don't worry!" Louise smiled brightly and gave her daughter a rare, and quick, hug. "And when we're all back in New York, we'll celebrate our new Director of Events."

"The board still has to vote on it." Between Caitlin's disapproval and the front-page news, Georgia could feel the promotion slipping through her fingers. No matter what her last name was.

Louise batted her hand like she was swatting away a gnat. "You're an Everett. We always come out on top. Ta ta!" The security guard held open the door and the head of Everett Enterprises disappeared into a waiting limo.

It's fine. Everything's fine. The parents of the groom didn't have to be there for the bridal luncheon or the groomsmen's round of golf. Or the intimate family meet and greet that would kick off the week of wedding festivities.

Georgia yanked the fabric of her blouse from her flaming skin, trying to create a little air circulation for the inferno inside her shirt.

Solomon, the night security guard, was eyeing her suspiciously. He already thought she was weird after the dove incident, because she'd run back to the office for a change of clothes. Apparently, it wasn't every day that the daughter of the CEO showed up looking tarred and feathered.

She practically ran to the lobby restroom, her shoes sliding on the polished floor. Once inside, she dropped her briefcase and leaned against the sink as she caught her breath. *It's fine. You're fine. Breathe. In and out. Two, three, four.*

Slowly, she raised her head and peeked one eye open. God, it was worse than she thought. Bright red splotches lined her neck like she was a teenager with a dozen hickeys. Not that anyone had ever given her a hickey. She'd been too focused on school for any recreational activities.

She pulled her shirt out and looked down at her chest. Welts had broken out across her breasts and stomach. It felt like the devil himself was trying to burrow into her body.

None of her normal calming techniques were cutting it. Fumbling in her purse, she found her earbuds and stuck them in. She sucked air in as she tapped the music app on her phone. The first strains of Ken Lionel's latest hit erupted from the speaker. Georgia switched it to the earbuds and collapsed on the small settee in the anteroom of the bathroom. By the chorus, she was breathing normally and was able to resist clawing her skin off.

I see you. Only you. And you are enough for me.

Music had always calmed her, but this song had been her solace lately.

Slow down.

Breathe.

Just be.

With me.

By the time the song ended, Georgia's breathing was even, and her skin was more salmon and less radish. She set the song to repeat and gathered her purse and briefcase. Slipping out the restroom door, she held her head high and pretended she was on the phone, so she didn't have to engage with Solomon.

The guard held the door as she exited the building, immediately hitting a wall of humidity combined with the rancid smell of rotting trash. Ah, summer in New York City.

It was three blocks to the subway, and the heat was compounding her already melting flesh. *Screw it.* She threw her hand up and a cab pulled over. Georgia rarely splurged on transportation—not heat, nor rain, nor snow—but she didn't think she could handle one more newspaper shouting at her. She'd grab a salad at the bodega on the corner and eat it while packing.

Tomorrow, she'd fly down to the Carolinas, where no one knew that her career was teetering on the edge.

www.ingramcontent.com/pod-product-compliance
Lightning Source LLC
Chambersburg PA
CBHW030150310726
48970CB00005B/1679